NO MAN'S LAND

Also by Sara Driscoll

Lone Wolf

Before It's Too Late

Storm Rising

NO MAN'S LAND

SARA DRISCOLL

KENSINGTON BOOKS
www.kensingtonbooks.com

KENSINGTON BOOKS are published by

Kensington Publishing Corp.
119 West 40th Street
New York, NY 10018

All Kensington titles, imprints and distributed lines are available at special quantity discounts for bulk purchases for sales promotion, premiums, fund-raising, educational or institutional use.

Special book excerpts or customized printings can also be created to fit specific needs. For details, write or phone the office of the Kensington Special Sales Manager: Kensington Publishing Corp., 119 West 40th Street, New York, NY 10018. Attn. Special Sales Department. Phone: 1-800-221-2647.

Library of Congress Card Catalogue Number: 2019944524

Kensington and the K logo Reg. U.S. Pat. & TM Off.

ISBN-13: 978-1-4967-2247-8
ISBN-10: 1-4967-2247-7
First Kensington Hardcover Edition: December 2019

ISBN-13: 978-1-4967-2248-5 (ebook)
ISBN-10: 1-4967-2248-5 (ebook)

10 9 8 7 6 5 4 3 2 1

Printed in the United States of America

NO MAN'S LAND

CHAPTER 1

Urbexing: Urban exploration, usually of abandoned or nearly inaccessible man-made structures.

Sunday, October 7, 10:47 AM
Massaponax Psychiatric Hospital
Fredericksburg, Virginia

"Is this how you usually get into these places?" Meg Jennings pushed through the ragged tear slicing diagonally across the lower half of the towering chain-link fence. She ducked low, to avoid the jagged edges that threatened to catch the long dark hair she'd tied into a ponytail and to tug at her backpack.

"This is easy, compared to some." District of Columbia Fire and Emergency Services firefighter Chuck Smaill grinned down at her. "It's a small price to pay to get a look at some truly creepy stuff."

"You're really selling it. And as a duly sworn member of the FBI, I won't even ask if we're trespassing. I think it's better if I'm left officially in the dark on that point." Meg straightened and turned to the man standing beside her. Several inches taller than her own nearly six feet, DCFEMS firefighter and paramedic Lieutenant Todd Webb had the build of a man used to physical work and the short-cut dark hair that spoke to how often he wore a firefighter's helmet. "Todd, give me a hand with the fence for Hawk?"

"Sure." Having preceded her through the gap, Webb grabbed one edge of the chain link and curled it back as Meg mirrored his actions on the opposite side.

"That's good. Okay, Hawk, come!"

The black Labrador trotted through the gap, his tail waving jauntily. Without his standard uniform of the FBI's Human Scent Evidence Team's navy-and-yellow vest, he sported only a bright red collar and rubber-soled Velcro boots to protect his paws.

Once he was through, Meg let go and the chain-link fencing vibrated back into place with a discordant metallic twang.

Smaill held his arms wide. "Welcome to no man's land."

Meg eyed the property around them. "No man's land?"

"It's an urbex term."

"Urban exploration has its own terms?"

"It has a language all its own. If you got on any of the urbex forums, you wouldn't understand half of what they say because they all use the lingo. Like 'blagging,' 'lift surfacing,' and 'tankcatting.' In this case, no man's land is the dead space between an outer security fence and the actual site or building. So, welcome to no man's land."

Meg took in the prickly weeds and overgrown grass, their lush green fading with autumn's cooling days. "Um . . . thanks?" She tipped her hand over her eyes, squinting past the open space to the red brick structure rising into the cloudless sky. "That's really fantastic Gothic Revival architecture. Such a shame it's practically falling down in real time."

Smaill's eyebrows shot up to disappear behind the sun-streaked blond hair that fell boyishly over his forehead. "You recognize the architecture?"

Webb laughed and bumped his shoulder affectionately to Meg's. "Oh yeah, she loves old buildings. I can't count the number of times she's had me pull to the side of the road so she can admire some old Victorian manor out her window. The older the better."

"Hey, at least I don't make you jog with me at six in the morning like I do Brian. He tends to pick parks for jogging, but I love going through the oldest neighborhoods in DC. Those classic houses have a special glow as the sun is just clearing the treetops." Meg considered the red brick structure. "And it's not hard to nail this one. See the decorative pointed brick crowns over the windows? The front-facing gables on the top floor in that steep roof? The main central castle tower? Classic Gothic Revival. But this building is more than its architecture. Do you know anything about it?"

"I always find out about a site before I visit," Smaill said. "Makes the hacking more interesting because you know what you're exploring. Also makes it safer because you get an idea of the setup and might foresee some of the hazards. When this place first went up in the decade following the Civil War, it was the Massaponax Insane Asylum. See how it's built? As a big center structure with the two wings on either side?"

"Yeah. The architect didn't quite get the symmetry down, though."

"He wasn't trying to. The wing on the left, the big one, that was the men's wing. The more modest wing was for the ladies."

"And here we are without McCord, the walking Civil War encyclopedia," Webb deadpanned. "Even without the numbers he could spout off the top of his head, I'm betting the Battle of Fredericksburg and the rest of the Civil War left a large proportion of the surviving male population with some nasty mental health issues."

"Got it in one," said Smaill. "Back then, they didn't know what was wrong with those men. PTSD wasn't defined until after the Second World War. In the First World War, they recognized the issue as 'shell shock,' but they still didn't know what to do about it. Now imagine how unprepared they were to handle it in the 1860s and 1870s after Sherman's March to the Sea, the destruction of South Carolina, and the retaking of Fort Sumter that ended the Civil War."

"So instead of dealing with it, they locked those men up here," Meg said. "Out of the public eye."

"Here and many other places. Hardly seems like the right way to treat veterans who barely survived the effort to protect their country. Granted, some days I'm not sure we do that much better now. Come on, let's get in there."

The group followed a scant path that cut across what was once a well-tended lawn, now given way to weeds and brambles dotted with fallen amber leaves.

When Smaill had invited Webb on one of his urbex outings, Webb had suggested that Meg and Hawk come as well. Having met Meg and Hawk six months before at the site of the National Mall bombing, and then being with her for several other cases, Webb knew urbex would be exactly the kind of search-and-rescue—or SAR—practice that kept Meg and Hawk at the top of their game. Meg agreed wholeheartedly. From then on, it was just a matter of matching schedules between a firefighter, a firefighter/paramedic, and a SAR team. A common day off between the first responders finally meant they could make the trip together from DC to Virginia.

"What's that mean?" Webb pointed to a faded metal sign attached to the brick near the front door featuring a yellow circle overlaid by a triad of downward-facing rust-colored triangles. "It's almost like a radiation hazard warning, but not quite."

"I've run into that one before," said Smaill. "It's the civil defense symbol for a fallout shelter from the Cold War."

"Duck and cover," Meg murmured. She scanned the lower windows—some were cracked but mostly intact; others were boarded up. "Can we get in the front door?"

"Last time I was here, someone had forced the lock on it and it was standing open. Hopefully no one has secured it since then. I'm not sure who owns the property now. I know there were rumors someone was going to buy it, gut it, and reno it into swanky condos, but clearly that hasn't happened yet."

"It's a great property." Meg scanned the front of the building, each floor marked by a horizontal stripe of white stone transecting the brick, and windows topped by decorative arches of alternating white and black blocks. "The outside is really stylish."

"And the inside is really a mess," Smaill countered. "But if they took it back to the studs and built it out again, it could be spectacular." Bracing one hand on the wrought iron railing, he climbed the stairs to the front door, with Meg, Hawk, and Webb following.

The heavy wood door formed a Gothic arch with a pointed apex. It stood open, leaving a gap of several feet to the doorjamb that allowed daylight to stream inside.

"When we're inside, be constantly conscious of your surroundings. For instance, places where the floor has given way can be treacherous. And if some spots have collapsed already, there are likely others that could go with only minimal stress. Eyes and ears open at all times. If anything looks dicey, don't push it." Smaill looked down at Hawk. "He's ready to go in?"

"All he needs are his boots. We can't afford for anything to injure his feet and risk taking him out of future searches. But he's used to working rubble wearing them. I'm going to keep him on lead unless I'm concerned he's going to get caught on it. Then I'll let him loose."

"There might be a few places where he'll do better without it, but you know best. He'll come when you call him if he's off leash?"

"Just you wait," Webb said before Meg could answer. "That dog is so well trained, he can practically bring you breakfast in bed. Don't worry, he'll be great."

Smaill pushed the door open a few more inches and stepped into the gloom. "Then let's do it."

They moved from the brilliant technicolor of fall into what was originally monochrome hospital beige, now spoiled by dark splotches of rust and mildew and brilliant palettes of paint. It took a minute for their eyes to adjust to the lower light, but then details began to emerge.

The foyer ceiling was at least twelve feet high, but the whitewashed patterned tin, originally lovely curling scrollwork, was torn apart with whole sections ripped clean away, and the remaining areas were invaded with creeping rust stains. Paint peeled in ribbons from the walls around slabs of plaster that had lost their battle with gravity and crumbled to the floor years ago. The floor, once a utilitarian linoleum, was now an uneven spongy layer that tore in soft spots under their steel-toed hiking boots and was littered with papers and scraps of wood. The wall opposite the door was covered in clashing colors of spray paint, with the most recent artistic offering, WRekeR, in large red block letters with a white border over older faded stylings.

Webb whistled. "You weren't kidding. It's a mess. It looked way better from outside."

"This is nothing," said Smaill. "Wait until you see some of the hospital wings. Come this way."

Turning to the right, they entered a cramped office with a rubble-covered floor. Open cubbyholes of worn, faded wood lined the walls above where desks once stood. Overhead, a gaping gash in the ceiling revealed a glimpse of the floor above, and pipework for the sprinkler system and wiring for the ceiling lights dangled, free-floating, overhead. A single intact bulb hung from a rusty fixture.

Meg and Hawk wandered over to where a pile of heavy, yellowed papers was tossed carelessly in a corner. She squatted down for a better look at reports edged with mildew. "When did this place close?"

"Sometime in 2003."

"These are handwritten ward reports from the 1970s. I'd have thought this stuff would have been destroyed because of privacy regulations."

"Apparently not."

Meg turned to her dog, who was pulling slightly against the leash, his head turned to peer down a long hallway stretching into the men's wing. "Do you smell something, buddy?"

"Mildew, dead critters, and rotting wood." Smaill picked up a curled black-and-white photo from inside one of the cubbies, holding it out by one corner for them to see. The picture showed a section of brain with a long, thin protrusion thrust deep inside. "For sure he smells something. You say you've explored ruined buildings before?"

"Yes, but usually freshly ruined. Explosions, fires, natural disasters. Nothing like this. It's something new, which is good for him." She gave his leash a light tug as she got to her feet and Hawk came to stand beside her. She pointed up at the ceiling and the rooms visible overhead. "Are we going up there?"

"You bet. Down into the basement too. It's pretty creepy down there."

"Lead the way."

They made their way down a hallway where paint curled from the walls as if bubbles had formed and popped, revealing the scarred wall beneath. Overhead, a line of rusted fluorescent lights marched in a drunken line along the gloomy ceiling. Weak daylight tumbled over the floor through open doorways leading to exam rooms.

"Hawk, come." Meg paused in the doorway of an exam room, scanning the interior. Lines of rust ran down one wall in rivulets to disappear behind a steel gurney. An overturned wheelchair with only one rubber wheel remaining sat beneath a cracked window. Beside it, ragged holes in a tangled pile of moldering blankets indicated the resident rodent population. A rippling, faded poster listing the classification criteria of *DSM-IV* mental disorders was still tacked to one wall, and a vacant doll head lay on top of a narrow white-laminate medical cabinet, the gash of its mouth grinning into eternity.

"That's creepy as hell."

Meg glanced over her shoulder to find Webb close behind her. "The doll?"

"The doll head. What happened to the rest of it? I thought this place was for adults."

"There were women," Smaill replied. "So there may have been kids too." He paused, frowning at the doll. "That's a nasty thought."

"Sure is."

Farther down the hallway, their progress abruptly halted at the gaping hole that stretched the width of the hall and dropped all the way down into the depths of the basement. Long slats of wood subfloor drooped into the gap, hanging nearly to the floor below.

Meg stopped a few feet back and was surprised when Hawk didn't stay with her but instead leaned toward the hole. A gentle tug at the leash brought him to her side. "How do we get around that?"

Smaill pushed open a door to their right that was nearly invisible in the gloom. "Up this way. Get out your flashlights and watch your step. Things are going to get a *lot* less stable. I'd recommend taking Hawk off his leash now. He's going to need complete freedom to navigate."

Meg pulled a flashlight from her backpack and shone it past Smaill. Not only was the stairwell beyond the doorway dark due to the lack of windows, but most of the middle of the staircase had collapsed, leaving a curl of steps clinging to the outer wall as it rose up into the shadows. She stepped into the stairwell to peer at the pile of torn wooden steps, fractured railings, and crumbling plaster. "That's more like what I thought we'd be dealing with. You're sure it's safe?"

"The steps are built right into the wall. Use your light, watch your step, stick to the wall, and you'll be fine. Don't trust the railing on the wall to hold you if you slip, or you'll end up on the pile below." Smaill gestured at Hawk. "He'll be able to manage?"

"Better than us. He has four feet and a lower center of gravity." She unhooked Hawk's leash, coiled it, and stuffed it in an outside pocket of her backpack. "Todd, you go first, and I'll send Hawk up after you."

Webb pulled a compact flashlight out of one of the pockets of his cargo pants and turned it on. He started up the stairs, his long legs carrying him easily over the first step piled high with rubble. The step groaned under his weight, but held. Keeping his light trained on the step above, Webb moved slowly and carefully into the dark. He stopped partway to push enough debris off the step to make room for his boot, and it tumbled onto the wreckage below with a crash. Halfway up, he turned around. "It's more stable than it looks. Send Hawk up."

"Hawk." Meg waited until the dog's gaze swung up to hers. "Go to Todd."

Hawk neatly jumped over the first step and then continued toward Webb, who shone his flashlight down on each step to guide the dog's way.

"You're right," Smaill said. "He's more sure-footed than I am. You next, and I'll bring up the rear."

Climbing the stairs was a slow, precise process. Place a foot, test your weight on the step, then transfer that weight. No sudden moves; just gradual, steady progress. But within three minutes they were on the upper landing gazing down at the ruins below.

"Are we going to be getting down the same way?" Webb asked.

"No. The other flight of stairs in this section is at the end of the wing. It's cut off from the main entrance by that cave-in, but there are a couple of emergency exits with crash bars on the ground floor we can force open to get out. Come on, things get interesting up here."

Smaill led them through the upper areas of the wing. Each room was lined with windows, and the light streaming in chased away the gloom. But the remnants of life here only accentuated the creepiness hinted at below:

A multistall bathroom where the sinks had been ripped from the wall and thrown to the floor in front of stalls so rusted, it were as if they'd been sprayed with blood.

A wooden prosthetic leg lying alone in a corner of the corridor, its painted surface so old and worn that it looked like mummified skin.

A ward room with the twisted remains of a bedstead crumpled near a pockmarked radiator sagging away from the crumbling wall.

A skeletal stainless steel table in the middle of a surgical suite, standing beneath a darkened lamp.

But creepiest of all was the morgue they discovered in the basement after they had descended a much sturdier flight of stairs. The room retained most of its working components, so it felt as if the staff had just stepped out and would return momentarily. A compartment door stood open, the stainless steel slab with its integrated neck support pulled out, ready to accept the next corpse. Sturdy glass organ jars were clustered on a nearby countertop beside heavy rubber gloves, tossed over the edge as if just removed. An organ scale dangled beside a deep sink, its needle several degrees off plumb as if ghostly flesh lay within its bowl.

But throughout their exploration, Hawk seemed distracted, his attention always focused down the corridor or out the nearest door. Meg was constantly calling him to her side when he wanted to wander away from the group.

"What's up with Hawk?" Webb crouched down beside the autopsy table and gave Hawk's back a good rub. "I've never seen him this distracted. Do you think he's picked up on something?"

"As Chuck said, I think he's smelling a dead rodent somewhere." She held still for a moment, considering her dog. "But his head is definitely not in the game. So why don't we let him show us?"

Webb straightened. "Let him lead the way?"

"Sure, why not? We don't have a set search plan here. We haven't found whatever he smells yet, so he'll only lead us somewhere new."

"That works for me, as long as it's safe," Smaill said. "And you said he'll come if you call him if he gets into trouble."

"Definitely. We're in the basement, so there shouldn't be any gaping holes dropping a story or two. But he's a wizard with voice commands, and on top of that, we have his 'don't mess with me' name."

Smaill glanced at the dog and then back at Meg. " 'Don't mess with me'?"

Webb laughed and clapped him on the shoulder. "Don't worry. This is your first foray into canine search-and-rescue. Spend time with Hawk and it'll become second nature."

"That's the name I use when Hawk has to follow my commands with zero hesitation, even if it looks like I'm throwing him straight into the path of danger," Meg said. "Like the time we were doing a search on a railway trestle and got caught near the middle of it with a train coming straight for us. We were closer to the side with the oncoming train, so I ordered him to sprint directly for it." She extended both arms to include herself and Hawk. "As you can see, we both made it. So if I think he's getting into trouble, I say 'Talon' "—Hawk jerked to attention and she laid her hand gently on his head in acknowledgment—"and he'll do whatever I say."

"Handy. I wish we could train our candidates at the house like that."

"Amen to that," Webb said with a grin.

Meg knelt down next to Hawk. "Hawk, something's got your attention. Find it."

Hawk's ears perked up and his head tilted at her.

"He's a little confused because he's not in his work vest," Meg explained to the men. "But he doesn't need it here. Come on, Hawk, we'll follow you. Find it."

Hawk turned and trotted through the open doorway melting into the darkness beyond.

CHAPTER 2

Cubed Location: An urbex route requiring different sequential exploration methods—for example, a tunnel ending in a basement hallway with a staircase leading to overhead scaffolding.

Sunday, October 7, 11:39 AM
Massaponax Psychiatric Hospital
Fredericksburg, Virginia

Pointing her flashlight to lead the way, Meg jogged into the gloom after Hawk, fearful of his running into unseen hazards. The heavy tread of hiking boots told her Webb and Smaill followed close behind. Alarm sparked for Meg when Hawk's pattern naturally fell into the easy back-and-forth zigzag of an outdoor search, where he would normally be looking for the edges of the scent cone to narrow his search pattern. His movements were subtle and wove around debris scattered over the floor, but he wasn't taking a truly straight path. Occasionally he would pause, sniff at a spot on the floor, and then keep going.

She tossed a quick glance over her shoulder. "He's definitely got something."

Webb watched Hawk for a moment. He'd worked with Meg and her dog often enough that he was now familiar with basic scent work techniques. "You don't think it's a dead animal."

"That's not what he's trained for." Meg left it at that, knowing he understood her meaning.

They jogged down the dank, gloomy corridor. On their right, massive, heavily rusted pipes lined the brick walls, and ancient electric light fixtures and wires hung down from the open metal gridwork of the ceiling. Water ran in thin, sluggish drizzles down to the floor, forming shallow puddles.

Meg tried to keep the flashlight beam in front of Hawk, but every time he sidestepped, he melted into the shadows. "If I'd known we were going to be doing this, I'd have brought my bigger flashlight from the SUV. Hawk, slow. It's dark and we don't want any missteps."

Webb adjusted his flashlight to fall ahead of Hawk, providing a dim glow to the oncoming hallway. "Does that help?"

"Yes, thanks. Although it looks like we're about to hit a dead end."

"Not a dead end," Smaill said. "Look, the corridor bends to the right."

"That's better. I was beginning to wonder where Hawk was going."

They turned the corner, the gloom easing as light came through the open doorway at the end of the hall. Hawk visibly brightened, his tail waving higher and his ears perking as he picked up his pace.

Meg moved from a fast walk to a light jog to keep up, and in seconds they were through the door.

Meg stopped dead, taking in the cavernous space. The room was easily two stories tall, running from the basement to the top of the first floor, where narrow windows near the ceiling let in traces of the brilliant fall sun through grimy glass. One whole side of the room consisted of massive floor-to-ceiling brick and steel furnaces, once the heat source for the entire complex. Metal struts wove across the ceiling, supporting a coal bin and a suspended crane used to transport the coal to the once-fiery furnaces.

Hawk, however, didn't spare a glance for the massive machinery, making a direct line to the far side of the room, where a rusted metal staircase rose to the roof. He didn't pause, but immediately started up the stairs.

"Hawk, stop."

He froze, looking back at Meg as she jogged to catch up.

"Sorry, buddy. But you need to wait."

Smaill moved underneath the staircase, his hands on his hips as he examined the metal. "This looks like a newer addition. The welds look solid."

Webb grasped the near railing and gave it a shake. When he pulled his palm away, it was black with coal dust. "It's filthy but stable. You can send him up."

"Hawk, find."

Hawk sprang up the stairs, quickly outdistancing the three humans following him. The staircase was an open-tread style of four zigzagging half-story flights until it reached the top, on level with a massive eight-foot-tall coal bin. The bin was built against the wall, near a graffiti-covered rolling garage-style door, no doubt the access point for the regular truck deliveries required to fill the bin and keep the furnaces running in the winter. From this height, there was no lifting of coal, which would instead be poured with the help of a movable crane directly into each furnace.

Hawk stopped in front of the coal bin and sat down, his face upturned to the upper lip of the container.

Meg cleared the top of the stairs. "Damn." She turned to Webb and Smaill as they stepped onto the upper platform. "He's alerting. There's someone in there. Can either of you see over the top?"

Smaill gamely tried a vertical jump. "Not really. It looks empty, but I can only see the first foot or so of wall."

"Hawk says it's not empty, and he's never wrong. Todd, can you give me a boost up?"

Webb wove his fingers together as a cradle and bent so Meg could brace herself on his shoulders and set her boot in his hands. "Ready? On three. One . . . two . . . three."

He lifted her as he straightened, and she stretched tall to reach for the top of the bin, her fingers curling over dented, blackened, rusted steel.

Leaning against the edge, she peered over the top. "Hang on, it's too dark inside." She pulled her flashlight out of her pocket, turned it on, and swept the beam down the length of the bin starting at one end. Inside, the massive container was empty except for a thin layer of coal shards covering the bottom.

Then a flash of color amidst the black.

Meg swung the full strength of the beam to the far end of the bin and froze when it landed on the still form. She swore quietly under her breath. She had known Hawk was right from the moment he started his search pattern. He was never wrong.

Sometimes she wished he would be.

A woman lay crumpled at the bottom of the bin, half slumped against the side wall. She was older, her face drawn with age and deeply lined, her silver hair cut short. The aqua track pants and jacket she wore were deeply smeared with coal dust, as were the beige, slip-on canvas loafers.

Then the edges of the smell that pooled in the container hit her. She knew that smell. She didn't have to deal with it often, but she knew the smell of death.

They weren't just late. They were days late.

Hawk whined and paced restlessly at Webb's feet.

Meg straightened and pushed away from the bin. "We're not in time. Not even close."

"It's a person?" Smaill asked.

"Yes, but she's gone."

"Are you sure about that?" Webb snapped into paramedic mode in the blink of an eye. "Hop down. I'll go in and check her out."

Meg braced her hands on his shoulders again, pressing in an imprint in coal dust, and jumped down. "She's dead. I recognize the scent of decomposition. And we don't want to contaminate or disturb the scene."

"Humor me, okay? I'm a paramedic; I just need to confirm patient status. I promise I won't disturb anything." Webb turned to Smaill. "What's in your pack?"

"Everything we need to get you out once you're in." Smaill wove his hands together just as Webb had and held them out.

Meg simply stepped back. There would be no stopping these two men until one of them had a look, up close and personal. First response was hardwired into them, so she let the scene play out. She crouched down beside Hawk and threw an arm over his back. "Good boy, Hawk. Smart boy. You found her. We wouldn't have known she was here if it wasn't for you." She kissed the top of his head, and he returned the affection with a long lick up her left cheek.

Webb braced his boot in Smaill's hands and then stepped up onto his shoulder, keeping a hand on the edge of the bin to steady himself as Smaill braced himself against it.

"Be careful," Meg advised. "You break a leg on a bad landing and you'll be hard to get out again."

"You don't know us firefighters very well if you think that." Strain laced Smaill's voice from the effort of carrying Webb's weight, then Webb jumped into the bin with a resounding thump, and Smaill straightened. He slammed the side of his fist twice against the metal wall. "Webb, you good?"

"Affirm." His voice echoed inside the metal box. "Give me a sec."

A glow flashed on inside the coal bin as he turned on his flashlight, followed by the sound of bits of coal shifting and crunching under his feet. The glow stopped at the end of the container.

Meg counted off the seconds of silence as she watched Smaill shrug out of his pack and dig through the contents.

"You're right." Webb's tone was flat. "I couldn't smell it out there, but I can in here. I'm no expert, but I'd guess she's been dead for a day or two max. How on earth did Hawk find her? He's not a cadaver dog."

"No, but death occurred recently enough that the scent still carries a human tang. Cadaver dogs are trained for more significant decomposition than this, all the way down to bare bones buried in soil." Meg straightened, turning toward Smaill. "How many people come through a place like this?"

"Surprisingly more than you'd think," Smaill said. "So, what made Hawk determined to track this one?"

"Would he zero in on the scent of blood?" Webb asked.

"He would, yes. He's used to tracking injured people, so that could explain it. Was she injured?"

"Not badly, but yes. There's some blood on her hands, but I don't want to move her to see where it's coming from. I can just see a medical ID bracelet under the left cuff of her jacket. Want me to look at it?"

"No." Meg said the word so fast he'd barely finished the question. "I need to call in law enforcement. If they consider it a crime scene, I don't want us to have touched anything. If it's there, they'll get details off it inside of a few hours."

"Okay. Let me grab a few photos of her so you can see what we have, then I'll get out of here. You may have found her, but I assume this isn't a federal case?"

"No. Definitely local."

They waited while Webb's camera flashed several times from inside the bin.

"Got what you need?" Smaill called.

The garbled response was unintelligible. Two more flashes.

"Sorry, was holding the butt of my flashlight in my teeth so my camera could focus. I'm ready to come out now."

Smaill pulled a harness and a coil of rope from his backpack and strapped on the harness. He unwound the coil, already secured with carabiner clips at both ends. "Heads-up." He tossed the weighted end over the far end of the bin. Then he snapped the end of the rope to the clip on his harness, braced himself, and took a hold of the line.

"Let me help." Meg grasped the rope three feet ahead of him and braced herself as ballast. "Okay, we're ready."

The length in their hands snapped tight and then dragged with Webb's weight as he used the rope to climb up the side of the bin until he could grab the top with his hands and drag himself up to the rim. Hooking a leg over the edge, he levered himself out of the bin to sit on the edge.

"Impressive," she said. "I don't think I could do that."

"Now you know why I spend so much time working out. It's not just the sixty-pound gear and the hundred-pound hoses. It's having the strength to save your partner's life if an active scene goes to hell." He jumped down to the floor below and straightened. "And that's why she didn't get out. She wouldn't have been able to manage it even if she'd had a rope. Especially at her age."

"Can I see your photos?" Meg asked. "I got an impression of age, but no real idea of how old."

Webb pulled his phone out of his back pocket, brought

up the photos he'd taken, and handed it to Meg. "I'd say she's eighty, possibly older."

Meg flipped through the series of photos, some full body, some straight on to the face. "I agree. Hopefully that medical ID will lead us to her identity. Don't they usually state the name?"

"Not always. If it's a registered one, it will have either her name and phone number or a membership number the cops can trace. But I've seen some crafty home-etched ones that give only medical information. Helpful from my perspective if I have someone unconscious and his bracelet says he's diabetic or epileptic or allergic to certain meds. Not so useful when you need to know identity."

Smaill had stripped out of the harness and was now coiling the rope to put back in his bag. "Finding out who she was is one thing, but I want to know how she got in there in the first place."

"Not on her own." Webb made a futile attempt to brush some of the coal dust off his cargo pants, then quickly gave up when the stains didn't budge. "The real question is, who put her there to die alone in the dark? Or was she already dead when she went in? And why?"

CHAPTER 3

Ninjors: Urbexers skilled at climbing who enter locations that cannot be accessed by doors, tunnels, or stairs.

Sunday, October 7, 6:25 PM
Jennings residence
Arlington, Virginia

So Hawk had been trying to tell you something all along." Meg's younger sister, Cara, a near carbon copy of Meg's black Irish coloring with her fair complexion, long black hair, and ice-blue eyes, held out her hand for Meg's wineglass.

Meg passed her the glass. "Yes. Mentally, I was off the clock and wasn't in search mode, but Hawk was." Her gaze wandered to where Hawk snuggled into a companionable pile on one of the dog beds with Cara's two dogs—Blink, a neurotic brindle greyhound, and Saki, a mini blue pit bull. "It was a novel location for him, and I assumed his interest was in the strange, musty smells, not what was essentially a familiar one."

"How long do they think the victim was there?"

"No more than a few days at most. That's why Hawk tracked her. Decomposition hadn't progressed very far and she still smelled human. And she'd been injured, so he was following the scent of blood. There may have even been blood drops to follow that we never saw. The floors were . . ."

"A mess?"

"That would be putting it kindly." Meg took back a full glass from Cara.

"Is this someone who was solo exploring and had a fall and couldn't get out?" Clay McCord asked from beside Cara. One of the *Washington Post*'s crack investigative reporters, McCord instinctively drilled down into any story.

"That's where it gets interesting." Webb sat back, draping his hand over the top of Meg's chair. "There's no way this woman got in there by herself."

"What makes you say that? Where did you find her?"

"Inside an eight-foot-tall open-topped coal bin on a raised floor overlooking a wall of massive old furnaces," Meg said. "The coal bin had no easy access from ground level. Todd got in by standing on Chuck's shoulders and jumping over the side."

McCord whistled. "So just getting into the bin if she was by herself would have been impossible."

"The other wrinkle is she was eighty-five," Webb said. "On top of that, she was in a part of the building that required a challenging path up to the second floor because the rest of the first floor was cut off by a cave-in right down to the basement. From the upper floor, there was a second, intact staircase down to the basement at the far end of the wing. And she had some significant health issues. A history of stroke and heart disease, and she was on anticoagulants. There's no way she didn't have assistance to get in there."

"Wait a second." Cara fixed Webb with a level stare. "I know you're an all-star paramedic, but how could you tell all that on someone with no vital signs?"

"She was wearing a medical ID bracelet with a 1-800 number. The cops called and reported her as deceased under suspicious circumstances and got her name and details so they could inform next of kin."

"That would do it. You called in the Fredericksburg PD?"

"Fire, police, and EMS to transport the deceased," Meg said. "Her name was Donna Parker. There was a roll-up garage door that was the original access for coal deliveries, and Todd and Chuck said that was the way for them to get in."

"Definitely more straightforward than our path," Webb said. "Smaill went out to meet them and brought them around the rear of the building. The Fredericksburg firefighters took care of the door with a K-12 saw in about two minutes. Then we helped the boys recover the body from the coal bin using ladders, ropes, and a rescue basket. Great guys." He scowled. "Better than the cops they sent us."

Meg rolled her eyes. "Todd's still irritated by one of the cops."

"The guy got in your face about trespassing and wants to call Beaumont and lodge a complaint."

"He knew you were FBI and still wanted to report you even though you just recovered a victim no one knew was on the property?" Cara sounded as outraged as Webb. "What a weasel."

Webb held out a fist and she fist-bumped him in solidarity.

"He was doing his job. And technically, he's not wrong," Meg reasoned.

The twist in Webb's lips telegraphed his disagreement. "His partner had all the same information and clearly recognized he had a group of first responders on a day off. He had no problem with it. Was grateful for the assistance, actually."

McCord set down his knife and fork, impatience radiating in the set of his shoulders and the way he ran his fingers through his dark blond hair, already subtly streaked with gray from life in both the newsroom and war zones. "Good cop, bad cop, yada yada. Let's get back to the real story. Someone put an elderly lady into a coal bin. Alive or dead?"

"We don't know," Meg said. "We're only ballparking how long she was in there, and we're certainly not experts. She was extracted and was sent to the ME's office in Richmond for a full autopsy."

"But even that's only going to give time of death," Webb added. "That's not going to say how long she was there before death, or whether she was even alive when she was brought into the asylum. Either way, she must have been carried in. Even if she was alive, there's no way she could have managed the stairs up to the second floor or then down to the basement."

"Or actually gotten into the bin," Cara added.

"And there's the real issue," Meg said. "McCord, can you please pass the garlic bread?" When McCord didn't move, Meg tried again. "McCord?" She looked at him more closely. His gaze was unfocused on the middle of the table. "Uh-oh, we've lost him." She snapped her fingers inches in front of his wire-rimmed glasses. "McCord!"

He blinked and looked at her as if he'd never seen her before. "What?"

"There you are. I was asking for the garlic bread, but now I'm asking what's on your mind. You weren't in there."

He passed her the bread basket. "Sorry, you got me thinking. You said this is someone quite elderly, found dead in a place she couldn't have climbed into on her own."

"It's *extremely* doubtful," Webb said.

McCord pulled his phone out of his pocket and pulled up his browser. "It's ringing bells."

"Wait a second." Meg set the basket down untouched. "Ringing bells as in it's happened before?"

"I think so. Give me a minute." Head bent, he started running search queries.

Meg sat back and turned to Webb. " 'Happened before' could indicate serial incidents."

"Don't get ahead of yourself. I know you're law enforcement, but there isn't a case in every incident."

"Agreed. But you have to admit this would be a somewhat strange situation."

"You've got me there. McCord?"

"Hang on." McCord's thumbs flew over his keypad. "I'm just about . . . there . . ." He paused, scanning an article, and then looked up. "I was right. It *has* happened before."

Meg leaned sideways, trying to read his screen. "Where? When?"

"About six months ago in an abandoned Gilded Age mansion outside of Trenton, New Jersey. The remains were extremely decomposed, but there were enough personal effects that they were finally able to make an ID. It was an eighty-three-year-old man."

"Cause of death?" Webb asked.

McCord shook his head. "Nothing listed. Advanced decomposition, so they may not have been able to make a credible guess at it." He set down his phone. "What if this is the beginning of a pattern?"

"Two data points don't make a pattern," Cara said.

"That's true, and normally I wouldn't suggest it, but look at the commonalities. Neither of these incidents can be coincidence."

"You're suggesting that someone is killing seniors and

dumping their bodies, or is taking them places they can't escape from and then leaving them to die?" Webb's expression clearly showed his disbelief. "Doesn't that seem a little far-fetched? Also, if someone is doing this purposely, he or she isn't even taking the trouble to hide the identities of the victims. With their identity known, the killer might be tracked from them. It doesn't make sense."

"I'm not disagreeing with you, but I've been able to find another case in under three minutes. What if there are others?"

"Then we'd have a stronger story." Meg took a sip of her wine and let the idea simmer for a moment. "You up to doing some research?"

McCord grinned. "I'm an investigative reporter. Research is my middle name."

"Then do it. We have a suspicious death in Virginia and another in New Jersey."

Cara made a small sound as she suddenly saw Meg's line of thought. "If it's a pattern, it just crossed state lines, and it would be an FBI case."

"Exactly." Meg drilled an index finger at McCord. "Get me more information. If someone is killing senior citizens or leaving them to die alone in condemned buildings, I can talk to Craig about opening an investigation so we can find the perp and nail his ass to the wall."

CHAPTER 4

Busted: Getting caught trespassing in an urbex site.

Monday, October 8, 9:12 AM
Forensic Canine Unit, J. Edgar Hoover Building
Washington, DC

Leaning on the doorjamb, Meg rapped her knuckles on the open door. "Craig? Got a minute?"

Craig Beaumont, the craggy-faced supervisory special-agent-in-charge who ran the Human Scent Evidence Team, looked up from his computer screen. "You're saving me from Brian's latest case report. Absolutely. Come on in."

Meg took a chair across from his desk, Hawk settling quietly at her feet. "Something happened over the weekend. Something weird that's bothering me."

"Something concerning the FBI?"

"No. Well, not yet, anyway." At Craig's raised eyebrows, she rushed to explain. "I was out exploring an old abandoned psychiatric institution in Virginia. It's been closed for about fifteen years, and urban explorers go through it for fun. One of the firefighters on Todd Webb's shift is into urbex, and he invited us to come along. Hawk and I went because I thought it would be good practice for him. All of the physical search challenges with none of the actual search."

Craig sat back in his chair and loosened his tie slightly. "I hear a 'but' coming."

"Um . . . yeah. We found someone."

"Someone who'd gotten lost while they were exploring the building?"

"Maybe. But definitely someone who died in the building or whose body was dumped there."

More raised eyebrows from Craig, but his silence directed her to continue her story.

"Hawk was distracted pretty much from the get-go. We were in an office full of old ward reports, examination rooms, a surgical suite, a morgue, and he was all over the place. It wasn't like him at all."

"He could smell the body." Craig's statement told Meg he had jumped ahead of her tale.

"You know he's not a trained cadaver dog. Corpses aren't his thing; that's the Victim Recovery Team's job." Meg ran a hand over Hawk's square head, and his tail thumped in response. "I wasn't in search-and-rescue mode, so I wasn't watching his body language for any signs of alerting. But, finally, even Todd questioned his distraction. He's worked enough cases with us that he knew something was off. I gave Hawk his head, and he led us deeper into the basement. And that's where we found her, in the back of the furnace room, in a coal store above these ancient furnaces. Craig, she was a frail, eighty-five-year-old woman. Maybe she was dead long before she was placed in the bin, but it's been bothering me that she might have died alone there because she certainly couldn't climb out in her condition. And then it gets more complicated. When Todd and I had dinner last night with McCord and Cara, it flipped a switch for McCord. He did a little fast research and found a similar case in New Jersey. This time it was an eighty-three-year-old man found in a condemned Gilded Age mansion near Trenton."

Craig's relaxed pose melted away as he leaned forward.

"Two elderly persons found dead in unlikely places they'd never be able to get into under their own power?"

"And certainly couldn't get out of," Meg confirmed. "I asked him to dig deeper and see if he found any other instances. I was going to wait until I heard from him before talking to you, but it's been bothering me all night."

"You're thinking we have a serial killer who is crossing state lines, killing the elderly."

"I know it sounds a little insane. Whoever is doing it isn't even trying to hide the victim's identity."

"What you're suggesting is entirely hypothetical, but that's where a lot of cases start. It's also where cases are missed if investigators don't start making connections. Maybe the killer doesn't need to worry about victim identification. If there's utterly no connection with the victim, he doesn't have to worry about being linked to him or her. To efficiently evade identification, he could remove the head and hands, but that's a lot of work. And that still leaves DNA. Why go to all that trouble if you don't have to?" He studied her thoughtfully for a moment, his fingertips drumming rhythmically on his desk. "I think you have traces of something here."

"Traces pretty much sums it up. This isn't enough for us to lay claim yet."

"No, but I could make some inquiries. Maybe between that and McCord's research, we'd have a better idea of what we're looking at."

"You'd do that? I know how busy you are."

Craig glanced down at the surface of his desk, which was covered with case reports, file folders, and requests for search-and-rescue teams, and winced. "I'm not so busy that I can't make a few phone calls and pull a few strings. Let me get back to you in a few days."

"Thank you." Meg stood, and Hawk jumped to his feet beside her. She took one step toward the door and stopped.

"Oh . . . uh . . . sorry, but you may get a call today from the Fredericksburg PD."

"About this case?"

"About your team members who were caught trespassing yesterday." She threw him a contrite smile. "One of the responding officers was extremely unhappy about that. And it felt like he was more focused on that than the body. Luckily, his partner had his eye on the real issue, but this guy . . ."

"Small-town cop, big power play?"

"Something like that."

"Don't worry, I'll make it go away."

"Thanks. Again, sorry." She started for the door but stopped in the doorway when Craig called her name. "Yes?"

He waved an aggrieved index finger in her direction. "It sounds like a fun outing, one I'd probably enjoy myself. But next time, try not to get caught. You know the locals hate us feds and love to rub stuff like this in."

"Yes, sir."

She was grinning when she left his office.

CHAPTER 5

Bricked Up: An entry point that has been blocked or made inaccessible in the past.

Wednesday, October 10, 4:37 PM
Forensic Canine Unit, J. Edgar Hoover Building
Washington, DC

"What on earth happened to you two?" Brian Foster's dark brows snapped together and his lip curled as he took in Meg's mud-soaked clothes and bedraggled hair. Hawk wandered in behind her, his fur tipped with mud. Brian's German shepherd Lacey jumped to her feet from where she lay beside his chair and ran to Hawk, sniffing him from head to toe while he wagged his tail in greeting.

"You should see the other guy." Meg dropped into her desk chair across from Brian and glanced down at her filthy clothes in disgust.

"You were fighting Mother Nature?"

"Just about." Meg ran a hand self-consciously through her hair and then shrugged and dropped her hand to her lap in resignation. "Are all the twigs and leaves out?"

"Close." Brian pushed out of his chair and crossed to her. He pulled first a small twig and then a mangled, brilliant red leaf from her ponytail and dropped them on her desk. He smoothed her disheveled hair away from her face. "Now they're all out. But you're still a mess."

Meg tipped her head against her chair back and laughed. Of all the handlers she worked with in the Forensic Canine Unit, Brian was her closest companion. Coworkers for years, and friends for almost as long, Brian was always her best ally, even if he regularly gave her a hard time for fun. Meg had been his strongest supporter and counted both Brian and his husband, Ryan, among her closest friends.

With a sigh and one last chuckle she looked up at him. "You're too good to me."

"Always." Brian's green eyes sparkled with laughter as he sat back in his chair and propped his feet on the corner of his desk. "Where did Craig send you?"

"Ellicott City."

That wiped the smile from his face. "Yeah, I can see that. They've barely recovered from the last round of flooding and here they are in it again. Looking for flash flood survivors?"

"Mudslide." She held out her hand for her dog. "Hawk, come." She ran a hand over his stiff, spiky fur. "I didn't do a very good job of toweling the mud off you." She pointed to the floor. "Down." Hawk settled on the floor with a long sigh. "He's exhausted, even with a power nap in the car on the way back. I know how he feels, and I didn't get a power nap. It was seriously hard physical work slogging through the mud looking for victims." She smiled. "But we found three, all alive, so it was worth it."

"Nice." He grinned at her, knowing full well the satisfaction of a successful search, as well as the sucking grief of finding victims they were too late to save. "But next time I recommend wearing coveralls."

She stuck her tongue out at him. "Funny man. I did wear coveralls. And when they became too saturated to move, I stripped down to street clothes. My mistake was in not bringing two sets of coveralls because then I . . ."

Brian stared at her questioningly when she trailed off. "Then you . . . what?"

But Meg wasn't listening to him. Her attention was fixed on Craig, who had left his office and was headed straight for them, a notepad in hand. "Incoming," she murmured. When he got closer, she said, "What's wrong?"

Craig pulled over a spare chair and sat down between Meg and Brian. "Why does something have to be wrong?"

"The look on your face. What don't we know?"

"I made those phone calls you asked for."

"About the elderly victims?"

"Yes."

"This is related to the asylum victim?" Brian asked. "And Clay McCord's possible connection?"

"Yes, though I'm thinking that 'possible' is becoming 'probable,' " Craig said.

Exhaustion rolled off Meg, and she sat bolt upright. "You found another one."

"Two."

"No way. You mean McCord was right?" Meg rolled her eyes. "There'll be no living with him after this." She held out her hand for Craig's notes. "What've you got?"

"Patience. You know you can't read my handwriting."

"Hieroglyphics," Brian muttered, earning a steely glare from his supervisor.

"Then tell me," Meg said. "What did you find?"

"Two seniors. One disappeared from a retirement home and was reported missing. The other disappeared from a private home, but because he has no family and was a bit of a recluse to begin with, no one knew he was gone until his body was found."

"No one should die alone and unnoticed like that," Brian said.

"I couldn't agree more." Craig scanned his notes. "The first one was found inside a movie theater in a shuttered mall in Martinsburg, West Virginia. The second was found inside an abandoned brewery in Smithton, Pennsylvania."

"Was an autopsy done on either of them?" Meg asked.

"I've only got minimal information at this point, so I don't know, but I'll find out. I suspect it would depend on the state of the remains when they were discovered. Both cases are listed as suspicious deaths, and both remain open."

"Can you get copies of the case files?"

"Already requested."

"This has piqued your interest, hasn't it?"

"I don't know if that's the correct term for it, but it has my attention, yes. I don't know if it's because the victims are my dad's age, but I find mistreatment of the elderly pisses me off. It's like taking advantage of a child. You don't prey on the helpless."

"And if you do," Meg said, "God help you, because we're coming for you. Thanks, Craig, this is a huge help."

"Hopefully, we'll get more on it soon. But that's not all."

"There's another victim?"

"Not definitively. But this new information made me think about who hasn't been found in an abandoned property. Who is simply missing. And there certainly are a number of missing senior citizens. Florida, Missouri, New Jersey, Maryland, Virginia, and others. Some have gone missing from retirement villas, some have disappeared from their own homes, some have disappeared while out on walks while out of town visiting family." Craig held up a hand. "And before you say it, not every missing senior is going to be related to this. The sad fact of the matter is that the elderly disappear by misadventure every day."

"They do, and that could cloud this, but you still might have a victim or two in that list, we just don't know it yet."

"Precisely. And many of these happened within the last six to nine months, so the trail has gone stone cold."

"Ah. I follow you now," Meg said. "You want to watch for new missing victims."

Brian nodded in agreement. "That makes sense. We have what looks like a multistate incident going on, and we know it's ongoing because the latest victim is so recent. What's to stop him or her from taking the next victim. Have you got alerts out?"

"I do," said Craig. "We'll see where this goes. If anyone goes missing, I'll hear about it and then we can decide if there's anything we can do with the information."

"And if there is, we'll go after the killer. Hopefully in time to save a life."

CHAPTER 6

Access Details: The information by which one selects and gains access to an urbex site.

Saturday, October 27, 9:12 AM
Jennings residence
Arlington, Virginia

"Good morning." Meg regarded Webb over the rim of her coffee cup, her smile broadening when he simply slid her a sideways glance and shuffled toward the coffeemaker. "Wow, this is a switch. Usually I'm the nonverbal one and you're all smiles and energy in the morning."

Webb poured coffee into the mug she'd left out for him and took two swallows, disregarding the heat. He set the cup down on the counter and closed his eyes, as if concentrating on the caffeine flowing into his veins. Then he opened his eyes, picked up his coffee, and wandered to the table. He paused long enough to bend and press a kiss just below her ear, chuckling at the surprised catch in her breath, and then straightened to push past the dogs. "Look out, Hawk. Blink, shift left. Saki, you too." He sidled around the pack of dogs surrounding Meg, pulled out a chair, and fell into it. "Have you already eaten?"

"No, I was waiting for you to regain consciousness. I figured you needed a decent breakfast after working all those hours yesterday. The dogs, however, seem to think it's a crime that I haven't fed them a second breakfast. Let me assure you, they got their own an hour ago." She pushed the *Washington Post* across the table to him. "You guys rated an above-the-fold story in this morning's edition."

"It's not often you get an industrial fire that hits five alarms, requires every firefighter in the city, and has compressed gas cylinders exploding every few minutes for extra excitement. When you have something like that, you don't clock out at end of shift, you keep going until it's out."

"And then you're too wired to actually fall asleep. You did about thirty-six hours before you finally crashed. And then you *crashed*. I'm lucky we got you into bed, because once you were out, there was no moving you."

Webb took another gulp of coffee. "Sorry. I know you wanted to go out last night."

Meg waved the apology away. "No need to apologize. We can do it another night." She pushed back her chair and stood. "Eggs work for you?"

"Perfect, thanks."

Cara appeared in the doorway, wearing a robe over her pajamas with her hair sleep rumpled. "Morning," she croaked. "Coffee?"

"Aren't you two a pair this morning." Meg pointed toward the coffeemaker. "Left a cup out for you. Pour and go. I knew you didn't have any classes this morning, and I wasn't sure if McCord stayed over last night, so there's one for him too."

"No, he was out covering some story for this morning's paper"—she threw a pointed look at Webb—"so he knew he'd be working late."

Meg pulled the paper closer and leaned over it to stare at the byline for the headline story. "Of course it's him. I should have known."

"He had a late deadline and he didn't want to drag Cody here in the middle of the night, or we'd have all the dogs in an uproar greeting each other in the wee hours of the morning."

"For which we are eternally grateful." Meg smirked at Webb. "Not that it likely would have woken you."

"Not a chance." Webb drained his coffee mug with three more swallows and pushed away from the table. "I think I'm conscious now. Let me give you a hand with breakfast."

Thirty minutes later, they lounged around the breakfast table with refilled mugs and empty plates. Webb took his last piece of bacon and tossed it to Blink.

Cara poked him in the biceps. "Stop feeding my dog at the table. You're teaching him bad habits."

"I'm trying to win him over. You notice he's not terrified of me anymore?"

"I have actually." She poked him again. "Stop feeding my dog at the table."

"Yes, ma'am."

"Now you're making me sound like my mother. I—"

Meg's phone rang from where it sat beside her plate. She glanced at the display. "It's Craig. I'm not on today, so maybe it's something big." She accepted the call. "Hi, Craig."

Craig eschewed a greeting to cut right to the chase. "A missing senior has just been reported."

"What? How did you find out?" Meg grasped Webb's forearm to get his attention and angled her phone outward so he and Cara could hear.

"I asked to be kept in the loop in case of any missing seniors, and one was reported missing yesterday afternoon in Allentown, Pennsylvania. Now, I know what you're thinking—"

"That this could be someone who is just confused, or who has wandered off and will be found in the next half hour."

"I know. I took two minutes to weigh this before calling you because it isn't an obvious abduction. The gentleman's name is Warren Roth, and he's missing from Park Ridge Residence retirement community. He was supposed to meet other residents at the community center for their weekly Friday night dinner. One of them had talked to him midafternoon and he had intended to go but then never showed. They knew where he kept a spare key, so they went into his place, but he wasn't at home. None of his family knows where he is. He's seventy-nine but has no major health issues given his age. A little high blood pressure, but that's about it."

"We don't even really know we have a case yet; we're just suspicious of one." Meg locked eyes with Webb, who nodded encouragingly. "On the other hand, I'm free today and I don't mind putting a little time into this. What's the worst that could happen? We find a confused elderly gentleman and get him home, or get him medical care if he needs it? Or we have a fun afternoon doing urbex at a new site?"

"That's why I called. There's no losing side to this equation as long as you want to put in the time and effort."

"I'm up for it. And I'll call Brian. Another team would be useful."

"That's fine with me. It's not up to me where my team members go on their days off."

"Keep you in the loop?"

"Absolutely."

"Thanks, Craig. Bye." She hung up and then immediately speed-dialed Brian, talking as soon as he answered. "Morning. Want in on some urbex?"

"For fun or for an actual search?"

"Possibly an actual search. I'm going to treat it like that, anyway. Craig just called. There's a missing senior in Allentown, Pennsylvania. I know it's your day off and you and Ryan might already have plans."

"I'm free. Ryan's about to head out to some special meeting at the Smithsonian, so he won't even notice I'm gone. Where are we searching?"

"No idea yet. Can you head over and we'll leave from here? I need to call a few more people. Then we need to brainstorm."

"I can be there in a half hour."

"Great. See you then." She hung up. "Brian and Lacey are in." Her phone alerted an incoming text, and she opened Craig's message. She finished her coffee in a few swallows as she turned the details over in her mind. "Chuck's on your shift? He's off duty today?"

"Unless he picked up some overtime, yeah."

"Think he'd be willing to help out? We could really use him. He's the expert at navigating urbex sites."

"I'll call him. Let me get my phone." Webb left the room, heading for Meg's bedroom.

"What about Clay?" Cara asked. "He's going to want in on it."

"He's the other person I wanted to contact. Honestly, we could use his on-the-fly research skills. I need to get dressed. Can you call him? Tell him we're headed to Pennsylvania and that if he's in, I need him to bring his laptop. Tell him he absolutely cannot bring his crazy dog with him."

"You think he'd want to?"

"I think he thinks search-and-rescue is pretty interesting, and maybe it's something Cody could work toward when he calms down a bit more, but now is not the time."

"He can leave Cody here with Blink and Saki and me."

"Which always makes him happy, so McCord won't feel guilty about leaving him." She stacked her dishes on top of Webb's and carried them to the sink. "I need to get ready. If he wants to come along, tell him I need him here inside of thirty minutes."

"Oh, he'll be here. He wouldn't miss this for the world. Now stop cleaning the kitchen. You might be saving a life. Get moving."

CHAPTER 7

Urban Adventure: An investigation of derelict structures focused on experience rather than sightseeing.

Saturday, October 27, 12:18 PM
I-95
Westminster, Maryland

"Talk to me, McCord. What are you thinking?"

"Give me a few more minutes." McCord's tinny voice came through Meg's cell phone speaker as her gaze shifted to the passenger side-view mirror, where she watched Brian's navy SUV follow them. McCord was the dark form sitting in the passenger seat.

"We've been on the road for two hours, so you must have an initial list. Now give. I want to bounce your ideas off Chuck for safety and feasibility."

Everyone had met at Meg's house and they'd been on the road since before ten-thirty. They'd quickly decided that Brian would take his SUV with his K-9 compartment carrying Hawk and Lacey with McCord, while Webb drove Meg and Smaill in his truck, which was already loaded with tools and basic rescue and emergency medical gear. McCord had his laptop with him and was using the drive time to research potential sites in the Allentown area.

When the dead air over the connection lasted more than fifteen seconds, Meg rolled her eyes and tried again. "McCord . . ."

"Yeah, yeah. Okay. I have a short list of five places, most of them in Allentown, but one outside of Allentown as well."

"Run them by me," Smaill said from the back of the king cab. "I've done some urbex in that area. Not a lot, but some, and I might be able to fill in some blanks."

"Great. Here they are in no particular order. Break in with comments at any time." McCord paused for a moment. "First up is Millford Middle School. Built in the nineteen twenties, the school was closed in the eighties after fire ripped through one wing. Been abandoned ever since."

"Possible," said Smaill, "but less likely. I've heard about it. The building is pretty unstable, and someone got hurt in there a few years ago, so they locked it down. Could make it harder to get inside, especially considering the perp isn't going in alone."

"Good to know. I'll move it down the list. The next is the Allentown Opera House."

"Allentown was big enough to have an opera house?" Meg asked.

"Third largest city in Pennsylvania and in a metropolitan area of nearly a million. It opened after World War II, during the boom years, and was a popular cultural hot spot for not only opera but the symphony and traveling Broadway shows. But it didn't make it to the millennium. Closed in 1998. Someone bought it to refurbish and reopen it, but that never happened. It's right in town and easily accessible."

"Probably also easily visible to anyone passing by wondering why someone is dragging an elderly man into an abandoned building," Webb said.

"There is that," Smaill agreed, "but I've been there before. It's a glorious mess of disintegrating velvet curtains and gold-leafed ceilings. A maze of rooms backstage, and I'm pretty sure the upper platforms for lighting are still intact. Definitely some places to strand someone with low mobility. Keep it at the top of the list."

McCord ran through other possibilities—a tool and die factory, a parish church, and an outdated hospital on the edge of town. "There's one other, but it's a little more out of the way."

"That's the last one?" Meg asked.

"Yeah. Bethlehem Steel."

Meg exchanged a look with Smaill, whose face lit up as if he'd had a sudden eureka moment. "There are alarm bells going off here. Chuck, have you been there?"

"No, I wasn't into urbex when it was accessible, but I've seen pictures, and the stories are legendary. So was the disappointment in the community when the land was sold. Bethlehem Steel was once an industry giant, the second biggest steel producer behind US Steel and the country's largest shipbuilder. But in the eighties and nineties, they couldn't compete with cheaper international goods and they filed for bankruptcy in . . . 2000?"

"Close," said McCord. "2001."

"OK, 2001. This huge industrial complex in Bethlehem on the banks of the Lehigh River has sat empty and rusting away since even before they declared bankruptcy, so it was a community favorite."

"Until it was bought in 2007."

"Right. The company that bought it razed part of the complex and built a casino. They hold outdoor concerts there now, but the majority of the original buildings are fenced off from the public. No more urbex from that point on. But there are many places your perp could abandon someone. Of course, now that the property is under new ownership, it will likely be harder to get inside."

"Could go either way," McCord said. "The company has turned the site into a tour opportunity and they've built walkways and platforms around the complex, but that's all outside. You can't go inside the buildings. However, they're working on restoring some of the buildings for inside tours."

"Which means there's access to the property somewhere."

"That's what I'm thinking, and that once we're in, we could move from building to building unencumbered."

"And think of the timing," Webb said. "Roth was taken on a Friday evening and could be transported and brought into the site after dark, and after any workers who are part of the restoration have gone home for the weekend."

"But if he's leaving Roth on-site, as long as he's not already dead, he could still be alive on Monday morning to be found by the workers." Brian's voice filtered through the speaker. "You said there was no evidence of cause of death on Donna Parker?"

"Nothing obvious," Meg confirmed. "She was injured. You know how fragile the elderly can be and how their skin can be like parchment. It looks like there was a struggle during the kidnapping and some of the skin on her arms tore, causing bleeding. But that was certainly not enough to cause her death."

"So, assuming they're going into the sites alive, how are they dying? It's October. It's not going to be heat exhaustion or hypothermia. Maybe the suspect hopes shock will bring on a heart attack?"

"Maybe he's got a pocket full of digoxin to help that along." Webb shoulder-checked and moved into the left lane to avoid a lumbering 18-wheeler. "That would induce heart failure and would look like a typical heart attack on the surface. If that's what he's doing, he might even be administering it before he gets to the dump site so he's lugging a dead body and not a struggling one. The elderly tend to be frail and wouldn't take much effort to move."

"Would a digoxin overdose show in an autopsy?" Meg asked.

"Sure would."

"Then I'll poke Craig to get us that information. Okay, McCord. What's our list?"

"Of the Allentown sites, you like the opera house best, Smaill?"

"Yes. But after that, I like Bethlehem Steel. It will also take much longer to search because of how big it is. Let's hit the opera house and then Bethlehem Steel. After that I'd say the hospital, the tool and die factory, and then the church. But I'm hoping we won't have to search all those. Warren Roth needs saving *now*."

"Agreed. Brian, stay with us. Hawk's okay with you?"

"Good as gold. He and Lacey are snoozing in Lacey's compartment. They're wearing their vests, so they know they're going to work and to rest while they can."

"Smart dogs." Meg flipped to her map app. "It's about fifty minutes until we get to Allentown. And I know it's going to make the trip take longer, but I want to stop at Mr. Roth's retirement community. Flash our badges, see if we can get a couple of pieces of laundry to use for scenting since there's a spare key floating around. Having items with his scent will reduce the possibility of the dogs tracking the wrong person and will be more efficient in the long run. We need to cover as much ground as we can as fast as we can."

"Roger that. Lead the way, we'll be right behind you." Brian ended the call.

Meg tucked her phone into the backpack at her feet and swiveled in her seat toward Smaill. "If the opera house doesn't pan out, how hard is the steel plant going to be?"

"Parts of it will be challenging, and it's just plain big. But we have two dogs. Can we split them up?"

"Absolutely. That's standard protocol for us."

"Then let's make two teams. Webb, you go with Meg, I'll go with Foster. If anyone gets into trouble, then we're there to lend a hand and will have gear on hand. McCord can decide who to go with. That way we can spread out and cover more ground."

"We can't assume Roth is dead," Meg said. "We have to run this as if we're on the clock and it's ticking down. Until the clock winds down to zero, we still have a chance to save him."

CHAPTER 8

Infiltration: Trespass and entry into an occupied site.

Saturday, October 27, 2:40 PM
Bethlehem Steel Works
Bethlehem, Pennsylvania

They struck out at the opera house.

A crumbling façade hid the beauty of a graceful interior of soaring ceilings adorned with gold-tipped Rococo flourishes. The main theater was still a sight to behold even with a faded mural ceiling; the remnants of a massive crystal chandelier; and the swag of what were once rich burgundy velvet curtains trimmed in gold brocade. Vermin had nibbled away the trim, and years of wear had taken the nap off the velvet, so the dull base weave bled through in patches.

A search backstage, both above and below, as well as the public corridors and restrooms, revealed nothing to interest the dogs. The teams met at the broken rear door where they originally entered, and jointly agreed the site was clear. It was time to move on to Bethlehem.

The area around Bethlehem Steel had seen a significant public makeover. Forty years before, the site had been strictly industrial—a sprawling iron giant located beside a river and sandwiched between a network of railway lines used to both pick up and discharge massive loads of materials. Now, the eastern end of the original property had been cleared to make room for a casino and outlet mall, while the land just south of the existing steel plant was converted to a concert stage adjacent to a visitor's center.

Wide parking lots surrounded the area, testifying to the expected crowds, but today, although the parking structure around the casino was full, the lots closer to the old steel mill and blast furnaces were mostly empty.

"We're lucky it's late in the year for outdoor activities," McCord said. "The place is mostly deserted."

"Did you look up as we were coming in?" Smaill pointed to the far side of the mill, where a raised concrete and steel platform hugged the south side of the property. "There's a tour going on up there now, probably twenty or so people in it."

"As long as they stay up there, we should be fine," Meg said.

The group walked along the rail lines, just outside the shiny, new chain-link fence separating the freshly paved parking lot from the rail land. During the drive from Allentown, McCord had selected a place for them to park, far from the abandoned steel mill, upriver behind a cold storage facility closed for business on the weekend. They were able to bend down an old section of fencing for the humans to climb and the dogs to easily jump over. From there, it was a brisk walk for a mile and a half down the packed gravel railway bed lining the tracks, skirting lines of boxcars, their gazes fixed on the tall rust-brown smoke and burn-off stacks towering over the complex. Everyone shouldered a backpack: Meg and Brian wore their standard go bags with everything they and the dogs needed for a prolonged search, McCord and Smaill carried tools and rescue gear, and Webb shouldered his paramedic pack in case Roth required medical assistance.

"Does anyone know what we're looking at?" Brian asked. "I don't know anything about industrial sites."

"I spent the last part of the trip boning up on this place and how it functioned," McCord said from the middle of the group, raising his voice to be heard. "Anyone else?" When no one spoke up, he said, "Looks like it's a good thing I did. Okay, we're looking at what little is left of what was once a massive steel plant." He swiveled and pointed behind them. "All the way over there, back to where we parked? That was originally Bethlehem Steel property. They razed huge sections of casting and storage buildings when they built the casino, the mall, and the rest. But they kept the iconic blast furnaces, the gas-blowing engine house, and one of the machine shops. The engine house is that long structure under the tour platform. Twelve tandem eighty-foot engines built in the 1890s that ran seven days a week, three hundred sixty-five days a year until the plant closed in 1998."

"They sure don't make 'em like they used to," quipped Brian.

"No kidding. If I get fifteen years out of a washing machine I buy today, I'll be lucky. Anyway, those engines pumped and compressed air for the blast furnaces. But I'd put searching that structure lower down on the list. One end of the building is open to allow visitors on the upper tour platform to see right in; it's unlikely anyone could be inside unnoticed. However, there is a lower level, so I wouldn't take it right off the list, just move it down toward the bottom. The machine shop is now part of the

National Museum of Industrial History, so that's even lower down the list since it's open for visitors as we speak. That leaves the blast furnaces."

Meg scanned the twisted mass of pipes, tanks, and smokestacks rising into the sky. "I assume that's what's in front of us?"

"Yes. Blast furnace primer in sixty seconds so you know what we're walking into. You can't make steel until you can make iron, so the point of a blast furnace is to mix and melt down the materials—ore, coke, and limestone—to make molten iron. You see the main structures that have those massive pipes and what looks like a cage at the top of them? Those are the blast furnaces. On the far side from us, each blast furnace has a steeply sloped ramp, or elevator, where carts full of the material would be pulled to the top of the furnace and then dumped in. The air from the gas-blowing engines would first go into those triplets of huge hot blast stove tanks for heating and then would be injected into the furnace about a third of the way up. As the materials drop through the heated furnace, they melt, producing waste gases that rise and are drawn off by the giant pipes you see up top, and then the molten iron pools in the bottom of the furnace. The waste gases go through scrubbers to clear out the particulate matter, and then the hot air is sent back into the blast stoves for reheating and then into the furnace again. Any residual waste gases are vented out through those tall smokestacks."

"Sounds like hot, miserable work," Smaill said.

"Oh, it was. But this is the company that first figured out how to mill I-beams. There'd be no Golden Gate or George Washington Bridges without them. Or the Empire State or Chrysler Buildings. Or the Hoover Dam. The steel for all of those projects came out of these five furnaces."

"Could someone be inside one of those furnaces?" Webb asked. "Are they accessible?"

"I don't think so. If the company needed access, they shut the whole furnace down and decommissioned it to get inside. These things are tightly sealed and pressure tested. There's no door in."

"So how does the molten metal get out?"

"There's a clay plug blocking a port at the bottom. When it's time, they drill the plug and the metal pours out. Pure molten iron is heavy, while the impurities, the slag, is lighter, so they literally skim the slag off the top and divert it to a separate collection spot. From what I understand, those two materials are collected underneath the furnaces. So we're going to need to search both levels."

"Got to get in first," Meg said. "Look at all these No Trespassing signs. In a place like this, there's got to be security we'll need to get around. I'm kind of worried we might get tagged."

"Maybe we should give Craig the heads-up," Brian suggested. "Not to clear our way ahead of time, there's no time for that, but in case we get caught."

Meg glanced over her shoulder at him and nodded in agreement. "That's a good idea." She pulled out her phone and speed-dialed Craig. When he came on the line, she explained why they'd chosen that location on the drive up and their concerns about security. "If we find Roth here, security is going to find out when we call in ambo and local PD support. I know we're here on our own time and not on an official case . . ."

"You get caught, or you find Roth, I'll clear the path for you. You're both carrying ID?"

"Yes."

"Good. Just try not to get caught. I'd rather call security

and report you found a kidnapping victim than have them call me to bellow about my teams."

"Understood. Thanks, Craig." Meg hung up. "He'll bail us out if we need it. But let's try not to. Okay, we're coming up on it now." They'd followed the rail lines behind the closed section of the property, and now Meg scanned the back of the stories-high metal structures and brick buildings that were part of the blast furnace complex. "I don't see any cameras. I see security lighting but no eyes in the sky."

"I don't either," Smaill said. "They likely use security patrols. It would be nearly impossible to effectively install security cameras in a place like this. Too complex, no uniform straight walls. Too many places to hide." He indicated the four-foot chain-link fence. "They didn't even try very hard here. They could have made this fence five or six feet high."

Webb flicked the thick, twisted wire pairs that topped the upper line of the fence. "Guess this is supposed to be a deterrent?"

Smaill let out a bark of a laugh. "Not to us." Then he stopped and looked down at the two dogs. "But what about them?"

"That's nothing," said Brian. "Meg, parkour style?"

Meg took in the two dogs, bright eyed and standing at attention. "That'll work."

"Here?"

Meg leaned over the fence and looked up and down the fence line. "Here's as good as anywhere. I'll go first." She shrugged out of her pack and thrust it into Webb's arms. "Hold this." Planting the toe of her boot into the fence, she quickly climbed it, hopping over the jagged top and landing lightly. She held out her arms to Webb. "Bag?" He tossed it to her, and she set it down a few feet away while quickly scanning the area for any sign of a security patrol. "Toss me your bag," she said to Brian, and then put it with hers out of the way. "Okay, do it."

Brian turned his back to Lacey and bent over, bending his knees slightly and bracing his hands on them. "Lacey, over!" The German shepherd retreated a few paces and then bolted for Brian, leaping onto his back and using him as a springboard to sail over the fence and land beside Meg.

McCord grinned at the dog prancing happily around Meg's feet. "Nice. More graceful than any of us."

"They tend to be. Hawk, over!" Meg commanded.

Hawk followed Lacey over the fence to land staring up at Meg with a happy grin and his tongue lolling from his mouth.

"Toss me your packs, then you guys are next."

Two minutes later, the group gathered behind one of the blast furnaces, the second in the long row of five.

Meg pulled out her cell phone. "First off, everyone's phones on vibrate. We'll need to communicate between the teams, but the last thing we need is someone's phone blaring 'The Boys Are Back in Town.' "

"Hey!" protested McCord. "Why am I the one giving us away?"

"Because you're an easy target. Now, let's stay in the same teams as at the opera house so each team has rescue gear in case anyone runs into trouble. I think we should start at the one end and work our way down the line."

"A systematic search is the best way to go," said Brian. "But to make the best use of the teams, let's start at opposite ends and work toward the middle. Each team clears a furnace and then moves on. We'll meet at that one." He pointed at the middle furnace and then dropped his hand to indicate the open lower level with large railcars underneath as if ready to catch their precious cargo. "Looks like we can gain entrance through the lower level."

"Sounds good. Okay, Brian—you, Lacey, and Chuck take the near furnace. Todd, McCord, and I will head for the far end, and we'll take it systematically. If you need to make contact, text first in case we can't get it right away. Then we can do a voice call if the coast is clear."

"Works for me," Brian said. "Come on, Lacey girl, let's see who we can find." He shouldered his pack, and then he and Smaill headed toward the easternmost furnace.

"Hawk, come." Meg headed west, with Webb and McCord falling into step beside her. They stayed close to the buildings, constantly watching for any sign of movement and listening for the slightest sound that might indicate a security patrol. They ducked under heavy metal scaffolding and around railcars and debris, darting between buildings until they made their way to the end. They had just cleared the last gap between furnaces when the sound of radio static buzzed through the quiet. Meg held up a fist for the men and gave Hawk the hand signal to hold as they all froze, barely breathing.

"Jack, is Larry in yet?" The man's voice held a note of disgust.

A radio crackled, then a disembodied voice said, "He just called in. Said he'll be another fifteen."

"Goddamn it. Of course he's late again. I'm going to do one more round past A and B, then I'll circle back to clock out. Tom out."

"He's coming this way," Meg hissed.

"Inside, quick." McCord ran toward the lower level of the furnace, disappearing between an I-beam coated in layers of dripping, solidified iron and a railcar holding what looked like two massive upside-down bells.

"Go!" Webb whispered as he gave her a push to follow McCord. "I'll make sure the coast is clear."

Meg gave Hawk's leash a tug and then ran with him to follow McCord. She ducked past the railcars and ran deeper into the building.

And was swallowed by darkness.

CHAPTER 9

Seccers: Urbex slang for security guards.

Saturday, October 27, 3:08 PM
Bethlehem Steel Works
Bethlehem, Pennsylvania

Meg slowed as the gloom closed in around her, far inside the lower level with open daylight seeming miles away. She tightened up on Hawk's leash and ducked under a metal staircase to crouch down, holding as still as possible. She strained to pick up any sound, but she heard only her own heart beating in her ears and her grating breath. Laying one hand on Hawk's back, she felt him quiver beneath her touch but otherwise remain motionless. She leaned out just far enough to see the entrance, feeling relatively secure there was no way anyone could see in far enough to spot her.

A dark form strolled by, transecting the distant block of light. After about forty-five seconds, the figure passed by again, this time in the opposite direction, and disappeared from view. Meg sank down beside Hawk, waiting until she could be sure the security guard was gone. A full minute passed, then she heard the scuff of a boot and "Meg? Webb?"

Meg stood and peered out again. Her eyes were becoming acclimatized to the lower light levels, and instead of blackness, now there were only shadows. "Here," she called quietly.

McCord popped out from behind a bank of heavy iron pipes with labeled valves. "Where's Webb?"

"Here." Webb stepped forward, framed by the light. "I stayed closer to the entrance to keep an eye on him. But he just passed right by, never even looking in. He went to the end of the property, turned around, and came back. If we assume this is furnace A, he's circling the one next to us and then heading to the security office, wherever that is."

"Hopefully not near the far end of the complex, or he may trip over Brian. But I'm going to let him know security is out and about, just in case." After sending Brian a quick text, Meg dug in her backpack to pull out the dirty sock sealed in a zippered bag, opened the bag, and offered the sock to Hawk. "Hawk, find Warren. Find." She loosened the leash and then stepped away to let her dog scent the air. He moved through the lower level in straight lines, telling Meg he didn't have the scent yet.

He stopped momentarily beside one of the railcars with the giant vats and gave a curious sniff.

"Could someone be inside?" Webb studied the open lip of the vat, easily ten or eleven feet in the air.

"Hawk's not saying there is. These things are massive. What were they for?"

"Liquid slag." McCord laid a hand on the cast-steel vat. "They'd take them by rail off to a distant pit and dump them. The solidified slag later became a component of cement. The other cars, the ones that look like mini subs with a hole in the top, those were for the molten iron and went for further smelting into steel. I don't think anyone would fit easily into one of those cars."

Webb watched Hawk cast about for a few moments. "He's not picking up on anything, is he?"

"No. We've done the circuit. Let's move up a level. Maybe try the flight of stairs I hid behind."

They had a bad moment when they came to a door at the top of the stairs that seemed locked, but it gave way as soon as Webb put his shoulder into it. It creaked open on long-disused hinges, and they squeezed through the smallest gap possible to avoid making any more noise than necessary.

Up on the first floor, they found themselves inside a large, open space where the body of the furnace rose up and out of sight through the metal roof. The furnace itself had a round base sitting on a squat, cylindrical stem encircled by coils of pipes and valves. A cracked rubber hose lay in a tangled pile at the base near an iron-splashed circular opening into the furnace. Under the port lay a deep channel cut into the floor that ran into the next room before splitting into two. A wide, retractable paddle hung on a lever at the Y to separate the slag from the molten iron before they flowed into separate vessels below.

"Has Hawk detected anything?" McCord asked.

Meg shook her head. Hawk wasn't showing any of his usual signs of alertness to signal he had the scent. She pulled the bagged laundry out again and offered it to him along with the hand signal for "find." He led the way around the furnace, trotting through a trail of sunlit dust motes filtering through a row of tagged water pipes lined up like jail bars. But his manner remained relaxed, his nose working, casting about for one particular scent. A scent Meg knew wasn't present.

They cleared the main level, exploring rusting catwalks of industrial mesh that vibrated with every carefully placed step, control rooms filled with graffiti-covered panels and buttons, and an abandoned office with a time clock forever frozen at 3:17 and a forgotten pair of safety glasses, set down as if the owner would be returning momentarily to pick them up and keep working. With great care, Webb inched his way up a half flight of the tiers of external steps that slunk up the outside of the blast furnace, using Meg's binoculars to peer along the open metal staircase. They didn't dare climb the steps, or send Hawk up, for fear of being spotted by security or a tour group, but Webb felt confident there was nothing up that staircase. And, as he rightfully stated, anyone going up there to abandon the victim would also be too visible for comfort.

Meg pulled out her phone and texted Brian:

Cleared first furnace. Moving on to second. Update?

A few minutes later, a return message:

Ditto. Already searching #2.

Moving between the furnaces on the upper level meant crossing a solid steel catwalk tucked behind a trio of massive blast stove tanks that rose so high they blocked the sun, sending an autumn chill down Meg's spine. The tanks separated the search team from the concrete tour platform, and the group had to freeze for several heart-thudding minutes that felt ten times as long when a tour guide's voice filtered through to them, describing the construction of the original blast furnace and stove tanks in 1914. Webb and McCord huddled together against the rail behind one tank while Meg crouched down next to Hawk behind the next. As the guide's voice droned on, repeating history she'd no doubt described hundreds of times previously, Meg found herself considering the oily, rainbow-like sheen that coated the outside of the tanks, the only spot of blooming color in an otherwise dull, rusted landscape.

Finally, the guide and her tour moved on, and the team waited a full two minutes before daring to continue without detection. Once inside the next structure, the search began anew.

They had just cleared the second furnace when the phone in Meg's pocket vibrated. She opened Brian's text.

We found him. Already gone.

Meg's muttered curse caught the attention of both men, who stopped to look at her.

"Brian found him. We weren't in time. Again." The single word was full of frustrated bitterness. Meg bent over her phone.

We'll come to you. Where are you?

Second blast furnace. Upper level. On one of the support maintenance catwalks for the furnace. I'll call Craig to let him know.

"We need to get to the second furnace in from their end," she said.

"It'll be easiest to get there from outside." McCord pointed to a three-sided railing grouped around a gap at the far end. "That's probably the staircase down. Then we need to skirt the back fence down the property."

"While not being seen." Webb stepped over a forlorn rubber boot, toppled and dust covered in the middle of the floor. "We're going to have to let security know, but it would be better not to be caught in the act."

"Agreed."

They found themselves downstairs in a familiar landscape of rail tracks, slag vats, and molten metal cars, and quickly moved through the rusted graveyard toward daylight.

McCord stopped at the outer boundary and held up a hand as he leaned out, scanning up and down the row. "We're clear."

They quickly covered the ground to the far end, stopping between complexes to watch for security guards while counting the towering rise of furnaces as they went.

"This should be it here." Webb stepped into the shade of the lower level. "Assuming they're all built similarly, we should be able to get up through a staircase here."

Minutes later, they stood beside the bulk of the blast furnace.

"I don't see them." McCord stared upwards, looking for the catwalk. "How high up are they?"

"Not sure. But Hawk will take us there. Hawk." Meg waited as Hawk looked up to meet her eyes. "Good boy. Find Lacey."

Hawk immediately trotted around the furnace, jumping over channels and around diverters. As they circled around to the far side of the furnace, Meg spotted a staircase that rose high into the pipes. Hawk arrowed directly for the steps and started up without hesitating. Meg paused at the bottom, one hand on the railing, and looked up to find Brian two stories above her, waving madly. She waved back and followed Hawk. The staircase wobbled with every step and had a decided air of instability.

Meg was just starting the second flight of steps when an ear-splitting *clang* rang out. She whipped around, keeping her balance with one hand clutching the grimy handrail, to find McCord behind her, frowning down over the railing. "What was that?" she hissed.

McCord grimaced. "Maybe a bolt came off the underside? I didn't kick anything. But these stairs feel as if they are coming apart at the seams. Hopefully security didn't hear it."

"If they did, I hope Craig has already told them we're on-site conducting an investigation."

They climbed the rest of the way without incident and met Brian, Lacey, and Smaill on the catwalk.

Meg looked past Brian to the floor of the catwalk. A slender, balding elderly man lay on his side on the platform near the upper level of the furnace, one hand dangling lifelessly over the edge, his skin a sickly gray. "Stupid question, but you've checked him for signs of life?"

"First thing we did." Brian laid his hand on Lacey's

head. "She led us right to him, with no hesitation as soon as we made it to this building. I tried for a pulse, then Smaill did, but there's no use. The body is cold to the touch. He's only been missing a day, but he's been dead for hours now, maybe even since last night. We backed off to preserve the crime scene."

"You got through to Craig?"

"Yes. He's alerting local authorities to come and take over. And he's calling security so they'll know they have people incoming."

"Thanks." Meg bent and stroked a hand down Lacey's silky fur, earning an enthusiastic tail wag. "Good job, Lacey girl."

"Security! Don't move!"

Meg froze, her hand partway down Lacey's back, but her eyes cut to the floor below them. A single man dressed in black stood, feet planted, his gun held in both hands and fixed on them unwaveringly.

She straightened slowly, raising both hands into the air. "FBI," she called down. "We're here on a case and have identification."

"You're trespassing."

"We're FBI," she repeated slowly. She glanced at Brian to find the same thought mirrored in his eyes. *Power-hungry rent-a-cop*. "Can I show you my identification?" She dropped one hand toward her pocket and her flip case.

"Keep them up!" the man bellowed, reaching for the radio on his belt. "I'm calling in backup."

He was raising the radio to his mouth when it crackled to life. "Larry, I need you to go to furnace D. The FBI just contacted us. There are two K-9 teams on-site for a murder investigation, and they've identified a victim on one of the catwalks. They'd like our support in bringing in Bethlehem PD and EMS."

"You said K-9 teams?"

"Yeah, you know, like dogs?"

Larry squinted up at them, and Meg quietly called Hawk over so he was visible from below.

"I'm there now," Larry said. "I have them. PD is coming?"

The radio crackled, and part of the first word was lost in static. "—mont said he was calling them next, but he wanted to make sure we knew they were on-site. He said he was sorry they didn't let us know before the teams got on-site, but they were following an active lead and didn't know where they'd end up."

"Ten-four. Larry out." He clipped his radio on his belt and looked up.

He hesitated briefly, and Meg could see the stubborn displeasure on his face before he finally lowered his gun. Only then did Meg lower her hands. *Seriously unhappy he's not going to be a hero today.* Turning back to the group, she rolled her eyes, then pasted on a bright smile. "Come on, Hawk. Come be an ambassador for the FBI." With her dog at her side, she started down the flight of stairs to meet the disgruntled security guard halfway.

CHAPTER 10

Chatière: Literally a "cat hole"; used to squeeze in or out of a tunnel.

Friday, November 2, 9:44 AM
14th Street NW
Washington, DC

Meg's cell phone rang as she was driving past the Washington Monument. A quick glance at the number displayed on her dash told her she didn't recognize the caller.

"Jennings."

"It's Mac Turner of the Bethlehem PD."

"Officer Turner, it's good to hear from you. Thank you again for your help last week. You smoothed over a very awkward situation."

"Just Mac, please. No need to stand on ceremony. And I know Larry. He's a good guy, just a little overzealous. He wanted to be a cop, but the stars didn't quite align for him there. He does this instead and takes it *very* seriously."

"He does, indeed. What can I do for you, Mac?"

"Actually, it's what I can do for you. I know the powers that be are still figuring out who this case belongs to, but I wanted to give you a heads-up; otherwise, you might not hear for days or weeks. We have the tox results back."

"Already? Who did you pay off?"

Turner's warm laugh carried clearly over the line. "That may be how you have to play it in DC, but we're a lot smaller here. Yes, there's a backlog, but we don't get so many suspicious deaths, so those cases get bumped way up the line. And, I admit, I called in a favor with this one to get the results faster."

"I'll say. We have a previous victim from almost a month ago, and I'm pretty sure results aren't back yet, because my SSA would let me know as soon as they hit his desk. So, what does the report say?"

"It lists cause of death as a chemical called difethialone."

"I'm not familiar with that one." Meg drove with the flow of traffic on Constitution Avenue and between the twin Federalist structures of the US Department of Commerce and the Ronald Reagan Building and International Trade Center. "That's a poison?"

"Essentially. It's an anticoagulant that in high doses is used as a poison. Specifically, a rat poison."

Some of Meg's positive energy drained away. "Rat poison? A common poison that's cheap, plentiful, and sold everywhere. In other words, untraceable."

"Most rat poison is exactly that. But, as I understand it, this stuff has been banned by the EPA since 2008 and off the residential market since then."

"You know a substance is bad news when the EPA bans it. Any information on why?"

"It was among a group of really nasty and long-lasting pesticides the EPA removed from residential use, so now it's available only to commercial exterminators."

Hope sparked in Meg again. "If it's a chemical with those kinds of restrictions, there's likely a way of tracing those purchases. Our killer may be someone who works with industrial pesticides."

"Maybe. Of course, it could also be someone who found an ancient can of the stuff in a corner of his garage and is using it to kill humans instead of rodents. If it has any stability, an old stock like that could remain active and toxic for a long time."

"Did your ME say how fast this stuff works? Or any theories on how it was delivered?"

"Stomach contents agreed with the evidence of his last meal we found in his kitchen," said Mac. "But on top of that, they found 190-proof grain alcohol. According to the ME, difethialone isn't soluble in water but is soluble in organic solvents."

"Meaning alcohol."

"And the higher the concentration, the better. The booze could also have the secondary side effect of possibly making the victim more pliable. Meg, this poison doesn't kill instantly. Depending on how much is given, it could take hours, or maybe even up to a day. Trace evidence on the clothes also shows low levels of difethialone."

"Meaning some of it spilled while the perp was forcing it down Mr. Roth's throat," Meg reasoned. She signaled her turn and made a right onto F Street NW. "We've been wondering all along if the victims were alive or dead when they were left in the urbex sites. Because of the time delay, this means it's almost a surety they were alive. But it's doubtful the suspect waited until arriving at the dump site to administer the poison. He probably gave the poison somewhere private, so by the time he got Roth to Bethlehem Steel, he was already unwell. Less chance he'd be able to escape and get to help."

"From what we've learned about Warren Roth, he was

mobile, so he should have been able to make it down those stairs."

"Further proof that he was already failing by the time he was abandoned. Goddamn it, I want this guy. Leaving the frail and defenseless to die alone in the dark in a strange place? A person's last minutes shouldn't be terrified and helpless. Have you got a copy of the report you can send me by email?"

"Sure do. Give me your email address and I'll do it now."

"I'll give you my SSA's as well." She spelled out both email addresses. "I'm headed into the office now, and we can discuss it as soon as I get to the unit."

"You going to make a run for jurisdiction?"

"We are. We're going to get it, too, based on what we have. I'll have my SSA put some pressure on getting the other autopsy results. If that's the same poison, or class of poison, then we have a solid case for cross-border killing, and that makes it ours."

"I've forwarded the ME's report to your email addresses. Good luck with it. If you have time, let me know how it goes. It may not be our case anymore, but I want to know Roth gets the justice he deserves."

"That's a promise, Mac. Thanks." Meg hung up and turned onto 10th Street NW, the massive bulk of the J. Edgar Hoover Building rising high on her left. She speed-dialed Craig and started talking as soon as he picked up. "Check your email. You should have the autopsy report for Warren Roth."

There was moment of silence, then, "I've got it."

"The ME says Roth was killed with rat poison. I'm pulling into the parking garage. Can we lean on autopsy results for Donna Parker? It's been about a month, and if these two victims line up, we can make a case for jurisdiction. I want this one, Craig."

"I hear you. I do, too. If we can match COD on both victims, I'll be able to make it happen. This may be too soon, though. You know most tox results take four to six weeks to come in."

"Do you think it will be an impediment if we can't tie together COD?"

"Maybe. Maybe not. There are enough similarities in the unique body dump sites with victims that I can make a case for the potential of a common killer. Let me make some calls. See you in a few." The line went dead.

Meg glanced into the back of her SUV, where Hawk sat, ears perked as if listening to the conversation while he gazed out the windshield through the open emergency exit between the cab and his compartment. "You hear that, Hawk, buddy? Craig's going to do the heavy lifting to make sure this is our case. Then we're going to get this killer."

CHAPTER 11

Abseiling: A controlled vertical descent by rope.

Friday, November 2, 2:35 PM
Forensic Canine Unit, J. Edgar Hoover Building
Washington, DC

"Meg? Got a minute?"

Meg looked up to see Craig leaning out his office door. "Sure." She pushed away from her desk and stood, Hawk coming to his feet to join her.

"Bring Brian, too." Craig scanned the office. "Anyone else here? Scott? Lauren?"

"No, but I can bring them up to speed if you want. Let me grab Brian and we'll be right in."

"Bring a chair with you." Craig rolled his eyes. "Someday, I swear, I'm going to get us a conference room."

"So you keep saying. Give us two minutes."

A few minutes later, Meg, Brian, and the dogs entered Craig's office to find him seated across from a petite brunette in a navy business suit. She stood and offered her hand with a wide smile. "Hi. Agent Kate Moore."

"Agent Moore." Meg shook hands. "I'm Meg Jennings. This"—she held out a hand to Brian, who entered the office behind her, pushing his desk chair—"is Brian Foster. And Hawk and Lacey."

Meg stood aside so the new agent and Brian could shake hands, and then Brian positioned his chair in the empty space by the door. Meg and Agent Moore took the two chairs opposite Craig's desk.

"My apologies for the small space," Craig said. "Most of the time we're meeting about cases out in the field, so this is the biggest room we have."

"This is just fine." Agent Moore's voice held a smoky, melodic quality with a gentle overlay of Tennessee. "Lots of room for us all." She looked down at the dogs, sitting quietly at their handlers' feet. "Can I say hi to the dogs?"

"Absolutely." Meg gave Hawk the hand signal to stand. "Hawk, go and say hi to Agent Moore."

Hawk politely sat in front of the agent and offered his right paw to her. She solemnly shook, then repeated the action with Lacey. "These guys put my dogs to shame."

"Dogs?" Meg accentuated the plural.

"I have two King Charles spaniels at home. They're well behaved, but not *this* well behaved." She looked up at Craig. "Would you like me to start?" When he gave her a wave to go ahead, she turned to face Meg and Brian. "First of all, call me Kate. We're going to be a team and working this case together, so we might as well start off on the right foot. I've been assigned the case concerning the kidnapping and murder of an as-yet-to-be-determined number of senior citizens."

Meg's gaze flicked to Craig, and he nodded in response. He'd come through for them again, not only getting an agent assigned but ensuring that his people stayed involved.

"I understand you were both involved in victim discovery?" Kate continued.

"Yes. Hawk and I found Donna Parker entirely by chance. But after we began to suspect that there might be more killings, Craig stayed on top of reports of missing seniors. When Warren Roth went missing, Brian and Lacey assisted with the search effort and were instrumental in recovering Mr. Roth's body." She glanced at Craig. "Were you able to get the tox results for Donna Parker?"

"I tried, but they're not ready yet. They'll send them as soon as they can."

"We can work around them until they come in." Kate opened the folder on her lap and flipped through the pages. "Brian, you and Lacey discovered Mr. Roth?"

"Yes." Brian rubbed Lacey's back. "Though Lacey did the heavy lifting."

"That was good work by y'all. SSA Beaumont brought this case forward with the information that one of Meg's contacts suggested other victims. I wasn't sure about the strength of the other information, but I used it as a springboard."

"My 'contact' is Clay McCord, an investigative reporter for the *Washington Post*," Meg said. "I'd say that information is pretty strong."

Kate pulled a pen out of her breast pocket and jotted down McCord's name on one of her notes. "I've heard of him, and I'd agree. We don't usually encourage reporters to be involved in our cases, though."

"McCord won't be a problem," Craig interjected. "He's worked with us on several cases in the past, he has solid contacts, and he knows how to keep his mouth shut until told otherwise. He can be . . . useful."

Meg chuckled. "I won't tell him you said that."

Kate watched the exchange with a cocked eyebrow. "I'll keep him in mind." Her smile melted away. "But I've already done some groundwork of my own, and it's not encouraging."

"That doesn't sound good," Brian said. "What do you mean?"

Kate pulled a list from the folder. "I found a number of missing seniors who have never been found, and others where the body was recovered under circumstances similar to the two victims we know about."

"How big a number?"

"Twenty-three."

Brian gave a low whistle and exchanged glances with Meg. "Surely that can't all be the work of one guy. That would be one hell of a spree if it was."

"Probably not," Meg agreed, "but some of them could be. Some of the others could be unfortunate events that haven't been resolved yet." She held out a hand to Kate. "May I see the list?"

"Sure." Kate handed the list to Meg. "I don't even know if that's all of them."

Meg scanned the list, a knot growing in her stomach over the number of names and locations. "Craig, have you still got that national map in your desk?"

Craig opened a drawer, rummaged for a moment, and pulled out the folded map. He extended it across his desk. "What do you want it for?"

"You'll see. Can I borrow some arrow flags, too?"

"Sure." He found those and handed them over as well.

"Tape?"

He didn't even comment, just pulled out a roll of Scotch tape.

Brian looked over Meg's shoulder at the list. Then he plucked the map out of her hands and stood.

"Where are you going?"

"I see what you're doing. I'm helping get started." Brian stepped over Lacey, picked a section of wall by the door, and unfolded the map, holding it in place while craning his neck to look back at Meg. "This good?"

"Perfect." While Brian taped the map to the wall, Meg handed the list to Kate. "Let's start at the top. Can you read them to me one by one?" The *thump* of a desk drawer shutting drew her gaze toward Craig.

He held a fine black marker across the desk to her. "Write the victim name and the date of disappearance on a flag for easy reference. Write the name and the date of discovery on a second color-matched flag. Those go on the locations where they disappeared and where they were found, if they were found. Hopefully you won't have similar colored multiple pairs in the same state."

Meg smiled her appreciation and took the marker.

They grouped around the map, Kate reading out each name and location and Meg writing down the name and dates on arrow flags, while Craig called up coordinates on his phone and Brian located them on the paper map. It took a full half hour, and when all the data were pinned on the map, they stood back.

Brian crossed his arms over his chest and stared at the map. "I know these may not all be our victims, but if even only a fraction of them are, added to our existing victims, we have a real problem."

Hawk bumped against Meg's legs, and she reached down to stroke her hand along his head. She knew his sensitive nature, and knew he was picking up on the sudden tension in the room. She dragged her chair around to face the map and sat down, letting Hawk settle between her knees while she studied the map.

Flags pierced the map from New Hampshire in the northeast, through Massachusetts, Rhode Island, Connecticut, New York, and Pennsylvania, then westward through Ohio, Kentucky, Indiana, and Illinois over an extended period.

Twenty-three possible victims. Ten states. Over four years.

"I know these may not all be case related, but as Brian said, if even a fraction of them are, it's a real problem. How did this stay under the radar for so long?"

Kate tucked a hank of her shoulder-length bob behind her ear. "Cross-border disappearances. Older victims who don't seem to generate the same outrage as younger ones. Some victims didn't have family support and weren't even noted as missing until after a body was found. And, as we've said, these may not all be victims related to this case."

"How many victims were recovered with actual physical remains?" Craig asked.

Kate ran a finger down her notes. "Eighteen."

"How many had autopsies? Better yet, how many had tox screens run?"

"I'm going to need to dig for that. I've just been assigned to the case, so what I have so far is really bare bones."

"Then you're not going to know this, either, but I wonder how many were buried versus cremated, and if we could get a court order to exhume them and run a tox screen?"

Kate made a note on the page in a flourishing hand. "I don't know, but I'm fixin' to find out." She took in the map. "This is big, and could easily be bigger than what we're looking at now."

Meg followed her gaze to the map. So many names, dates, and places.

How many more would there be before they caught the person responsible?

CHAPTER 12

First Service: The time of the first passenger train departure in the morning. Access to abandoned underground rail sites becomes much more dangerous once scheduled service begins, since rail platforms are crowded with commuters and the third rail providing power to electric trains is energized.

Monday, November 5, 8:47 AM
Jennings residence
Arlington, Virginia

Meg's cell phone rang as she was loading her breakfast dishes into the dishwasher. Cara scooped it up and slid it across the island to her.

"Thanks." Meg glanced at the caller ID on the screen—Kate Moore. "Morning, Kate."

"Morning. Where are you?"

Meg's gaze flicked to Cara at the abrupt end of pleasantries. "I'm at home still. What's happened?"

"We have a missing senior. A resident of Hampden Manor, on the outskirts of Baltimore. They specialize in Alzheimer's patients. One of their residents, seventy-three-year-old Mrs. Bahni Devar, had breakfast with other residents at their first seating at seven this morning. She missed an eight-fifteen appointment with a social worker but wasn't in her room, and they couldn't locate her in common areas. They did a grounds search because their residents sometimes wander the property a bit. They're not overly mobile, so they can't get far, but some of them can get confused and turned around, so they wanted to find her quickly. One of the staff thought to check the security cameras to give them a direction if she'd just wandered off."

"She didn't just wander off, did she?" Anticipating the direction of the conversation, Meg went to the mudroom and grabbed her hiking boots and her go bag, then carried them back into the kitchen. Wedging her phone between her ear and her shoulder, she opened the bag and sorted through it, double-checking the contents.

"No. The camera recorded her being led out of a side door of the building by a workman in coveralls, wearing a baseball hat pulled down low so his face was hidden."

"Where did they go?"

"They walked out of camera range."

Meg's head snapped up so fast she had to juggle the phone to keep it from slipping. "On foot? You have a direction?"

"Yes and yes. Can you go?"

"Hawk and I can leave from here." At the sound of his name, Hawk's head rose from where he dozed on the dog bed in the corner of the kitchen. She gave him the hand signal to come. "Can you text me the address?"

"Yes. And let me call Craig for you. I'll clear it with him that you're heading out."

"Thanks. Call me if you have any problems with him. Otherwise, if I don't hear from you, I'll assume he green-lit the search." She glanced at the clock on the stove. "At this time of the morning, it's going to take me a good hour and a half to get there."

"Do you need anyone else to help?"

"It's up to Craig to manage the deployment, and I'm not

even sure who else is available. It may literally just be me. Do me one more thing?"

"Name it."

"Call Hampden Manor and ask them to collect a few small pieces of dirty laundry from Mrs. Devar's room. A shirt, a pair of socks, anything, but it needs to have been worn. Clean won't help us. We'll use it to give Hawk her scent. Tell them also to use gloves so they don't get their own scent on it, and to seal it in a zippered plastic bag."

"Laundry. Gloves. Bag. Check."

Meg zipped her bag shut. "Thanks. Hawk and I are walking out the door now."

"Good hunting." Kate hung up.

Meg pulled out a chair and sat to lace up her hiking boots.

"Someone else has disappeared?" Cara asked.

"Just this morning. Was escorted out of the building by a worker, or someone posing as one."

"You think that's the perp?"

"I think there's a good chance it is. We'll start there, but if this situation is anything like the others, he's already transporting her somewhere else. The question is, where?" Meg looked up as she jammed her foot into the second boot. "I'm going to call McCord to see if he can make any suggestions. I'd call Chuck, but he's on shift this morning with Todd, and I know how that goes. They don't sit around the firehouse much. If McCord can't come up with anything, then I'll call Chuck."

"Knowing Clay, he'll hit some urbex boards and get you everything you need."

"I'm counting on it." Meg stood and shouldered her pack.

"Here." Cara handed her a travel mug of coffee. "For an extra boost on the road."

Meg grinned at her. "Who needs a wife? A sister is much better."

Minutes later, she and Hawk were in the SUV, headed for I-395 to start their journey northeast. Using the hands-free controls in the SUV, Meg called McCord. He answered on the third ring, and she could hear the buzz of the *Washington Post* newsroom behind him. "It's Meg. Have you got a minute? Or thirty?"

"Nothing on the books for the morning. What do you need?"

"We have a missing senior. I'm en route to the facility she disappeared from—an Alzheimer's residence. But I need some remote research help while I'm on the road."

"I'm your man. What do you know so far?"

Meg updated him on the little she knew. "I'm betting there's essentially zero chance we're going to find Mrs. Devar on-site. If she's going to be poisoned with the same rat poison as Warren Roth, then there's a window, but it's a small one. I need a list of places in the area where the suspect might leave her."

"I can do that. Search radius?"

Meg pictured the map that still hung in Craig's office with its color-matched flags and the distance between them. "Twenty miles is probably more than enough, but let's say twenty-five, just in case. Unfortunately, that's going to include all of Baltimore." She could hear the click of McCord's keyboard as he made notes.

"That's definitely going to make the list longer. How much time do I have?"

Meg glanced at the dash. "I'm an hour out, maybe more if I hit traffic. Hawk and I will start the search as soon as we get there, and that could take anywhere from ten minutes to an hour."

"I'll have a list ready for you in ninety minutes, with a

prioritized search order like last time. Is anyone else with you?"

"So far it's just me. Let's assume it stays that way until you hear otherwise."

"Got it. Call me when you can." Then he was gone.

Meg merged onto I-395 and promptly had to slow down with the increased traffic. Pushing away the urge to hammer her horn—she needed to move, damn it—she settled for darting through traffic, desperately trying for the fastest route. But every few minutes she found herself sneaking glances at the dashboard clock, the knot in her stomach growing tighter as the minutes ticked past.

CHAPTER 13

Step Irons: Metal rungs built into a masonry wall to act as a ladder.

Monday, November 5, 10:06 AM
Hampden Manor
Baltimore, Maryland

Hawk picked up the scent on the walkway immediately, leaving Meg to jog behind, still clutching the plastic bag containing several pieces of dirty laundry in one hand and his leash in the other. She let the lead play out, giving Hawk full freedom to weave back and forth across the scent cone, trying to locate the outer edges. The closer they got to the source, the narrower the cone would become, funneling them directly to their goal.

From the side door, Hawk skirted a patio filled with tables and padded lounge chairs, heading for the tree line that bordered the property to the west. Meg glanced at her watch, noting how much faster they'd arrived than originally anticipated. When she'd been pulled over for doing seventy-five miles per hour in a fifty-five zone on the Baltimore-Washington Parkway, she thought she'd made a grave error that would cost entirely too much time. But a fast explanation, a flash of her FBI badge, and a quick glance at Hawk's FBI vest was all that was needed to earn her a Maryland State Police escort to the Hampden neighborhood of Baltimore, complete with lights and siren. Losing four minutes had gained her twenty.

Hawk darted into the forest, down a path so narrow that Meg would have missed it had she been doing a visual search. But his nose led them where her eyes could not, and soon Meg was pushing through branches, many of which were snapped off three or four feet above the ground. Fall's brilliant colors sparkled all around them, and the air was rich with the earthy scents of fallen leaves and autumn rain. Dry leaves crunched under her boots, and small animals scurried in the bushes as they prepared for the coming winter.

Meg paused briefly to examine the branch of a sapling, dangling drunkenly from where it was broken nearly in two, observing the green wood beneath the torn bark. *Someone's been through here recently. Or, more likely, two someones.*

Hawk paused momentarily in a small area where the undergrowth gave way to ground cover, now mostly carpeted in bright leaves. But when he was about to continue, Meg stopped him with a single command. She pulled out her phone and took a quick photo of the area, taking ten seconds to observe the disturbed leaves, pushed aside to reveal the moist earth and protruding roots below. More tellingly, she noted the single handprint pressed into the mud.

You struggled away from him here and fell. You fought him before he got you under control again. Meg felt a flush of pride for the spirit of the older woman, likely confused and scared out of her mind but still showing a spark of gutsy spunk. *Hang on, Mrs. Devar. We're coming for you.*

"Hawk, find her."

Hawk resumed his sprint through the forest.

Three minutes later, they broke out of the trees onto a

back road, the tarmac surface rippled and cracked. Hawk banked right and followed the gravel shoulder for thirty feet, then stopped, casting about for the scent. He looked up at Meg and whined.

She crouched down next to him. "You've lost her, haven't you?" As she stroked a hand over Hawk's exercise-warmed fur, she studied the road around them. And froze when she realized they were standing in the middle of the evidence. She slowly stood. "Hawk, come." Carefully stepping onto the solid surface of the road in overlarge strides, Meg turned to look again at the shoulder. Twin ruts dug into the gravel with clearly defined bare spots where the tires had spun, leaving behind a spray of rocks. It was the distinct signature of a vehicle, parked off-road and leaving in a rush.

"Hawk, sit. Stay." Meg dropped the leash to pool at his feet and walked fifteen feet down the road, studying the pavement. Crouching down, she examined the dark smears marring the surface. The tire tread patterns were clear, and between that and the ruts in the gravel, Meg knew a sharp team of crime scene techs could determine chassis size and tire type, and might even be able to come back with vehicle identification. "Gotcha, you bastard."

She straightened and pulled out her cell phone to text McCord.

Vic is gone, taken in a vehicle. Will call in 10 mins. Be ready with the list.

Next she called Craig to request a crime scene team to process the site, telling him she wouldn't be able to wait for them. She gave him the exact coordinates and described the scene. After hanging up, she followed his request to take and forward pictures of the scene in case anyone disturbed the area before the techs arrived.

Less than ten minutes later, Meg and Hawk had retraced their steps through the trees and were back in the SUV.

She called McCord. "Talk to me, McCord, where am I going?"

"You want the whole list?"

"I want the first one so I can put the address in my phone and get started. I'm two or three hours behind them. I'm never going to catch the suspect, but Mrs. Devar might still be saved."

"Then I'm going to send you to the Bowie Meat Packing Plant in Lansdowne. You're only twenty minutes away." He rattled off the address, which Meg typed into her phone and then had Google Maps direct her route as they sped down the driveway.

"I'm on the way. Tell me about this plant and why it's number one. Chuck says it helps him to know about a place before he goes in. Gives him an idea of the setup and potential hazards before he steps into it. And, for now, I'm on my own, so I want everything you can give me."

"This may be more info than you need, but better to know too much than too little in this case. The Bowie Meat Packing Company was founded in the 1860s at a time when refrigeration was a challenge, to say the least. To expedite transport of meats while they were still fresh, the main plant was located in Chicago as part of the city's massive stockyards. Served by the rail lines, they processed up to fifty thousand hogs a day."

Meg was struck silent for a moment. "Fifty thousand. That's hard to wrap your head around."

"Sure is, especially when you consider it was done one hundred percent by hand, and that number doesn't include beef processing. The company pioneered the assembly line and is generally credited for giving Henry Ford the idea how to set up his car plant in Detroit. Anyway, they had some smaller locations, always situated beside rail lines to allow for the transport of live animals in and butchered meats out. They located their Baltimore plant beside the old

Baltimore and Ohio rail line. Move the animals in, slaughter and process them, and then pack the butchered meat into refrigerated railcars and move it out."

"You just said refrigeration was hard to come by."

"This was decades later. By the early twentieth century, when this plant opened, they'd figured out how to make ice for industrial refrigeration. The plant opened in 1903 and went gangbusters until the Great Depression. Then the company nearly folded. They had to let go of most of their workforce, but they managed to stay in business. They hit their stride again during World War II, when canned meat became a military staple. But the jobs were nonunion and low paying, so workers went elsewhere. In the end they couldn't pay more and stay competitive, and the plant finally closed in 1966."

"It's been closed for half a century? That seems hard to believe."

"Hard or not, there you have it. It's a pretty big complex. Several connected brick buildings and its own power generation plant with double smokestacks because this was before municipal power grids. Huge steam engines powered the refrigeration units. It's going to be a lot of area to cover. Will you be on your own?"

"Yes. Everyone else is already out on other search calls, but Craig's going to redirect them to me if they become free in the next little while. So why this place specifically?"

"As opposed to the others on the list? Partly because of its location—it's in an industrial area, southwest of town with a few other shuttered businesses, so it's probably not too difficult to get in and out of unnoticed. Add to that, if Mrs. Devar actually managed to escape the building, there isn't a neighborhood full of people around for assistance—just a few huge properties spread far apart. Also, that section of the B&O rail line was sold to a big transportation company, so it's used only for industrial rail transport and not passengers. The other factor that puts this one at the top of my list is how old it is and how long it's been closed. It's considered to be a dangerous place for urbex—rotten floors, collapsing staircases, etcetera. In fact, it's due for demolition in the near future to make way for some new warehouse that will benefit from the proximity to the rail lines."

"If it was that treacherous, you'd think that would be a draw to the people who do urban exploration."

"You mean urbexers."

"Urbexers?"

"Yeah, urbexers. People who do it for fun and the challenge. I've been forced to pick up the lingo. They also have their own slogan: Pics or it didn't happen. Which has been great, because I can check out these places remotely to see if they'd be good body dump sites. Anyway, you're right, the danger is a definite draw to some, but this happens to be the site of an urbexer death a few years ago, so they consider the place to have bad juju."

"They're superstitious?"

"They can be."

"What happened? So I know what to avoid while we're in there."

"As long as you don't climb the smokestack, you should be fine. And as impressive as Hawk is, he's not so amazing that he'd be able to climb iron rungs mortared into brick as a ladder. The two smokestacks are each over two hundred feet tall. An urbexer climbed one, and just as he reached the top, one of the rungs came loose. He had most of his weight on it and couldn't catch himself when it gave way. Fell about eighteen stories, landed on the roof, went right through it, and fell another four or five stories down. He was gone by the time his buddies found him. But considering you're going in there alone, you need to be careful. Really careful.

If you want me to stay on the line with you as a virtual spotter, I'm here."

"That might not be a bad idea. I can keep you updated as to where we are, and if we run into trouble, you'll know immediately and can call for assistance. What other places are on the list if the meat-packing plant doesn't pan out?"

"I have another four locations picked out—a hotel, a clinic, and two more industrial sites, but let's start here. It's really the most likely site for the killer's task."

"That works for me. I estimate arriving in fifteen minutes. Let me call you when I get there."

"I'll be here. When you get there, you'll have to park on the road in front, as it's completely fenced, but according to blog sites, you'll find a break in the fence line around the back of the complex, which will give you access to the whole site."

"Great, thanks. Talk to you when I'm on the property."

"Ten-four." He hung up.

Meg glanced at the map, gauged the time it would take at the calculated speed limit, imagined the terrified older woman slowly bleeding out, and pressed down harder on the accelerator.

Hang on. Don't let go.

We're coming.

CHAPTER 14

Edgework: Undertaking a life-threatening risk for no reason other than to feel "the edge."

Monday, November 5, 10:55 AM
Bowie Meat Packing Plant
Lansdowne, Maryland

"I'm here." Meg settled her pack more securely onto her shoulders as she looked up at the connected buildings that comprised the plant. Made of red brick, the largest part of the structure looked to be about five stories tall, topped by two towering brick smokestacks. The name BOWIE was emblazoned on them in vertical block letters, once a bright white, now faded to a ghostly gray.

"How does it look?"

"Like if the Big Bad Wolf were here, he could huff and puff and blow the place down." Meg eyed the crumbling brick, broken windows, sagging roofline, and nearly waist-high weeds that stood between Hawk and his goal. "Seriously, it's a mess."

"And you're on your own."

"Yes. I called Craig and told him I was going in with you on the line. He wasn't happy."

"He wouldn't be."

"He didn't even bother to tell me to wait for backup, because he knows if Hawk catches the scent, I'm following because time is not on our side. He's not thrilled, but he gets it."

"I want to stay with you, but will talking to me be a problem? You'll need both hands free for you and Hawk."

"Both hands are free. I'm talking to you over my Bluetooth earbuds." She opened the zippered plastic bag and offered it to Hawk once more. "Hawk, this is Mrs. Devar." She waited while he scented the article. "Find Mrs. Devar."

Hawk swung toward the buildings, his nose in the air, trying to find even a molecule of scent.

"Here we go." Meg closed the bag and stuffed it into one of the side pockets of her backpack. "I'm giving him a second to catch the scent. There are several buildings, and it would save a lot of time if he has an idea where to go. If not we'll . . ." Her voice trailed off as she studied Hawk's posture. His spine stiffened as his tail rose high into the air, his ears perked. "McCord, you did it. Hawk has her scent."

"Already?"

"You know how good he is." Hawk pushed through the tangles of overgrown grass toward the largest of the three structures, the building with the smokestacks. "He's headed for the structure with the smokestacks."

"That's the refrigeration plant. It opened a few years after the main processing plant. A room full of boilers fed steam into the flywheel steam engines that powered overhead condensers. They cooled the air for the massive plant refrigeration unit. The smokestacks carried away the exhaust from the engines."

"Look at you, learning all about industrial operations."

"I'm a quick study. You have to be in this job. And I

thought if you knew roughly how the building worked originally, you'd have an idea what's what once you're inside."

Hawk pushed through the grass, winding his way toward the building with a quick, sure stride, Meg following in his wake. "There's an opening into the building across from here, so access isn't going to be a problem."

"I'm going to follow along virtually via photos and blueprints, so I can try to tell you where you're going. Thank God for multiple monitors."

"Good thing you're not at home on your laptop. Okay, we're getting closer now and he's . . . he's . . . uh-oh."

"What?"

Hawk slowed his pace and started casting about in the grass.

"He's lost the scent already."

"As you got closer to the building? Could the body be outside instead?"

Meg scanned the scraggly grass and weeds on what had once no doubt been a beautifully cultivated lawn. "Maybe? But that seems unlikely. Why go all this way, come to a site like this, and then dump the victim outside?"

McCord let out a hum of displeasure. "You're right, that doesn't make sense. Are you going to take Hawk in and hope he catches the scent again?"

Meg studied her dog for a moment. Hawk moved jerkily, trying to catch the scent on brief gusts of wind. He looked up at her and whined. "No, I'm going to backtrack a bit. Hawk, come." She retreated with him about fifteen feet, and then his head shot up, nose in the breeze. "He has it again. Hawk, find her." They turned toward the building, but ten feet along he whined once more. "Lost it again. Hawk, buddy, what's going on?"

"He's having trouble?"

"Not exactly. It's not him, it's the scent. He's reporting what he picks up on, but the scent is disappearing on him. Now why is that? Hawk, come." She led him back again to where he had detected the scent twice, and she could tell from his change in alertness the moment he picked it up. "He has it again. So why here?" She studied the building, cataloging windows and doors, anywhere scent could be leaking from the structure. Then she looked up. "Wait a second."

"What?"

"I've got it." She squinted at the trees at the near end of the building. For more than fifty years, the property had gone untouched, and nature had reclaimed it with a vengeance. Trees grew in uneven clumps toward the end of the property, their multicolored leaves waving in the vigorous breeze. She stuck her index finger in her mouth and held it over her head. "It's the wind."

"Blowing the scent? But wouldn't you expect that? Isn't that how scent tracking works?"

"You're right, anytime you're doing an external search, the wind is what carries the target's scent to you. But obstacles can play hell with air currents, and what's a building but a giant obstacle? The air flow is coming over the building and falling on the far side fifty-odd feet from the near wall. The wind isn't too strong today. A harder breeze would have the scent landing farther out, and he might have missed it altogether. It's called a chimney effect. Walk too close to the obstacle and you're actually walking out of the scent trail."

"So the vic is on the other side of the building?"

One hand shading her eyes from the glare of the sun, Meg peered up at the roofline over the lines of broken windows. "Could be, but again, too easy. I think she's on the roof. The breeze is blowing her scent off the roof toward us."

"Until you get too close."

"Exactly. He's not picking up a fresh trail on this side of the building at ground level, which likely means the suspect took her in on the far side. If he's scouted out the building, he may have known the easiest way to enter when carrying a burden. If we go in on this side, it may save us time, and Hawk will reconnect with the scent inside when we cross their path." She stared up at the roof, brilliantly backlit by sun and clouds, and let out a shaky breath. "Assuming my theory is correct, we need to find a way up there. And if the inside of the building is in the same shape as the outside, that may be a problem."

"I'm looking at pictures. It's not good. You're going to need to be even more careful if you're not staying on terra firma. Not to mention your love of heights."

A shudder snaked through Meg. Ever since she was six, when she nearly fell off the roof of her grandparents' cottage after the railing on the widow's walk gave way, Meg had had a blinding terror of heights. She never sought them out, but sometimes a search forced her to meet her fear head-on.

She had a bad feeling about this search.

"Oh yeah, I *love* them." There was no mistaking the sarcasm. "I'll try not to let you hear my knees knocking when I'm up there."

"No need to hide it from me. I know all about facing things that scare the living daylights out of you . . . and doing them anyway."

Meg thought about his time as a war correspondent in Iraq, and how many years he'd remained when a lesser man would have returned home. "Yeah," she said quietly. "You do." She cleared her throat. "Okay, McCord, you gonna be my wingman?"

"Always. Let's do this!"

"Actually, can you do something for me while we get started? Contact Baltimore EMS and give them a heads-up that we need a team on standby. I don't want to tie them up coming all the way out here if we've lost her already, but if we haven't, I'll need them double quick. They can have a local team identified and ready to roll, if needed."

"Can do."

Meg looked down at Hawk, sitting quietly at her feet, gazing up at her. "Hawk, come. This time I'm going to lead for a bit. Heel."

Together they slogged through the long grass, heading directly for an opening the size of a double door. As they got closer, she was able to see large sections of plywood that once covered the opening laying in a shattered pile inside the door. Broken by time or explorers, she wasn't sure.

She tightened the leash and gave Hawk a quick check to make sure his protective vest and search boots were securely in place. Then they stepped into the gloom.

It took only a moment for her eyes to adjust to the lower lighting, since the interior was lined with grimy windows, some shattered, letting in ambient light. She found herself in a room filled with a long row of rusted tanks approximately four or five thousand gallons each. "I'm inside, in a room with about a dozen enormous tanks."

"If I'm reading this right, you're in the room next to the steam engines. Those tanks would have been filled with liquid ammonia circulated through condensers to produce the cold air for refrigeration."

"That's a lot of ammonia." She glanced down at Hawk's relaxed stance. "Hawk doesn't have the scent yet. I'll make a pass through and then move on." They passed through the room of tanks, winding around broken brick, shattered glass, and old rusted tools. "Moving into the next room." Meg paused for a moment in the doorway, taking in the huge airy space, easily three stories high and brightly lit from a skylight that covered the entire length of the room, opening it up to the sky, the inset glass long gone. Multicolored graffiti covered the lower sections of the walls that rose upward to steel I-beams that spanned the skylight. Valve-studded pipes of varying diameters ran overhead through the wall, leading into the next room. "Now we're in a big room with a ton of pipes and machinery. We're going to have to be careful in here. The floor is covered with scraps of rusted sheet metal and glass. It's a tetanus wonderland."

"You've had your shot?"

"Always up to date on tetanus in my line of work. No vaccine for dogs, but Hawk's wearing his boots. We'll be careful, and I'll check him over afterward. Speaking of Hawk, he's still not telling me he smells anything."

"Any stairs?"

"No. There are windows on both sides of this room, up on what is likely the third floor, but no way to get there that we've found yet. Huge holes in the floor looking down into the basement, though, so we'll watch our footing." They stuck to the solid concrete floor in the middle of the room, following a cleared area flanked by rows of rusted barrels on one side and massive engines on the other. "There's some sort of giant engine with two ten-foot flywheels in here. Two of them, actually."

"Those are very cool antiques. Early twentieth-century steam engines used to power the condensers and refrigerators. Get to the far end of the room. It looks like there should be a doorway into the next section, the boiler room. The boilers produced the steam needed to run the engines."

"You have done your research."

"At your service, ma'am. That's what I do."

Meg and Hawk left the engine room and entered a darker space beyond. The floor here was originally comprised of steel mesh, but parts of the mesh had crumbled or were missing altogether. Large sheets of plywood had been lain down to cover the worst areas. The windows were covered by clear plastic sheeting, once attached to the walls by wide orange tape, but now they drifted lazily on the incoming breeze. Along the right side of the corridor, yellow caution tape warned trespassers against the most treacherous areas. "We're in the boiler room. There are huge floor-to-ceiling steel structures in here, and lots of internal piping. A whole section is taped off with caution tape."

Beside her, Hawk suddenly shot to attention, his nose in the air and his tail waving like a triumphant flag. "Bingo. Hawk has her. Somewhere in here, I bet there's a flight of stairs."

Hawk trotted down the corridor and angled under the caution tape at the first gap between the massive structures. Meg lifted the tape and slipped underneath. "We're past the caution tape now. And here's a narrow flight of stairs." She traced the upward path of the metal steps. "Looks like it goes up at least a few stories, not sure about all the way."

"Keep talking to me. This is when things could get dicey. If you run into trouble, I need to know."

"Wouldn't do it without you. Hawk is heading right for the stairs." Meg tightened the leash slightly, drawing him a little closer. "Stay with me, Hawk, I don't want you getting too far ahead and running into trouble."

A single width of stair treads led down into the depth of the basement in front of them, but Hawk didn't even give it a glance, instead circling the staircase to the far side. Meg followed him up steps lined at the edges with scraps of wood and brick and shards of glass. She cast a quick glance upward, not daring a long look while jogging behind her dog, but even that brief view was enough to show that this skylight had not fared well and that blue sky and drifting clouds were directly overhead.

Hawk hit the first level and followed the catwalk around the corner, running between the railing on one side and dented, rusted ductwork on the other. Approaching the end of the catwalk, he slowed. Decades ago, curving around the corner to the next flight of steps would have been elementary. Now, a large section of the meshwork had collapsed, leaving an airy drop to the walkway one story below between the I-beams that supported the staircase.

"Hawk, stop," Meg commanded, giving her time to catch up with him. She came to the edge of the gap, calculating the distance. For herself, she could step out a foot, balance on the two-inch-wide I-beam, turn one hundred eighty degrees, and step another foot onto the lowest tread of the next flight of stairs.

But you can't explain that to a dog.

No help for it, they were going to have to do it in two jumps. The first, over the gap to the far side of the walkway, and then the second, back and onto the section of the stairway.

"Meg, talk to me, what's going on?"

McCord's voice reminded Meg she had a virtual search partner she'd been ignoring. "Sorry. We just hit a gap on the catwalk right where we need to do a one-eighty onto the next flight of stairs. I can't talk Hawk through it, so we're going to have to jump over it, and then jump back."

"How wide is the gap?"

"Four feet?"

"That's pretty far. Be careful."

"Luckily this platform seems solid. Let's hope the guardrails on the far side are as well, because that's what's going to catch me. Hawk, come." She backed up several paces, Hawk heeling at her side. "Now stay." She held up a hand, palm out and fingers spread to him as reinforcement, and then unclipped his leash from his vest and stuffed it in her jacket pocket. "Here goes." She took a run at it and then leaped over the gap, landing with a *clang* on the far side as she held out her hands to catch herself on the rough guardrail. She hit the guardrail hard, but the sturdy metal held. "Made it," she said to McCord. "Hawk, your turn. Come here, boy. Jump!"

Hawk stayed motionless for a moment, his eyes calmly fixed on Meg; then he sprang forward, his powerful hind legs pushing off as he arced through the air toward her. His booted feet hit the metal, and he slid a few inches before Meg caught him. "Good boy!" She rubbed a hand down his back. "Now we do it again, but we not only have to make the jump, we have to land up a step. This is going to be easier for me than it will be for you, buddy. Stay here, Hawk." She pressed against the guardrail. "No real room to take a run at it, but here goes attempt number two." Meg gave herself an extra boost by launching off the guardrail.

She landed heavily on the step, reaching out with both hands to grasp the stair rail and catch her balance. Puffing slightly, she turned to her dog. "Hawk, come." She patted her palms twice on her thighs. "Jump."

Hawk pulled back as far as he could, took a few steps, and then leaped across the divide. Three feet landed on the first and second steps, but his fourth foot landed where the metal flooring should have been, and he scrambled to catch his balance. Meg was ready and leaned out, one hand clutching the stair rail and the other grabbing for the handle strap running across the back of his vest. Catching it, she leaned back on the steps, purposefully overbalancing to drag him up the stairs with her. His boots scrabbled for a hold, and then he was steady on the steps beside her. "Hoo boy, that was a close one. Hawk almost missed that last jump. But we made it and we're moving on."

"Well done."

Meg pushed to her feet. "Hawk, heel. No leash this time, so we're not tied together if either of us runs into trouble. Heel." She started up the stairs again.

Another flight of steps, and another landing to cross to get to the next section. This section held massive tanks, similar to the ammonia tanks below. Each level became brighter as they worked their way up toward the roof. Meg confirmed they were still on the right track by Hawk's posture; everything about his stance told her he was still tracking Mrs. Devar.

The last flight of stairs was heavily covered with shards of vaguely green skylight glass and carried them over a chain of deep coal hoppers, now empty but once full of tons of coal to stoke the massive boilers. They continued up, the bulk of a red brick smokestack, easily thirty feet in diameter, rising up beside them to pierce the roof beside the skylight. Then they were through an empty doorway and out on the roof, startling a small flock of roosting pigeons into the air in a burst of sound and feathers. Forest and industrial buildings spread out around them, with railroad tracks running behind the building. In the distance, cars hurtled along I-895 running north toward Baltimore or south to DC.

The chilly autumn breeze was stronger here, but Hawk needed only a second to refocus the search. He circled the skylight and headed past the towering smokestack and toward the center of the building.

"We're on the roof," Meg reported, "and Hawk still has the scent. She's here somewhere."

"I'm looking at a Google Maps aerial view," McCord said. "Where are you?"

"We came out on the roof on the south side, by the

southernmost skylight and smokestack. Hawk's taking us north, back across the roof again."

"From this photo, it looks as if there's a skylight that runs the length of the middle of the building. Do you need to get around that?"

"Not sure yet."

"If you do, one end is blocked by the second smokestack, but there's a section of open roof at the east end."

"I'm not sure yet where we're going, but that's good to know."

They cautiously hurried across a roof covered with a fine, pebble-like gravel under shattered bricks from the crumbling stacks, glass from the skylight, and roofing shingles. Swampy puddles of water gathered in low-lying areas tinted green with a mossy lining. Hawk crossed the roof in a nearly straight line.

Strong scent. We must be practically on top of her.

When he reached the bisecting skylight, Hawk abruptly sat down and barked.

"He's alerting. She's on the other side of the skylight."

"Can you see her?" McCord asked.

"No, but if Hawk says she's . . . No wait, maybe I do see her. There's a raised section on the far side, under some sort of stone structure and I can see a bit of color over there. Hang on, let me circle around the skylight to her. Hawk, come." Meg glanced at the tall smokestack, covered in graffiti at the bottom and rising high overhead but clearly blocking her way to the far side. She turned away from it to run down the length of the roof to the end of the skylight. As she got closer, she could see a narrow band of roof between the end of the skylight and the wall. The roof was sunken and uneven, with water gathered in the depression. "I'm not sure about this. The roof is in rough shape."

"It hasn't been maintained since 1966 at the latest.

That's a lot of time for a roof to collapse. From this aerial shot, parts of it around the plant already have."

"And me with no rope, harness, or buddy."

"Do not go out there unless you're sure it's safe."

"I have to get across, McCord. I don't even know if she's alive. Hold on, I'm going to try it. Hawk, sit. Stay. I'm not risking you on this roof."

Meg stepped carefully onto that section of the roof, the soggy materials shifting under her boot, collapsing and compressing. One step. Two. Three—

The roof gave way beneath her foot, and she leaped back as the area she'd been about to cross disintegrated, falling with a harsh crash, stories below.

"What was that?" McCord called.

"No need to yell, I'm right here." The displeasure in Meg's voice was less for McCord than the situation. "I can't get through this way. Parts of the roof have given way; the rest looks precarious. Which leaves me with two choices. The brick wall at the outer edge of the building—"

"I don't like that," McCord interjected. "That must be a five-story drop if you slip, and that brickwork is *not* secure."

"—or walking across the skylight." Meg turned and motioned for Hawk to follow her back to the skylight.

"Walking across the glass?" McCord's tone told her he thought she'd lost her mind.

"No, the glass is long gone. There are double I-beams about every twenty feet down the length of the skylight. I could walk across one of those."

"You, the woman who is terrified of heights. Again, isn't this about five stories up?"

Meg's mouth went desert dry. "Something like that."

"And if you fell, you'd land on . . . ?"

Meg sidled closer to the edge of the abyss and forced

herself to look down. *Way* down. "Those cool antique steam engines."

"You can't do it."

"How can I *not* do it? McCord, if I call the fire department to stage a rescue, it will take too long. I need to get to her now and find out if she's even alive. Walking over steel will be more secure than over crumbling brick. If she's alive, I'll get Craig to arrange for a flight crew to airlift her off the roof. But I have to get there first. If the perp did it, carrying the victim, I can do it."

"I don't like this."

The laugh that escaped Meg was entirely humorless. "Trust me, I don't either." She shrugged out of her pack and dropped it on the roof next to Hawk. "If something happens to me, you need to call the authorities. Tell them what happened. Tell them there's a victim who needs assistance. They'll also need to rescue Hawk and take him to Cara."

"Meg." The single word was heavy with warning. "That's crazy talk. If Webb were there—"

"He'd be climbing out on the I-beam with me, and you know it. And if you were here, you'd be right behind him." She crouched down next to Hawk, running her hands over him, trying to absorb his energy and confidence. "Hawk, buddy, you have to stay here. I have to cross to the other side of the roof, but I'll be back. Stay." She dropped a kiss on the top of his head and forced herself to stand. Forced herself to walk to the edge of the skylight.

The rusted I-beams sat a foot below the roof, stretching about twenty-five feet across the chasm. *Might as well be twenty-five miles*. Meg's heart was beating so hard, she thought she was going to have a panic attack. She forced herself to take a few deep breaths, to try to settle some of the terror burning through her veins like fire.

"McCord, I'm going to climb down to the I-beam and then make my way across it."

"Can you do it sliding across on your ass? Better that than walking it."

"That's not going to work. It'll take too long, and the I-beam is covered with glass that would cut through my pants and then me. That would increase my chances of falling off. I have to walk it."

"Meg, I—"

"No. I'm doing it. And I need you to stay dead quiet while I do. If you break my concentration . . . it won't end well. Can I count on you to stay quiet, or do I need to end this phone call?"

"Hell, no. I'm here. I'll shut up, but I am not going anywhere."

A small smile tugged at her lips at his stubborn tone. "Thanks." She sat down on the edge of the roof, being careful not to cut herself on any of the thick shards of glass surrounding the edge of the skylight, and swung her legs out so her booted feet rested on the I-beams. She lifted one foot and banged it into the steel as hard as she could, but it held firm, no wobbling and only limited vibration.

"Okay, McCord. Starting now."

"Good luck. Shutting up, but I'm with you every step of the way."

She took one more breath and slowly let it out through pursed lips. Then she pushed off the edge of the roof to stand at the edge of the beam.

Fixing her eyes three feet in front of her so she wasn't staring down into the deadly drop, she extended her arms for balance and stepped out into thin air.

CHAPTER 15

Grills: Metal bars found in the roof or sides of a drain. Grills allow rainwater to flow into sewers during a storm.

Monday, November 5, 11:18 AM
Bowie Meat Packing Plant
Lansdowne, Maryland

As Meg set her boot down on the I-beam, she felt the sole slip fractionally, and froze. The metal was intact, but storms and age had weathered the surface, crumbling the outer layer and giving it a gritty slickness that could spell doom. She started to hyperventilate as she wobbled slightly in the breeze.

Unbidden, but entirely welcome, a voice called to her from her memory—a voice she hadn't heard since middle school. *Jennings! We've gone over this before. Stay centered on the beam. Steady breath. Tighten that stomach. It's no different than walking a line on the floor. The fear is only in your head. Now do it!*

She closed her eyes for a moment, gathering herself briefly. Then she opened them, tightened her core, straightened her spine, and took another step.

Glass crunched underfoot, and her gaze flicked down to the shards littering the beam. With the toe of her boot, she pushed a couple of bigger pieces off, and seconds later they crashed to the ground. The distance implied by the time it took to hit bottom made cold sweat dampen her skin.

Maybe it wasn't such a great idea to remind yourself how far down it is.

Another step, then another, as the far side of the skylight frame inched ever closer.

A gust of wind made her teeter slightly, but she stiffened, stretching her arms out to reclaim her balance.

You're doing this. Keep going.

Four steps.

Five.

Six.

She was just over halfway there when her boot landed on several stacked pieces of glass, and half of the pile crumbled beneath her weight. Even that miniscule shift was enough to offset her balance, and she started to lean to one side. Panic washed over her, and she instinctively jerked the other way to compensate, making her stagger.

She gave a muffled cry as she teetered dangerously, fifty feet in the air above solid concrete and steel. In some far-off part of her brain, Meg registered McCord's harsh, in-drawn breath, but she pushed it aside.

Jennings, catch your balance before you fall! Lower your center of gravity and reset the routine.

Instinctively she curled in and down, crouching over the beam, her left knee coming down onto broken glass beside her right boot. Half stifling another cry, this time of pain as fire lanced through her knee, she leaned forward and grasped the edges of the I-beam. She rested her forehead on her right knee and let her breath come hard through gritted teeth as she held on for dear life. Her gaze fell on the room below, over barrels, engines, and a maze of pipes, all so small, so distant at this height, and she snapped her eyes shut. She raised her head to look forward and only then opened her eyes, staring unblinkingly at the far end of the I-beam.

Pull it together, Jennings. Finish it.

She could do this. She *would* do this.

Ensuring she had her balance, she grasped the edges of the I-beam tighter and then straightened her back knee. Sliding her hands toward her boots, she held a forward fold position for a moment and then slowly straightened, extending her arms.

One foot in front of the other. Go.

She took the first slow step, testing the footing of each boot before trusting her weight to it. Step by step, she inched across the beam.

The roof loomed close now. *One more step and you're there.* She took the step and then launched herself at the roof, not able to stand another second suspended over the drop. She scrambled for the edge, pushing up onto the rough surface, throwing herself forward onto the roof. She hit the gravel with enough force to knock the wind out of her, then just lay there, her fingers clutching handfuls of grit and stones as she tried to pull air into lungs that had forgotten how to function.

It's over. It's over. It's over.

Thank you, Mr. Wilmont.

She pushed herself onto hands and knees and crawled forward a few feet, not wanting to be anywhere near that skylight again. Sitting back on her haunches, she raised a hand to Hawk, reinforcing the command to stay but also letting him know she wasn't hurt.

She pressed her loosened earbuds more firmly into her ears. "McCord." Her voice was hoarse with strain, so she swallowed and tried again. "McCord, I made it."

"Oh, thank God. That took forever. And I thought you ran into trouble."

"That's an understatement. And it can't have been more

than a few minutes, but it sure felt like forever." She struggled to her feet on legs that shook and winced as pain shot through her knee, but her attention was already fixed on the body lying no more than twenty feet away. "Going for Mrs. Devar now." Not trusting the roof, she crossed it as fast as she dared and hopped up the short brick wall. Scrubby trees and shrubs sprouted in clumps wherever they could take hold in cracked stone and between bricks. And nestled among the greenery was a petite, white-haired woman with South Asian coloring. She was curled on her side, her eyes closed and her face slack.

Meg fell to her knees beside her and tipped the older woman's chin up so she could slide two fingers along her neck, searching for a pulse. The woman's skin was only slightly chilled, and Meg hoped that was simply from exposure here on the windy roof in cooling November temperatures.

"She's still warm. If we've lost her, I've just . . . wait . . . wait! She has a pulse. McCord, she's still with us. You found her and saved her."

"Glory hallelujah, finally. What can I do?"

"Call and cancel the EMS request. I'm going to call Craig now and have him arrange for an air ambulance to get her off this roof. I'll call you back when I can, but it may not be for a while."

"When you can. Go." McCord hung up, ending the call.

Meg speed-dialed Craig. "I found her. But I need medical assistance. I'm on the roof of the old Bowie Meat Packing Plant, just off I-895 in south Baltimore. I need you to get me an air ambulance."

"For her or both of you?"

"I'm a bit scraped up but don't need air rescue. I'll get it looked at later. Craig, I need them here now. I'm not sure how long before she bleeds out internally."

"Got it. I'll call you back."

Meg dropped her phone into her lap and took one of the woman's hands in hers. "Mrs. Devar, can you hear me? I'm Meg, and I'm with the FBI. We have you, and help is on the way. Please hold on. Help is coming."

Sudden exhaustion made her limbs feel as if they were filled with lead, and she collapsed back to lean against a pillar. Looking over her shoulder, she studied the wide expanse of the skylight and her dog on the far side of it.

"I can't believe I did that." Then, leaning forward, she considered the I-beam anew. "I can't believe *he* did that." Mrs. Devar might be slight, but she was still a significant load to sling across his shoulders and carry over that kind of gap. Even if she'd been unconscious, any shift in weight could have been suicide for the suspect. And if she'd been conscious . . . she was sure Hawk would have led her to two broken bodies below as soon as they'd arrived. "He's willing to die to pull this off." She looked back at Mrs. Devar. "Maybe you'll be the key. Maybe you'll be able to tell us why someone would risk his life to help you meet the end of yours. What does he gain from this that's so important he'd be willing to die to get it?"

CHAPTER 16

Labyrinth: A series of connected tunnels that were originally constructed for different purposes (e.g., joined storm and sanitary sewers, shared passenger and freight train tunnels, etc.).

Monday, November 5, 3:03 PM
Jennings residence
Arlington, Virginia

"You didn't have to come all the way into Arlington just for this."

Webb looked up from where he bent over Meg's lacerated knee, cleaning her ragged, bloody wound. "You would've gone to the hospital to make sure you hadn't seriously damaged your quadriceps or patellar tendons?"

Meg's face warmed under his pointed stare. "Probably not. I was just going to give it a good cleaning and figured that would do it. I mean, it hurts, but it's not that bad. Well, not at first, anyway. Hurt like a mother later, once they had Mrs. Devar loaded into the helicopter and gave me an airlift to the other side of the roof, where Hawk was still patiently waiting. Thank God for that, because I don't think I could have made that walk a second time."

"That's what I thought. Considering the stunt you just pulled and the probability of repeating it in the near future and needing to be at full strength, I thought I'd better check you out personally."

"And?"

"You sliced up the skin pretty nicely, but your tendons and ligaments seem intact. You could use a few stitches, but I can go one better." He broke open a blister pack and pulled out a tiny single-use tube. "Surgical glue."

"You're going to glue me back together?"

"You'd prefer that I sew the laceration? I can do it, if that's your preference."

Meg shuddered. "No, glue will be fine."

"It will also do better in a joint that sees lots of action." He opened the tube. "Now hold still."

Heavy knocking sounded at the front door just before it thumped open and a voice called, "Anyone home?"

Meg looked over her shoulder to where Cara was making coffee in the kitchen. "Guess who."

"You thought he wasn't going to show up? In here," Cara called, walking to meet him at the doorway. "Hey, you." She reached up on tiptoe, pulled his glasses off with one hand, and pulled his head down to hers with the other for a kiss lasting so long that Webb cocked an eyebrow at Meg at the display.

Cara finally pulled away, slid his glasses back into place, and dropped down to the floor with a smile. "That's for your hard work this afternoon. The first live recovery."

McCord blinked at her a few times, as if she'd slightly scrambled his brains, and then grinned. "Thanks. It took us long enough, but we finally won this one." McCord shrugged out of his leather jacket and hung it on the back of a kitchen chair. "Do I smell coffee?"

"You do. Go sit with Meg. I'll bring it out."

McCord wandered into the open concept living room adjoining the kitchen. "Hey." He slowly sat down beside Meg, taking care not to jostle her, then leaned in to study Webb's work. "That looks good. Really neat."

Without raising his head, Webb shot McCord a sidelong glance. "Not my first rodeo. Not even my first one with her."

"No, sir." McCord flopped against the couch cushions. "You nearly fell off the beam today, didn't you?"

Meg threw him a dirty glare as Webb's head shot up to pin her with accusing eyes. "You had to let that slip, didn't you?"

"You did. I thought so. It was hard to tell what was going on when all I could hear was the wind blowing and your breathing. But there was a moment there when I was sure you were going over. Is that when you got this?" McCord pointed at her knee, revealed below the rolled-up leg of her yoga pants.

"That's why I got this. I told you there were shards of glass littering the I-beam. A few of them crumbled underfoot, shifting my weight, and I started to lose my balance." She looked up as Cara came in with the coffee tray. "You know who saved my life?"

Cara set the tray down. "Is this a trick question? I'm going to go with you, since you were the only one there."

"Mr. Wilmont."

Cara recoiled slightly, her nose and forehead wrinkled in confusion. "Mr. Wilmont. Our eighth-grade terror of a gym teacher?"

"Exactly that Mr. Wilmont. Do you remember how he used to yell at us?"

"Do I ever." Cara dropped into a chair opposite Meg and fixed herself a cup of coffee. " 'Jennings! Tuck that head in when you roll. You can't hold the ball like that—that's traveling! Only sissies underhand serve, Jennings.

Serve overhand!' Oh yeah, I remember him. I'm pretty sure he didn't think any of us had first names."

"That's definitely him. Remember how I used to balk at getting on the balance beam, and he would force me up there and then bellow instructions? The beam was four feet off the floor and surrounded by mats, and I was still terrified to be that far off the ground."

"Your fear of heights was so bad you couldn't manage that?" McCord asked.

"I'm better now, but back then, the fall was still pretty fresh in my mind. He made me face my fear. When I was up there, panicking because I was losing control, fifty feet in the air over a drop that absolutely would have killed me, it was his voice I heard in my head. His voice telling me what to do, how to recover and not fall. That and your yoga saved my life."

Cara froze in the act of stirring sugar into her coffee. "My yoga?"

"All those mornings I wanted to sleep in, or Hawk and I had just come in from a run and you made me join you? That core strength I developed doing yoga may have saved my life. That being said, if I ever have to do another forward fold in midair on a steel I-beam, I'm never doing yoga again."

Cara settled in with her coffee and a self-satisfied grin. "I always told you yoga was good for you."

Webb finished smoothing a bandage over Meg's knee and rolled her pant leg down. "Can I suggest next time not doing yoga on broken glass. It would be a lot less painful, and you won't need surgical glue."

"I can get behind that." Meg gave the knee an experimental bend, winced slightly, and stretched her leg out again. "Thanks for fixing me up. It seems like you're always doing that."

"You're welcome. And in your line of work, that's not overly surprising. Any news on your victim?"

"I'm going to check in with the hospital in a few hours, but Craig gave the air rescue team a heads-up about the type of poison, so they were prepared to start treatment while they stabilized her on the way to the ER. Her initial vitals weren't too bad, so I hope she'll pull through. I'd love to talk to her, but I'm not sure how that will go."

Webb snagged a mug of black coffee off the tray. "You think family will get in the way?"

"No, I think she might, but not intentionally. Sorry, I haven't filled you in on the details. She was taken from a facility that specializes in Alzheimer's patients. I don't know how bad she is, and I know she had enough strength to fight him during the abduction, but I don't know if that was simply sheer terror because she was confused, or if she knew enough about what was happening to be rightfully scared of her abductor. She may not be able to tell us anything about him. And the security cameras from the residence didn't capture anything more useful than height and weight, so that still leaves the field wide open."

"Depending on how far the disease has progressed, she may not retain anything from the entire incident," Webb said. "Some patients forget things five minutes after you tell them. I've met some dementia nurses. They have a tough job and carry it off with grace and patience as they repeatedly tell patients the same thing several times a day, if not several times an hour."

"So we may not be lucky there. Although if she can't remember the incident, that may be a blessing for her." Meg scooted to the end of the sofa cushion and pulled the coffee tray a little closer. "I'll make sure we know a little better where we stand later tonight. Kate will already be looking into her background."

"Who's Kate?" McCord asked.

"The FBI agent assigned to this case. The Human Scent Evidence Team doesn't spearhead investigations on our own, and, minus Craig, we're not actual agents. But in his current role as our SSA, he's not supposed to investigate on his own, either. He arranges for us to work in conjunction with field agents and liaises with other departments. Normally we get called in to a case. This time we brought the case to him, and he had to work backward to get us a field agent. Enter Agent Kate Moore. She's running the investigation now and will be the one getting information on the evidence found at the abduction site."

"Anything useful?" Webb asked.

"Nothing definitive, but some of it might help. Tire tracks in gravel where he left his vehicle, and then actual tread impressions on the pavement from where he took off. Looks like a biggish vehicle. Not as big as a van, but maybe a large SUV."

"He's grabbing adults," McCord said dryly. "You have to know he's not using a smart car."

Webb raised his coffee cup to McCord in a mock toast. "The crack reporter strikes again."

"Kate will let us know if they get anything from the evidence." Meg poked McCord in the biceps. "I've already told her about you."

"Only nice things, of course."

"Of course. She knows you've been involved in the searches and may be useful for future contacts."

"Good, because I've already been doing some digging. I don't have access to the kind of personal information she does, but I do have a theory." He grabbed the last mug of coffee, poured cream into it, and stirred.

Cara leaned forward and smacked him on the shoulder. "Don't leave us hanging. Your theory is . . ."

"Weird. Outlandish." He took a sip of coffee and relaxed against the cushions. "But something that's definitely grounded in reality."

"I'll bite." Meg pulled her uninjured leg up on the couch and twisted to face him. "Let's have it."

"You asked for it. This all goes back to a story I did . . . four? Five years ago? It was one of those longer weekend-edition stories, when people have more time to read. The story was about senior care in immigrant populations, specifically the Asian diaspora. It's about how some young people are here, but their aging parents are there, and how they handle that situation. Some people go home again. Some support their parents from afar. And some bring their parents here. I didn't include it in the story, but I found out about a kind of horrific side aspect. In some cultures, specifically the Tamils of India, there is a rare additional option. It's called thalaikoothal."

"Come again?" Cara rotated her index finger in the air in a back-it-up motion. "I didn't catch that last word."

"Thalaikoothal. Ritual elder killing."

Meg stared at McCord as if he'd lost his mind. "You think this is some sort of ethnic elder killing? En masse? Spread over multiple states? Doesn't that seem far-fetched?"

"I said it was weird and outlandish. I wasn't kidding."

"What on earth would steer you in that direction in the first place?"

"Because social media is a wonderful thing, and I've been using it to follow the victims and their relatives."

Meg's brows drew together in disapproval. "Internet stalking, McCord?"

"What do you think investigative reporting is other than glorified stalking? In person, through contacts, from documents, or online research."

"Hmmm. You have a point."

"Of course I do. When you don't have the resources of law enforcement, you have to get inventive. All I have to go on is public record, but you might be surprised what you can dig up just from that. A lot of people are either not savvy about their privacy or know sacrificing it is a risk they take the moment they set foot on the Internet, so they consider themselves open books. They figure if they aren't doing anything wrong, what is there worth hiding? It's been pretty useful. In this case, I've found that the victims are too separated to know one another. They don't appear to be related. They didn't work for the same company or in the same field. There's even a twelve-year age gap between oldest and youngest. But I did find a common thread in the end."

Meg squashed the urge to shake him and yell *Get on with it!* She'd worked with McCord enough times to know that his slow explanations were often due to his forming links in his head, and she didn't want to interrupt that process in case he lost the thread.

"Which is?" Cara, however, was happy to give him a push.

"They seem to be linked by some degree to the Indian subcontinent. Mrs. Devar's family comes from Chennai in southern India. Warren Roth's late wife was Indian. Donna Parker was adopted into an Indian family as a girl. Before she got married, her maiden name was Achari. They are all either Indian or have a connection to someone who is."

"And you think they were killed because of that connection?"

"I can hear the skepticism in your voice. Just remember, my far-fetched ideas have saved your sister's life and several others."

"You've got me there. I have nothing but respect for your ability to . . . uh . . . stalk on my behalf."

McCord gave her a dirty look. "Way to butter me up, Jennings."

"It's what I do." She gave him a wink. "Okay, I won't give you a hard time anymore. Explain this thal . . . thala . . ."

"Thalaikoothal."

"That. Explain it to me, and how it might be involved, and I swear I won't discount it outright."

"Fair enough. It's an ancient Tamil practice that is essentially either a mercy killing or a form of geronticide, depending on the health of the victim. Rarely done at the behest of the victim, it's something a family does to its elders, often as a ritual with the whole community involved. In a nutshell, traditionally, they would force-feed an elderly person tender coconut water—the coconut water from inside an immature coconut. It's one of those new health fads these days, because it's full of electrolytes, especially potassium."

"Give a frail elderly person a large amount of that, and you'll definitely induce renal failure," Webb said. "Depending on the health of the victim going in, it would cause irreparable damage to the kidneys and they'd die within a day. Maybe two at most. And no traceable poison."

"And lots of coconuts grown in India, especially in Tamil Nadu."

"But why would anyone do that?" Cara asked. "That's awful."

"Not all cultures revere their elders. Some see them as a monetary burden who require resources they can't or don't want to provide. It's illegal in India, but it still goes on under the radar. Some stats I've seen lately suggest that possibly more than one hundred people still die every year because of the practice."

Meg considered McCord over the top of her mug as she sipped her coffee. "You're suggesting we have an Indian Tamil killer who moved here and is continuing an ethnic ritual killing. I understand the motives as you've outlined it for a family committing such a murder." She paused for a second. "Scratch that, I don't understand it, it's horrifying—"

"I've got it," McCord interrupted. "You understand it on an intellectual basis, not an emotional one."

"Right. But I'm having trouble seeing why someone would come here to do it. If there are a hundred victims a year lost to this ritual in a southern Indian state, it's because someone is turning a blind eye to it. That wouldn't happen here. No one would be sympathetic to that kind of killing."

"Maybe, but the reasons could be a Western version of what McCord described." Webb set his empty coffee mug down on the tray. "If there's life insurance, the motive could be straight-up monetary. Same thing if retirement or nursing home care is too expensive or is no longer available. Perhaps some families aren't able to pay for required lifesaving drugs. Or some may find the elderly to be too big a burden physically or emotionally. Especially if the younger generation works full time, who's going to give up their career to look after Grandma?"

Meg fixed him with a stare that conveyed her disgust.

He held up both hands, palms out in surrender. "I'm not saying I agree with it, I'm just saying there are some who would."

"I guess. Let me get this straight, McCord. For this theory to hold water, you're saying there's a killer, some guy who families can contract out to do the killing for them, which is why there doesn't seem to be a direct connection between the victims. Somehow, word is out there in the community that someone will carry out this traditional kill for a price, and he's being hired by the families. Then, instead of tender coconut water, which isn't readily available here as it is in India, he uses common rat poison. Easily available and causes the same kind of slow death."

"The other piece of information that's missing here is the number of Tamils living along the eastern seaboard," McCord said. "There are large populations of Tamils in Maryland, Delaware, Pennsylvania, New Jersey, New York, and DC. Even though they're now here, where it's flat-out illegal, in their ethnic background this is considered an acceptable practice."

"While it's not acceptable here by any stretch of the imagination, you're suggesting the killer may have brought the practice, or something based on it, with him when he immigrated," Meg clarified. "Either that or a family did, and they've hired him to carry out the practice for them. I'm still not sure I buy that, but leaving that aspect aside, why the urbex sites? That's not part of the ritualistic killing."

"I have a theory on that," Webb said. "The murderer isn't using ricin or arsenic or cyanide, or another of the fast killers. If he poisoned the victims in their own homes, they could call for help or crawl to find it. To get around that, he's taking them somewhere out of the way, somewhere they can't escape and where the chances of someone stumbling across them right away are low."

"But that actually means that the killer could be someone inside the urbex community," Cara said. "Maybe that's how you could track him down."

McCord leaned forward to pull out the notepad and pen he always carried in his back pocket. He flipped open the pad and started making notes. "That's a really good angle. I like it."

"I do, too," Meg agreed. "You don't have me sold on

motive, but I do think we may be onto something when it comes to the killer. This isn't just some guy off the street. This is someone who's handpicking locations from places he likely already knows. Someone who has visited, maybe even scouted, each location ahead of time so he knows where he's going and how to get in as fast as possible with his victim, and then back out again undetected. Though I question his sanity with the meat-packing plant and carrying Mrs. Devar over that drop. I wonder . . ." Palms pressed together, she brought her hands up to press her index fingers against her lips as she stared sightlessly at the table.

Webb tapped her shin. "Earth to Meg. What are you thinking?"

"I'm thinking of a couple of people who could be pretty useful right now. First off is Chuck. He knows these people. Maybe he could suggest some possibilities or do a little digging inside his community."

"I can ask him. I don't think he'd say no. What else? You said a couple of people. Who else?"

"SSA Rutherford, the profiler who worked with us on the Garber case. He might have some insight that would be extremely useful. He certainly made a big impact the first time we worked with him."

"Would you need Beaumont's approval to pull him in?"

"The case has been handed off to Agent Moore, so I think it would need to be her, but Craig would be onboard and could help to convince her. I'll call him later and run the suggestion by him. See what he thinks. On the bright side, we scored one for our side today, which is the best we've done so far in this case." She clinked her coffee mug against McCord's. "Good job, partner. We make a good team."

McCord grinned at her. "Have since the beginning. And I'm not done yet. I'm going to keep digging. See what I can come up with."

"That's good, because while we won this round, there's no guarantee that will happen next time. And for sure, there will be a next time. It's just a matter of who, where, and when."

CHAPTER 17

Usufruct: The right to enjoy or profit from another's legal property as long as you don't destroy it.

Tuesday, November 6, 3:58 PM
Behavioral Analysis Unit
Quantico, Virginia

Meg knocked on the closed door and was rewarded with a muffled "Come in."

She pushed the door open to find Agent Rutherford behind his desk. He looked up and smiled in recognition. "Ms. Jennings, it's nice to see you again." He stood, extending his hand in greeting.

Meg shook hands with him, having to look up to make eye contact with the tall African American. As always, Rutherford was immaculately dressed, wearing a dark suit, white shirt, and a maroon tie. "Thank you for making time in your schedule to see us." She moved over a step. "Agent Rutherford, this is Agent Moore, the field agent running this case."

Kate stepped forward and held out a hand. "Nice to meet you."

"You as well. Please, come in." Rutherford's gaze dropped down to where Hawk stood patiently at Meg's feet. "I remember you. It's Hawk, right?"

"It is. I hope it's okay he's here. We're basically inseparable. Part of the job is the constant connection."

"That's perfectly fine." He circled his desk and sat down. "Please have a seat." He waited while Meg and Kate sat down and Meg settled Hawk at her feet. "What can I do for you?"

"It was my idea to bring you into our case," Meg began. "You were instrumental to our understanding of the suspect in the Garber case, so I proposed to Agent Moore that you might be able to shed some light on our current suspect. Considering the serial nature of the case, and the fact that we have practically nothing to go on, we can use all the help we can get, hopefully before he strikes again."

"You know it's a man?"

"We don't," Kate clarified. "We have some indications that lean toward male based on size and strength, not to mention the fact that most serial killers are male, so we're using the masculine pronoun as a placeholder. But we know the killer could be a woman."

Rutherford turned to his computer and opened a blank document. "I understand you have three definite victims, one of whom survived, and the possibility of a number of others. I'd like you to send me the detailed case notes and photos, but for now let's go over what you know so I can ask any questions that come to mind at this stage. Then once I get the case file, I'll put together a profile for you."

Kate glanced at Meg, who nodded at her in encouragement. "That sounds great. How long does it take to put together a profile? I don't mean to rush you, but—"

"But your next victim could go missing at any time. I understand. We're used to working quickly and revising our profile as new information becomes available. Start from the beginning of the case as you know it, and we'll go from there."

"I'm going to let Meg start since she inadvertently found the body."

Rutherford quirked a single eyebrow at this new aspect of the case but simply looked expectantly at Meg.

Meg took him through the case, starting with Hawk's discovery of Donna Parker at the Massaponax Psychiatric Hospital. The deployment of the search teams looking for Warren Roth at Bethlehem Steel. The identification of difethialone as the deadly poison. Kate's introduction into the case and her discovery of the greater potential scope of the murders. The disappearance of Bahni Devar, the team's first chance to rescue a victim before the poison was fatal. Deciding which site to investigate and their success at the Bowie plant. And finally, McCord's theory about a possible connection between the deaths and disappearances.

Rutherford sat back, scanning his notes for a moment before turning to the women. "This McCord. That's the same gentleman who was involved in the Garber case? The investigative reporter whose involvement got you suspended from duty?"

Out of the corner of her eye, Meg saw Kate's questioning look. "Yes."

"Also the same gentleman who brilliantly figured out the body drop locations once the coded messages were decrypted?"

"Yes."

"Good man. He seemed to be right then and was apparently right about the body drops this time as well."

"He's like a dog with a bone when it comes to research. That's his real superpower."

A slow smile creased Rutherford's face. "Research as a superpower. I like it. Is there anything else you want to add to this?"

"No," Kate said. "I don't think we've missed anything, but all the details will be in the case file. If you have any questions, please let me know. I feel like there are multiple factors clouding our view of this case, and I know we're fighting the clock."

"Can you get me the file this afternoon?"

"I can send it as soon as I get to my office in the Hoover Building."

"I'll bump it up my list. Give me tomorrow to work on it. Can we plan to meet on Thursday?" He pulled up his calendar, checking his schedule. "In the morning? Say, ten?"

Kate pulled out her phone, checked her own schedule. "That works." She looked at Meg. "What about you?"

"My schedule isn't that regimented. As long as we're not called off-site to an incident, I'll be there, though that's really Craig Beaumont's call. But I know Craig, and I suspect he'll want me there, and likely the rest of the team as well. Brian Foster has taken part in one of the searches, and while Lauren Wycliffe and Scott Park haven't been involved yet, as part of the team, they could be the next SAR teams sent out depending on who is already deployed at the time of a victim disappearance. He'll likely want everyone to be in the loop so anyone can step into the case as needed. I'll run this all by him."

"Let me know what he thinks." Kate glanced at her watch and stood. "We won't take up any more of your time now. I'll get the case file to you in the next hour or so. I look forward to hearing your opinion on Thursday."

Meg followed her out of the office. As she pulled the door closed behind her, she caught a last glimpse of Rutherford, sitting back in his chair, staring at his notes on the case, his eyes narrowed in thought, already conjuring the deviousness of the perpetrator of such heinous crimes.

CHAPTER 18

Third Rail: The rigid conductor rail used to provide power to subway trains.

Thursday, November 8, 10:03 AM
Fourth-floor conference room, J. Edgar Hoover Building
Washington, DC

Brian came into the conference room with Lacey at his side, spotted Meg, and circled the long table to take the chair beside her. He nodded across the table at the rest of the team.

Tall, blond, and lanky, Scott Park slouched in a chair, his bloodhound, Theo, flopping at his feet and looking as relaxed as Scott did. Beside him, Lauren Wycliffe sat straight, one hand idly stroking the black and white head of Rocco, her border collie. As always, Lauren was poised and polished, but she was always ready at a moment's notice to kick off her Italian designer shoes, lace on her hiking boots, and wade into a search.

"Where's everyone else?" Brian asked Meg.

"On their way. I saw Rutherford in Craig's office as I was leaving, so they'll be here shortly. Kate was coming right from her office. She wants to do a general update of the case with everyone while Rutherford is here in case any new evidence will affect his current profile. That way he can adjust it on the fly."

"Good plan. While we're all in the room together, that makes sense."

Meg looked up as the door opened and her SSA and the BAU profiler came in and took their seats. A minute later, Kate Moore rushed in clutching a thick file folder.

"Sorry I'm late." She pulled out a chair and sat down, laying the folder on the table in front of her. "I was waiting on a report from the crime scene techs, and it came at the last second." She tapped the papers lying on top of the file. "I thought since we are all in one room, it would be good to bring everyone up to speed." She turned to Rutherford. "I don't think I'll be able to add anything that will change your profile, but this is new information that wasn't in the case file I sent you Tuesday."

"The more information, the better. And let me be the judge of what might alter the profile. Small details can make a big difference—you'd be surprised."

Kate opened the file. "Let's run through the forensics we have so far. First of all, the techs have gone through the dump sites with a fine-toothed comb and didn't find anything definitive. They were looking for hair and fibers and any commonalities between sites, but the problem is really too much trace versus too little."

"The sites are absolutely filthy," Meg said. "Is that causing part of the problem?"

"That's definitely part of it. Dust and grime, layers of it, make it hard to collect trace evidence without taking everything else along with it. Then that stuff needs to be separated out, which isn't entirely possible. The other issue is that a lot of those places have had a surprising amount of traffic. When they dusted for prints, they found hundreds of fingerprints and handprints, and they are working their way through IAFIS, but the problem is they're actually getting way too many hits. Urbexers love these sites, but when push comes to shove, they're trespassing. Many of them have been caught trespassing in the past and have been convicted on minor charges. But they're there, so we need to check each and every one."

"If we're leaning toward the possibility that one of those urbexers could be the suspect—and that makes sense considering where we're finding the bodies—then you may have already found him," Brian said.

"That's exactly what I'm thinking, so we're going to have to do a lot of interviewing and alibi confirmations. Now, if the guy is smart and is wearing gloves when he's in these sites, then he's the one we're *not* going to find this way. However, we do have some directly related evidence from the roadside location Meg found behind Hampden Manor, Bahni Devar's residence. Due to the nature of the site, we have several types of evidence. The vehicle was parked in the gravel on the shoulder of the road. When the vehicle left the shoulder, it did so at a high rate of speed, which gave us some good information." She opened the file folder and flipped through several pieces of paper. "First, the driver floored the gas pedal, causing the tires to spin. This left distinct marks in the gravel right down to the dirt substratum beneath all four tires. That allowed the techs to calculate the wheelbase, the measurement between the midpoint of the front and rear tires. It also let them determine the track size between the front and back tires. Keep in mind this isn't an exact science—it wasn't a tire impression on pavement. It's in gravel, so the measurements won't be precise, but it leads them in a definite direction. The tire tracks combined with the approximate wheelbase measurement have a best fit with the current Ford D-class platform. So we're potentially looking at a Ford Explorer, Ford Flex, or the Lincoln MKT."

"A vehicle big enough to put an adult victim in the back

seat or back compartment," Craig said. "Also, those vehicles often have tinted rear windows, decreasing the chance of anyone spotting the victim."

"I should tell you that also in this class is the Police Interceptor, the law enforcement version of the Explorer."

"Are you suggesting this could be a law enforcement officer?" Brian asked.

"We don't have any evidence to suggest that at this time, so I'm just putting it out there for the full picture. Based on the tire tread pattern, these vehicles are supported by the make and model of tires at the scene, which would be found as original equipment. The tires also hadn't seen much wear, suggesting this is a late-model vehicle." She flipped through a few more pages. "As far as other evidence goes, we have the security footage from Hampden Manor. The techs estimate the suspect is approximately six foot three and two-twenty. Body shape indicates a muscular build. We have no visual record of his face."

"That weight makes sense considering the load he needs to carry during the abductions," Meg stated. "I know these people are elderly, and probably slim and frail, but he needs to subdue and transport them through difficult urbex sites without dropping them or risking himself. Has anyone done staff interviews at Hampden Manor?"

"I did that personally," Kate said. "I interviewed staff members who were on duty not just that day but on prior days. Multiple people from different shifts recognized the workman's uniform. It's from an outside company that the home contracts to do their maintenance work. As a result, workmen are there on a regular basis. If something in the building needs attention, it's reported to management, who contact the maintenance company and they send workmen out ASAP. They've worked with the company for years and never had any trouble."

"I'm sure you checked, but I bet our guy doesn't work

for that company. He just used a uniform that made him essentially invisible," Lauren said. "It's the perfect way to hide in plain sight. But how did he get that uniform?"

"I checked with the company. They had a break-in a few weeks ago that went unreported. They came in one morning and found the door forced, but nothing appeared to be missing."

"Because they were cataloging valuables or electronics that might have been stolen," Scott suggested. "They wouldn't have been counting how many spare uniforms they had in the back room. This guy really did his prep work. He must have watched Hampden Manor beforehand to find the best way to get in without attracting attention." He looked at Rutherford for confirmation and received a nod in response.

"All contracted workers for that company are alibied for the time of the sighting," Kate stated. "Management doesn't have any repairs on record for that day or the few days leading up to the abduction. Of course, the nursing staff wouldn't have known that, so they didn't blink at yet another workman carrying tools, making his way through the place."

"Wait," Meg interrupted. "Tools?"

"Yes, tools. They were found in Mrs. Devar's room after the abduction." She held up a hand to forestall Meg's question. "And before you ask, the techs dusted for prints, and every piece was clean. Looked brand-new, in fact. There weren't even that many in the tool bag, just enough to give it some heft and to make it look real. In the video, the suspect is seen wearing work gloves, so that likely explains the lack of prints. From conversations with several staffers, it's clear he was there several times over the previous few days, doing 'repairs' in Mrs. Devar's room, and had been spotted going in and out a few times."

"But no one got close enough to see his face?" Brian asked.

"No. He always kept his head down. By and large, the workmen aren't really visible to the staff. They come in, they do their thing, they go out. Unless they cause trouble, they're kind of like wallpaper—there, but basically unnoticed."

Meg glanced down at Hawk, who caught her movement and looked up at her from his place beside Lacey, lazily thumping his tail a few times. "Any idea how he got Mrs. Devar out of the building so Hawk and I had a trail to follow?"

"I asked the staff about that as well," Kate said. "No one saw her leave with him, and no one heard anything. So she didn't go out kicking and screaming, but for all we know, she also may have been drugged. They did a tox screen on her at the hospital, but we don't have results yet."

"I think the profile will speak to how he got her out of the residence," Rutherford said. "If you're ready to move on to that."

"Just about. One more thing to add. I visited Mrs. Devar in the hospital, and I was not able to get a victim statement. She is fairly far along in her dementia and was very confused. Very pleasant, but I think she's back in the 1970s. She doesn't appear to remember anything of her experience, including anything about the man who abducted her."

"Bad for us," Meg said, "a godsend for her."

"I agree. She has enough challenges." Kate closed the file folder and pushed it a few inches away. "That's everything I have so far. SSA Rutherford, I'm interested in what you've been able to determine from the little we've been able to gather."

"It's a lot more than you think. And no, this information doesn't change the profile. It simply confirms it." Rutherford picked up a folder from the table in front of him and stood. "Bear with me while I lay the case out from the beginning. I know you're all familiar with the progression, but it helps paint a clear picture of how the evidence leads to and supports the profile. There's no hocus-pocus in a suspect profile, just minute details, some psychology, and the ability to put yourself in the suspect's shoes." He pulled out the first photograph and tacked it to the board on the wall. "This is Donna Parker. She was found deceased by Ms. Jennings and Hawk when they were trespassing in the abandoned Massaponax Psychiatric Hospital in Fredericksburg, Virginia."

At the word "trespassing," Meg sunk a little lower in her chair.

Rutherford hung a photo of the Massaponax Psychiatric Hospital beside the victim. "Mrs. Parker was eighty-five years of age and a widow who lived alone in Fredericksburg. According to the police report made by her son, she was fiercely independent and insisted on having her own place. But they compromised, and her son got an apartment in the same building. They talked daily and he knew her schedule, so when she didn't answer his phone calls, he was worried she was ill or had fallen. He went up to her apartment, but it was deserted. He reported her missing right away."

He pulled out a second photo and mounted it below the first, following up with a photo of the Bethlehem Steel furnaces. "This is Warren Roth, also found deceased, this time in a restricted section of the decommissioned Bethlehem Steel plant in Bethlehem, Pennsylvania, by Mr. Foster and Lacey. Mr. Roth was seventy-nine and disappeared from his retirement community in Allentown. He was supposed to meet friends for dinner, and intended to as of that afternoon, then failed to appear. When they went to his house, his car was still in the driveway, but there was no sign of him at home. His family was also not able to locate him and reported him missing. Cause of death was found to be difethialone, a rat poison, widely available for both commercial and residential use for many years, but it's been off the residential market for a decade. The difethialone was suspended in 190-proof grain alcohol."

"Moonshine?" Lauren's tone conveyed her distaste.

"Moonshine would do it," Rutherford agreed, "but the chemical composition in this case is too pure. It's Everclear, a widely available grain alcohol."

"Isn't that banned in some states?" Scott asked.

"It is. West Virginia, for instance. But you can buy it in New York, Maryland, Virginia, Ohio, and right here in DC. Wherever home base is for our killer, he could find multiple outlets for it and then bring it back across state lines.

"We got lucky when our third victim, Bahni Devar, was taken from Hampden Manor, outside of Baltimore, Maryland. Hampden Manor is a long-term care facility for persons suffering from dementia, and specifically Alzheimer's, so they monitor their residents closely. They knew shortly after she was taken that she was missing, and sounded the alarm. As Agent Moore described, Mrs. Devar was escorted out of the residence by the suspect, lead through the backwoods behind the building, and transferred to a vehicle parked and waiting for them off-road. She was driven about twenty minutes away to the abandoned site of the former Bowie Meat Packing Plant." Photos of Mrs. Devar and the location were tacked to the board. "The body drop site could be reached only following a hazardous climb, which the suspect managed while carrying Mrs. Devar, who was then left on the roof to die. However, Ms. Jennings and Hawk arrived before the anticoagulant properties of the poison killed Mrs. Devar, called for assistance, and an air ambulance responded. Mrs. Devar is currently recovering in hospital.

"I understand there are three additional potential victims found previously in New Jersey, West Virginia, and Pennsylvania. However, in this short time period I wanted to concentrate on the current victims because I didn't want to muddy the profile if any of the additional three are not truly connected. More information is being gathered there, so they will be added into the profile when and if it makes sense. And then there's this." Rutherford pulled a list out of the file folder and held it up. "The list of a number of other senior citizens, any or all of whom could also be victims. Twenty-three additional individuals, eighteen of whom were eventually found." He turned to Kate. "Have you considered exhuming those eighteen to test for difethialone?"

"We're working on exhumation orders for ten of those victims. The other eight were cremated, so we won't be able to do toxicological testing. But if any of those ten have difethialone in their system, we'll be expanding our victim pool."

"Then that aspect of the case may be updated as the case progresses. For now, we're going to work solely with these three victims. And, more specifically, on the killer. What do we know so far from the evidence and the established incidents? He drives a large late-model vehicle, possibly one picked out for this specific activity. He's organized, a planner, and he's willing to put in the time to make certain the abduction is successful. Consider the last abduction. He selected the victim, observed her in her environment, determined that the best way to perform the abduction was by entering the residence, and then devised a foolproof way to gain access not only to the manor but to the victim herself. To do that, he had to actually enter the building and determine her location. After that, he was seen going into her room several times, so he may have been offering 'friendliness' "—he mimed air quotes around the word—"to try to win her over. Of course, given her state of dementia, that might have been a futile effort. In total, all this might have taken weeks to work out. But he was willing to put in both the time and the effort."

"You said he selected the victim," Meg said. "You don't think the victims are being selected for him?"

Brian stared at her questioningly. "You mean like a contract killer being hired to carry out a hit?"

Meg nodded. "McCord developed a theory that's way out there, but we have to consider it."

"Right, the thalaikoothal theory." Rutherford left the board and came closer to the table. "Let's talk about that. Part of what he's laid out is correct, without question. Mr. McCord dug into the publicly available background of the three victims and discovered that they all have ties to India. They are of Indian descent, married someone of Indian background, or were adopted into Indian families. India is a large country, and there does seem to be a trend in victim connection with the southern states of the country, especially Tamil Nadu. And that's where Mr. McCord's theory comes into play. There is a historical Indian Tamil practice of geronticide, the killing of family elders through a ritual called thalaikoothal. It is usually carried out by the family and, in practice, can be a community ritual."

"By the . . ." Brian seemed briefly at a loss for words. "By the family? They kill their own relatives? That's barbaric."

"There are stories of seniors who get wind of the planning and then flee their own homes to save themselves. It doesn't happen often today in India, but it does still occur. There are recent stories online highlighting the practice. McCord questioned whether that's what this is. But I don't think it is."

"You think there's a more basic motive than simply age?"

"I do. It's a centuries-old established practice there, and people, including the authorities, are willing to look the other way. But that's not going to happen here. It would be a huge risk to take for relatively little reward. And perhaps you might find some people in the community who would want to do this, but we have three in less than a month and possibly twenty-six over a longer time frame. Yes, there are communities of Tamil diaspora living in many US states, but not that many. Not to mention in an affluent country like America, we have other options to take care of our elderly, including social security, Medicaid or Medicare for citizens, and family members who are likely earning more money and are better able to care for their elderly family members. Parts of India are devastatingly poor, and for some, they may see it as the only way to keep the remaining family intact."

"Still barbaric." Brian shook his head in disgust.

"It is, without a doubt. I do think Mr. McCord is onto something with the connection, though. This case has all the hallmarks of a single killer, so something has to be linking the deaths."

"You don't think this is a contract killer?"

"I don't. Let's talk about the killer's personality. What do we see in his kills? For example, consider the abduction of Mrs. Devar. We know the most about this case. He controls the situation, inserting himself into the environment as someone who can freely walk the hallways of a residence of vulnerable people. He manipulates the victim into walking out of the residence with him. There is some resistance—we know she struggled with him from the trail that Ms. Jennings and Hawk followed and from the evidence left behind. During that fight, he dominated her and maintained that control until he abandoned her to die. Control. Manipulation. Dominance—the three cornerstones of serial killer behavior. But what is his motive? It's not the kill. Killers who find pleasure in killing do it themselves, often by hand so they can watch the life fade out of the victims' eyes. It makes them feel powerful. This strikes me as more like a business transaction. He puts in the work, days or weeks of planning, carries out an abduction that puts him at risk of being caught, especially now that several other fatalities have been discovered and have made headlines in the media, and then enters what has to be a preselected body dump site that puts him at physical risk. But then he doesn't stay to ensure the kill is successful?"

"Do you think that's so he can be somewhere else at the time of death?" Scott asked. "Giving him an alibi?"

Rutherford walked to the board and stood for a moment staring at the victims' faces. "No, I don't. He has to know that in a suspicious death, the first thing we're going to do is an autopsy. Then we'll know cause of death, and the kind of window required for it, and will work backward through the time line. Not to mention we have him on the security camera at Hampden Manor removing the victim from the facility. He can't toy with that time line. That leaves us with a killer who is killing not for pleasure but for a different motive. This is what we classify as a Hedonistic: Comfort Killer."

There was a moment of silence as the room absorbed the label. It was Meg who finally broke the silence. "He finds comfort in the kill?"

"Not in the way you think. Let me break it down a bit further. Hedonistic killers kill for a variety of reasons, but it's always grounded in self-indulgence. Lust killers have an overwhelming need to kill because that's how they find sexual gratification. Thrill killers are sometimes hard to tell from lust killers, but in their case, although they are motivated by sexual gratification, what they get out of the kill is pleasure derived from the victim's terror. These two categories are almost exclusively men. The third kind of hedonistic killer is the comfort killer, and you can find women in this group. They kill for something that brings *them* comfort, not the victim, and most of the time that involves money. Contract killers would fit into this category as well, but I think there is too much connection in this case for contract killing. We're simply missing the actual connection and the trigger for the case. Once we figure out those two issues, then we'll have the complete picture. But the victims and the killer show all the classic traits of this kind of kill: organization, controlled crime scene, specifically known victim. These killers typically leave the weapon at the scene, which is not relevant here due to the cause of death. They also tend to concentrate their kills in one geographic area, but something else is at play here that is spreading them out geographically. And that's tied to the motive, which we have yet to discern.

"What happens during a crime like this speaks volumes about the perpetrator, and this raises another point about the killer—because of the incentive, which may be monetary, I don't sense a focus on the victim. The victims are really trivial to the mission. He spends time figuring out the abduction, but once he has the victim, he or she seems to be secondary. Retain, subdue, poison, abandon. There's no pleasure in the kill, or any concern about a protracted death."

"The victim is essentially a means to some yet unknown end," Craig said.

"Exactly."

"Taking all this into account, can you give us a breakdown of the person we're looking for?" Meg asked.

"I can. We're looking at a white male between twenty-five and thirty-five years of age. He's physically strong, which is why he chooses such demanding sites to abandon his victims. You'll find that he came from a stable home, with a father who was steadily and responsibly employed. He's likely the firstborn. He's of average to above-average intelligence and both socially and sexually competent. He likely holds down a skilled job, one requiring a substantial education, but given the nature of his crimes, he is either salaried and on his own time or a telecommuter with flexible hours, has some other type of employment flexibility that allows him to be out of the office for extended periods, or is self-employed. He's one hundred percent in control from the moment he selects his victims to the moment he abandons them. And he's going to be involved in the urbex community somehow. The average Joe on the street doesn't pick the locations in which you've found victims, because they don't know they exist. And even if they did, they wouldn't have the knowledge to move through the locations with his competence."

"That's a pretty good outline of our killer."

"It will be more helpful once you have a group of suspects to compare it to. Right now, it doesn't point to anyone in particular. Oh, one more thing. He's going to be the type who will follow along on media reporting of his crime. Knowing that could be useful for you at some point. After all, you do have Mr. McCord at your disposal."

"We've used him for that before, and he and his editor are always willing as long as they get the exclusive on the story once the case is closed. It's an option, if we need it."

"Excellent."

"This is extremely helpful," Kate said. "Really gives a better picture of the man we're up against. But I assume he's not done?"

"Impossible to say, really. There's a reason he's going

after these specific victims. When that reason is fulfilled, he'll disappear."

"Because the kills aren't the actual point. You don't foresee any devolution of the suspect or escalation in the kills?"

"I don't believe there will be. This is another reason you need to stop him soon. Not only to save the life of his next victim, if there is one, but because I suspect he'll vanish once the job is finished. This type of personality tends to compartmentalize these activities, and he'll simply move on and not look back when he's done. That will make the job of bringing him to justice that much harder, because there likely won't be another crime downstream to bring him to law enforcement's attention."

"Considering the effort required to plan these kills, do you think there's some time before his next one, or will he be ready to move on right away?"

"That entirely depends on how much prep work he's done in advance. If he has a location list of his victims ahead of time, the urbex sites may already be scouted. Keeping that in mind, as dangerous as those sites are, they would only be more treacherous once the snow flies, so I anticipate he'll want to have his kills completed by winter, or he may pause his activities at that point. Nothing like leaving a clearly traceable set of footprints in the snow to yell 'Here I am!' He's much too organized to make that mistake. Assuming he has more victims in mind, I suspect he'll move on to the next one within the next week or two." He closed the file folder. "As always, the profile will be amended as more information becomes available. And my door is always open if you want to run anything by me."

The group broke up as Kate rose to shake Rutherford's hand.

Brian leaned close to Meg. "The way this guy works it's like his victims are nothing more than notches on a bedpost. If only he'd get his DNA analyzed. Or someone in his family would. Then we might get lucky, like they did with the Golden State Killer."

"We've never been that lucky," she said. "We always seem to pick the hard way to end a case, and I have a feeling this one won't be any different."

CHAPTER 19

Rooftopping: A high-risk, unsecured climb to the top of a building or other structure in order to get a panoramic view.

Friday, November 9, 7:47 AM
Jennings residence
Arlington, Virginia

"Kate Moore."

Meg's reticence dissipated slightly with the alertness in the FBI agent's voice. "Hi, Kate, it's Meg Jennings. Sorry to call so early."

"No worries, I've been up for hours and am getting ready to head into the office. What's up?"

"I have a suggestion I want to run by you."

"Shoot."

"I know you went to Hampden Manor to interview the staff, but did they let you talk to any of the residents?"

"I discussed the possibility with them, but they weren't overly encouraging. A lot of the residents are not well. Strangers tend to scare them and they get confused. We agreed it likely wouldn't lead to any positive results and could actually harm some of the residents."

"I think it would be great to talk to some of them, though. Some of them are likely more lucid than others and may be able to help us."

"I agree." Exasperation crept into Kate's tone. "But we just went over why I couldn't."

"I think I can."

"How would you be different?"

"Because I have a therapy dog."

Kate was silent for a moment. "You think that would make a difference?"

"I do. My sister, Cara, has a certified therapy dog she takes to hospitals, retirement homes, and nursing homes. Patients who most of the time exist in a stupor often come alive when they're with a dog. Something about animal contact speaks to them at a deeper level. With your permission, I'd like to try."

"Are there any risks involved?"

"To the residents? None. You've seen Hawk a few times now. He's very calm and is as gentle as a lamb with the elderly and infirm. I'd also like to bring Cara and her therapy dog, Saki."

"I've heard about this sister. She's the one who likes to get involved in your cases."

Meg winced. "Actually, she's come into the cases because I've asked her to. Because she has a skill I can't find anywhere else. And this is a perfect example. If we find anyone who saw the suspect, I'll do the questioning. Cara will just be there to help narrow the field and to give us a variety of dogs, because sometimes you find someone who had that kind of dog earlier in life and they latch on to it."

A long sigh came down the line. "Okay, you've sold me. But I have some reservations about bringing your sister into this."

"She'll be one hundred percent my responsibility. And she'll likely have a better hand at this than me because she does this kind of therapy all the time."

"All right. Would it help if I called and officially cleared it with the staff? Told them you're coming and why you think you can make the residents comfortable with your visit so they'll talk to you?"

"It would, thanks. Tell them we can be there around ten a.m."

"Will do. Let me know as soon as you're out of there if you get any leads."

"I will. Thanks, Kate. It's frustrating to sit here waiting for someone to disappear. I really want to do something proactive."

"Let me assure you, I understand. I'll call them now. If there's a problem, I'll let you know, but assume you have a green light."

"Thanks." Meg hung up and turned to Cara, who had been sitting beside her for the entire conversation. "You're in. She's a bit nervous about it, but I convinced her."

"Good thing she doesn't know it was my idea." Cara gave her an overly wide grin, complete with batting eyelashes.

"It's a good one, and you're absolutely right that it could well be worth the effort. And I *am* frustrated at sitting here waiting for the next shoe to drop." She stood and called the dogs. "Hawk, Saki, you're up. Let's see if you can make a breakthrough for us."

Friday, November 9, 10:11 AM
Hampden Manor
Baltimore, Maryland

"I think we picked the perfect time to come," Meg said.

"Mornings are always best," Cara replied. "Especially

for dementia patients. They've had breakfast, their energy level is high after a night's rest, and if you can get them some sunlight, you can almost see them come to life. If they're going to be perky, this is when it happens. And this room is perfect. Cheerful, bright. A ton of natural light."

Flanked by their dogs, the women stood in the doorway of a large, comfortable sitting room, brilliantly lit by banks of wide windows that looked out onto overflowing gardens, now showing the sparseness of fall. In the distance, the trees bordering the well-manicured lawn glowed in flaming tones of yellow, red, and orange.

Meg glanced down at the leashed dogs. Hawk wore a simple red collar, and stubby little Saki wore her bright blue therapy group vest with several badges, including the Canine Good Citizen patch denoting her training. "You're the expert. Where do we start?"

"Pick someone to talk to," Cara said. "We've already caught a few eyes. Start with someone who looks interested. Then you'll find it snowballs from there, and people will come near to pet and talk to the dog. *You* may have trouble getting anyone's attention because you're not the star of the show today."

"You know what questions we're asking?"

"I do. If I find anyone who seems promising, I'll let you know right away. Come on, Saki, my love. Let's go make some new friends." Cara led Saki toward a couch occupied by two older ladies.

"Hawk, let's see what we can do." Meg headed in the opposite direction from her sister and approached a wizened old man, sitting by himself opposite a large, cold fireplace. "Hi, I'm Meg. Would you like to meet Hawk? Hawk, sit." Hawk obediently sat at the man's knee, looking up at him. When he continued to stare blankly into the cold fireplace,

Hawk touched his nose to the gnarled hand that rested on his knee.

The man blinked and looked down at the black Lab sitting beside his chair. A smile curved his parted lips, revealing several missing teeth.

"Would you like to pet him?" Meg asked, running her hand over Hawk's head and down his back to demonstrate.

The hand that rose trembled but settled with infinite care on Hawk's head, and the man's eyes closed in bliss. When he opened them, they were bright with unshed tears.

Meg looked over at Cara, who gave her an encouraging smile and a thumbs-up.

The first twenty minutes told Meg it was doubtful they were going to get anywhere and that she had greatly overestimated the ability of many of Hampden's residents to observe the world around them, retain it, and then be able to actually report on it. Hawk was a hit, but most of the residents were only barely verbal with a child's vocabulary, or they spoke gibberish. But their appreciation of Hawk was crystal clear.

A worthwhile trip, though not in the way I'd hoped.

"Meg."

Cara's call brought her head up from watching Hawk with one of the social workers and a nonverbal resident, who was slowly coming alive in his presence. Looking over at her sister, who sat with a woman on a love seat, she caught Cara's hand motions. *Dogs stay, you and I switch.*

Meg nodded at her sister, then bent low to Hawk as she dropped the leash on the floor at his feet. "Stay," she commanded. She met her sister halfway across the room. "Got something?"

"The woman sitting with Saki. She's the sharpest one in the room. Knows the residents and the nurses. She may have noticed a stranger."

"If she can recall seeing one and can tell us about them, that will be a gold mine, because I've come up empty so far. Thanks."

The sisters continued on, and Meg looked back in time to see Cara kneel down on the floor beside Hawk, pick up his leash, and start talking to the elderly gentleman.

"Hello." Meg took Saki's leash as she sat down carefully on the love seat beside the frail woman. She looked to be in her late eighties and leaned heavily on one elbow on the couch but repeatedly stroked the back of Saki's neck as the dog sat quietly beneath the woman's touch. "My name is Meg. Is Saki being a good girl?"

"A very good girl." The woman's voice held a tremor, but her words were clear.

"I'm so glad, Mrs. . . ."

"Lovett. Mrs. Lovett."

"I'm so glad, Mrs. Lovett. Saki loves meeting new people. Do you get many visitors here?"

"A few. Not me, though. I'm on my own."

"I'm sorry to hear that. I'm especially glad then that we could bring Saki to visit with you." She let a few seconds tick by as the woman continued to pet Saki. "You seem to be very aware of what's going on around here."

"More than most people. They're angry and only look inward. Or are just plain daft."

Meg struggled to keep the surprise off her face.

Mrs. Lovett pursed her lips. "Did I shock you? At my age I don't have time to waste. I just speak my mind."

"That's . . . refreshing. Don't stop on my account."

Mrs. Lovett gave a cackle of laughter and patted Meg's hand. "I like you, honey."

"I like you, too, Mrs. Lovett. Could I ask you a question?"

"Of course, dear. As long as I get to sit here with this pretty dog, you can ask questions for as long as you like."

Meg made a mental note to thank her sister again for this idea. "Did you know one of Hampden's residents, Mrs. Devar, left with someone a few days ago?"

Mrs. Lovett's smile faded. "Yes. That was when they put the security guards on the outside doors. They look very stern."

"They won't hurt you. They're here for your protection. But before the security guards came, do you remember any workmen in the residence?"

"There are often workmen here."

"Anyone specific you noticed? Someone who was working in Mrs. Devar's room?"

"You mean the workman who took her for a walk?"

For a moment, Meg simply blinked at her. "You saw her with him?"

"He was helping her. She wasn't always steady on her feet."

"Was she going with him willingly?" Meg asked.

"It looked like it. She was childlike." She frowned. "That's luckier than some. Some people here are violent. But at least they don't really know what's going on. I hope I won't when it's my turn."

Meg knew a reply was required but wasn't quite sure what to say and didn't want to do anything to jeopardize the fragile relationship she was building with Mrs. Lovett. So she went with gently repeating the statement. "Your turn?"

"It happens to all of us here. Everyone is here because of the dementia." When Meg couldn't find the words to answer, she continued. "I know why I'm here. I'm here earlier than some because I was on my own, with no children, no family, and could pay for my own care. And they've recently put me on some new drug that keeps me clear. But it won't last. Soon I'll be childlike like Mrs. Devar. Or worse. But I probably won't know it."

"I'm so sorry."

Mrs. Lovett smiled down at Saki. "Sweet girl. Such a blessing." The eyes she turned to Meg glistened with moisture. "I've been luckier than most. Had over fifty years with my Robert, but now he's gone." The hand that bore a dull gold wedding ring folded into a fist. "I don't want to lose him." She tapped her temple with her knuckles. "He's still here. I don't want him to go."

When Meg didn't know what to say, she simply took the woman's hand, squeezing back at the surprising strength. "Mrs. Lovett, could I ask a really big favor?"

"What's that?"

"You said you saw the workman. Would you be able to tell me what he looked like?"

"Why would you want to know?"

Meg pulled out the FBI flip case she'd thought to bring in case anyone questioned why they were there. She held her finger to her lips and then flipped the case open so only Mrs. Lovett could see it. "I'm here on a case. I'm here to help Mrs. Devar."

"You're an FBI agent?"

"I work for the FBI." Meg kept her explanation simple since she didn't want to confuse the older woman with an explanation of field agents versus canine handlers.

Mrs. Lovett studied the badge for a moment and then nodded. "What can I do?"

"We've seen security footage of the man with Mrs. Devar, but no one saw his face. Did you?"

"Of course. I was sitting in the big comfy chair in the main lobby. He walked right past me on his way to her room."

"Could you describe him to me?"

Mrs. Lovett looked thoughtful for a moment. "He was about my Robert's height, maybe six foot two. He was white, quite fair, actually. The kind that needs to wear sunscreen or they burn lobster red. Fair hair, with some red in it. Freckles across the bridge of his nose. Light eyes, not sure if they were blue or green. A birthmark on his neck, just above the collar of his shirt. Looked like a crescent moon."

Her answer sent Meg scrambling for her phone. "That's amazing. Would you mind repeating it so I could record it? I don't want to miss any details." She cued up her voice recorder app and then held her phone high so Mrs. Lovett could speak directly into it, grinning at her the whole time.

"Did I do all right?" the older woman asked after she had repeated the description.

"Did you ever! Mrs. Lovett, I could hug you." When the older woman blushed with pleasure, Meg did just that. "You could do one more thing, if you think you'd be up to it. Do you think you could work with one of our sketch artists to come up with a likeness of the man you saw?"

Confusion creased Mrs. Lovett's face. "You mean, you want me to draw him?"

"No, no, that's the artist's job. He or she will ask you questions—what are the shape of his eyes, was his nose this broad or that narrow, that kind of thing—and then they'll draw the face you saw. It's amazing to watch, actually."

"I think I could do that."

"I'll call and see if I can get someone to come here today while it's fresh in your mind. Are you free later this morning or this afternoon?"

"I was going to have my hair done, but for this, I think it can wait."

"You're a trooper, Mrs. Lovett." Meg stood. "I have to go now to make arrangements, but hopefully you'll see the artist later today."

The older woman's face fell. "That's the end of my visit?"

"For now. Maybe we could come back sometime soon. And you could meet my dog, Hawk." She pointed across the room to where Cara had moved farther down. "That's him over there. He's a sweet, gentle boy. I think you'd like him."

"That would be lovely." She bent and kissed Saki on the top of the head. "Bye, Saki. You come back, too."

Meg gave Cara a wave and led Saki out of the room and toward the main desk, where she flashed her badge at the new nurse who was stationed there. "Meg Jennings, FBI. I'm here investigating Mrs. Devar's abduction."

"Yes, they told me you were here. Did you have any luck?"

"I did, actually. Mrs. Lovett not only saw the man responsible but gave me a detailed description. After my first fifteen minutes with your residents, I didn't think we'd get any reliable information, but she's amazingly sharp."

"Some of the new drugs available now make such a difference. Not forever, but for months and sometimes even a year or more. And some days are better than others, but it sounds like she's having one of her good days."

"She has agreed to a sketch artist coming in today to work with her, so I'll set that up. I'll make sure you know the name of the individual, who will also be carrying identification, so you can confirm they are from the Bureau. If you'd like the home social worker to be present to ensure that Mrs. Lovett isn't overwhelmed or scared, that would be fine."

"Thank you, I think that would make us feel better. And

we'll make sure Mrs. Lovett has whatever time is needed with the artist."

"Thank you." Meg turned to find Cara and Hawk entering the lobby. "Hey."

"Did she work out?"

"Did she ever. Not only saw him but gave a detailed description. I'm calling Kate now to ask her for a sketch artist." They exchanged leashes, and Meg moved to a quiet corner of the lobby with Hawk as Cara knelt down to praise her dog for a job well done. She dialed Kate's number.

"Agent Moore."

"Kate, it's Meg. I'm at Hampden Manor and I've found a witness."

"Really? That's unexpected. Reliable?"

"I think so. She gave me a detailed description. White guy, fair skinned, strawberry blond, light eyes, freckles, about six-two, crescent-shaped birthmark on his neck."

"Definitely not of Tamil background."

"That was my first thought, too. There goes McCord's theory."

"Theories were made to be busted. We deal in facts."

"We do. To add to the description, she's willing to work with a sketch artist to come up with a sketch. Can you arrange that?"

"I can. When?"

"As soon as possible today. She has Alzheimer's, but she's having a good day and we need to take advantage of it. Just let me know who you get so I can let the staff know to expect them, and tell the artist to bring ID. Needless to say, considering what's happened here recently, they've increased security."

"No surprise there. Good work, Meg. Seriously. We'll be able to use the face in a comparison against our databases. If we need to, we'll put the sketch up for general distribution through the media, if we think it won't scare him off for good. Maybe we'll finally get some traction while we're sitting around waiting for him to make his next move. Let me get back to you in a few minutes with arrangements." She ended the call.

Meg slipped her phone into her pocket and grinned across the lobby at her sister.

Progress. Finally.

CHAPTER 20

Group Shot: A photographic record of every participant in a search or exploration.

Friday, November 9, 11:24 PM
Webb residence
Washington, DC

Meg stretched her legs out on the ottoman as the end credits scrolled down the wide flat-panel TV. "That was good. Goofy and mindless. I needed that. It's been a long few weeks." She laid her head back down on Webb's shoulder and let out a long sigh. "I really think we turned a corner today."

"Cara had a great idea, using the dogs as a way to get residents to talk to you."

"Sure was. And both dogs were great." Meg looked over to where Hawk lay on a dog bed, his torso twisted so his hind legs butted the wall with his belly in the air while the front half of him tipped onto his side. His favorite toy, a chubby, squeaky red dragon with yellow wings, was protectively tucked between his front legs. "I have no idea how that can be comfortable, but he does it all the time, so it must be." A gentle snore came from the dog, and she chuckled. "He sure does like that bed you got him."

She surveyed Webb's living room. Before they became a couple, his compact downtown DC apartment, just a stone's throw away from his fire station, was always neat and organized. Now there was a dog bed beside his flat screen, bags of treats in his pantry, and a scattering of tug and chew toys spread between his living room and bedroom. "You know, it's just struck me how much mess we brought into your life."

He looked at her sideways. "You mean you, Hawk, or both?"

"Mostly Hawk, but it's not really a bachelor pad anymore."

"I can live with that. Actually . . ." He leaned a little away so he could make eye contact. "I wanted to talk to you about that."

"About what?"

"My nonbachelor pad. What if we made that official, and you and Hawk moved in here?"

For a moment, Meg stared at him in silence, not even daring to blink. "With you?" As his eyes went flat and his expression became guarded, she mentally kicked herself. *Of course, with him. Who else?*

"That was the idea, yeah."

She could sense the walls going up between them, both mentally and physically from the way he pulled back as the relaxation in his frame dissipated, replaced with an uncomfortable stiffness. She reached for his hand. "That came out wrong."

"You think? Look, if the idea doesn't work for you, forget I brought it up. Besides, you're in the middle of a case and it's a dumb time for me to suggest it, so—" He started to pull his hand from her grasp.

"Wait." She clamped down on his fingers. "*Wait.* Give me a second. You're catching me off guard."

He fixed her with an unwavering stare but held still.

She let out a sigh and closed her eyes for a moment, gathering her thoughts. Then she took a breath and looked him straight in the eye. "It's clear you've given this some thought, and I admit I haven't." She frowned. "I'm going to say it's not you, it's me."

The laugh that escaped Webb had a razor-sharp edge.

"I knew that wouldn't go over well, because it's a cliché. But I actually mean it. I'm happy with how things are going. Cara's my sister, and I love her, and we do well together. I love living outside the city with a big backyard and having all the dogs together, because that makes Hawk happy. I also love you and having you in my life. Somewhere in the back of my mind, I've known this was going to come up, and I've been pushing it away because I know there's no way to have it all. Cara and I share a house, and it's one thing when our guys spend the night, but neither of us would expect the other to live with them. Not to mention that I live in another city, whereas this place works for you. It's close to the firehouse, and you love living in the city. But it wouldn't work for me full time. For us, really, because you know Hawk and I are a package deal."

"Which is why I suggested you both move in here. I would never ask you to leave him behind. You'd both suffer for it. Not to mention, I like Hawk. He's a great dog."

She turned to smile at her partner, sound asleep and oblivious to everything going on around him. "Yeah, he is." She turned back to Webb. "How long have we been together now? Six months?"

"Yeah."

"We're not teenagers anymore, and it's unreasonable for me to ask you to wait three or four years to settle down. What we have works."

"And could work even better. Look, I'm a firefighter. We're a practical bunch. We don't beat around the bush, so let me lay it out for you. I'd like to commit to something more than what we have now, and I'd like you to do the same." When she started to speak, he cut her off. "If living together here isn't what's going to work for you, then let's figure out a way that will. It doesn't have to be now, during this case, or even this month, but are you interested in moving forward?"

"Of course I am."

"Then think about it. This wasn't supposed to pressure you. I've been thinking about it, and I wanted you to know that. It can be the start of the conversation; it doesn't have to be the final decision. I—" He broke off as Meg's phone rang where it sat on the end table on her side of the couch. "We'll finish this later. You better get that. Any call at this time of night is never good news."

Meg reached for her phone. "Especially in the middle of a case like this." She glanced at the screen—Agent Kate Moore showed on the display—and answered it. "Jennings."

"Meg, it's Kate. He's taken another one."

Meg shot upright, pushing away from Webb. "Already? That makes the last two only four days apart. How long ago did it happen?"

"Around ten-thirty. This time the abduction didn't go the way he wanted it. He picked up Vikram Pillai as he was walking his dog. If he'd just grabbed the guy and stuffed him in his vehicle, it might have gone fine, but Pillai fought him and the dog pitched a fit. Considering the planning that went into Mrs. Devar, he'd probably watched Mr. Pillai and decided this would be the easiest way to quickly grab him while he was alone and out in the open, but he didn't count on the dog. Just a little fluffball Pomeranian, but it barked up a storm, attracting attention. No one got close enough to see more than a dark SUV, but a couple of teenagers managed to catch the dog. No tags, but they called the cops. The cops took the dog to the nearest emergency vet, and it had a microchip with the owner's full name and address. It's given us a big leg up this time."

"I'll say. Where was the victim abducted?"

"Germantown, Maryland. Info is still coming in, so I'll text you more details shortly."

"Thanks. I'd like to get Chuck Smaill involved again. We don't have time for McCord to research sites. I need someone who knows them off the top of his head if he's familiar with the area. You good with that?"

"Smaill was the one you were with during the first and second searches?"

"Yes."

"No objections."

"You realize that once I bring him in, I may not be able to shake him for this search."

"Just find him. You have my permission to use whatever resources you need. Bring this one back alive."

"Done. I'll let you know how things are going when I can." She ended the call and stood. "Hawk, come. I'm sorry, I have to go. Another senior was taken tonight, but it was witnessed so we're way in front of the curve on this one." She grabbed her hiking boots and glanced back at Webb. And froze. "What are you doing?"

"What does it look like I'm doing? I'm putting on my boots."

"Why?"

"Because I'm coming with you."

"You can't. I know you came before, but now this is officially an FBI case. Remember what happened the last time I got outsiders involved in an FBI case?"

" 'You have my permission to use whatever resources you need.' " When Meg stared at him, he said, "I could hear every word, and I followed the whole conversation. I'll bring my pack. I'm your medical resource."

"Good point." She jammed her feet in her hiking boots. "Germantown is about forty minutes away, so we need to get on the road now. Let's call Smaill from my SUV."

Three minutes later, they were speeding through DC's quiet downtown streets following the mapped route on Webb's phone. "Can you call Chuck on my phone?"

"Sure." Webb called up the number on his phone and then keyed it into hers so the call came through her hands-free system.

It rang several times and then Smaill picked up. "Hello?" He sounded clear and sharp. *Not in bed yet.*

Webb held up a finger to tell Meg he'd take the lead. "It's Webb. I'm here with Meg, and I have a favor to ask."

"Whatever you need."

"Meg just got a call. Another victim was kidnapped an hour ago. We're hoping to be able to pick your brain about possible search sites."

"I'll do my best. Where was the victim taken?"

"Germantown, Maryland."

Smaill whistled, and Meg and Webb exchanged cautious glances.

"What does that mean?" Webb asked.

"There's one really obvious place just outside of Germantown. The Old Montgomery County Jail. But that's going to be a hell of a search at this time of night."

"Why?" Meg asked.

"Because it's seriously falling apart. It was built in the mid-nineteenth century and only closed about a decade ago, but one of the buildings was condemned about twenty years ago and they worked around it as it decayed in real time. The key to urbex is to make explorations as safe as possible, and that means daytime searches with plenty of natural light. Sometimes you explore basements, but you make sure you have a really good light source for that. When you're in a place where the floors could give way and the ceilings could cave in on your head, you take every safety precaution or you stay out."

"We don't have time to wait for a daylight search, or we'll lose this victim for sure. What else is in the area? Where else might he go?"

"That's definitely the closest, but it's also the most treacherous place to leave a victim. Otherwise, this area is too built up and too close to the nation's capital. Most places are torn down as soon as they aren't useful."

"Why not this place, then, if that's the case?"

"Because there's a huge fight going on between the county and the historical society. The historical society wants it, or parts of it, saved because of its history as the main jail for DC for more than a century and because the original building is some old Italianate Victorian monstrosity. The county says it's a dangerous eyesore and wants it gone. So while the court battle rages, it sits there decaying. Seriously, though, it's a challenging urbex in the daylight. It could be deadly at night."

"Damn it." Meg took the turn to loop them around and onto the Francis Scott Key Bridge over the Potomac a little too fast, and she heard the scrape of Hawk's nails on his compartment flooring as he slid to one side. "Sorry, Hawk," she murmured. She eased off the accelerator. "Unfortunately, we don't have a choice. This could be our chance to catch him and end it all now."

"It's a big complex. Your chances of catching one man may not be very good."

"It'll be better with four dog teams. Webb's with me, too."

"If you need me, I can come. I've been there before, though it's been a while and I'm not sure how much it's degraded in the meantime. But I might be able to help."

Meg glanced at Webb, who nodded in encouragement. "Okay," she said. "We're on our way and will meet you there."

"I'll gather my equipment and be on my way." The call ended with a click.

"This place doesn't sound promising," said Webb. "Is it worth endangering the teams this way?"

"We'll be careful, but we have to try. I'm glad we talked to Chuck so we're going in with our eyes open. And having him on-site will be even better. But when push comes to shove, you guys shouldn't take any chances. This is our job, not yours."

When Webb didn't say anything, she glanced sideways at him. He was staring at her unblinkingly, his eyes narrowed and his jaw set in a mulish line.

She slumped on a sigh and turned back to the dark road ahead. "I'm doing really well tonight. I'm an idiot, aren't I?"

"You just told a firefighter not to take any chances. What do you think?"

"Yup. I'm an idiot. Look, you know what I mean. Taking chances is what you do day in and day out. I shouldn't be adding to that."

"Smaill and I are offering our help. Our skilled help.

We're carrying medical gear and rescue equipment and know how to use both. Not to mention about twenty years of experience between us. You're actually safer going in there with us than without us if this rescue goes to hell."

"Of course we are. Sorry. Last time I tried to blur the lines I got smacked down, and I guess I'm still a little sensitive to it."

"You got permission already. There are no lines to blur."

"You're right." She flicked a glance in his direction, some of her tension melting away when she took in his more relaxed expression. "Are we okay, or are you pissed at me? Because you need to put that away for now, if you are."

"We're fine, and I'm not pissed at you. Just remember, you're not in this alone."

She briefly squeezed his hand, where it rested on his thigh. "When I forget, because I probably will, be sure to remind me." Then she put both hands on the wheel and placed her next call.

"Craig Beaumont."

"Craig, it's Meg. He's taken another one. This time in Germantown, Maryland."

"When?"

"This is the kicker. It was only about an hour ago. I need everyone."

"Damn straight you do. This is the chance to nail this bastard if you can catch him on-site. Have you got a list of places?"

"Chuck Smaill says there's only one place that makes sense. Old Montgomery County Jail."

"Whoa. That place is a disaster. I've seen pictures."

"That's why I need everyone. And Kate has cleared any additional assistance I need, so Todd Webb is already with me, and Chuck Smaill is on his way. Both have emergency equipment, and Todd has his medical pack in case we need to treat the victim on-site. But I need Brian, Lauren, and Scott. And tell them to carry. If we run into the guy, we may need to be armed. And can you pass on a message to Brian?"

"Sure."

"Tell him I need his spare piece with the holster. I wasn't at home when I got the call, so my firearm is still locked in my gun safe."

"I'll call them now and I'll pass that on to Brian."

"Thanks. I'll let you know how it goes."

"No need. I'm on my way as well as soon as I make the calls. I can't help with the search, but I can help coordinate the teams on-site. I'll see you there." He ended the call.

"Now *that* I didn't expect," Meg said. "He usually coordinates from a distance."

"Better too many people on hand than too few. But you realize what that also gives you? An extra man outside the facility in case this guy gets past everyone inside."

"That's a good point."

"McCord is going to be pissed at you for missing this one."

"I know. But this site is too dangerous, and the last thing I need is him running into the suspect. He can give me a hard time about it later. Cara, on the other hand, will thank me. I wish we could take the time to get a personal article from Mr. Pillai for the dogs so we could do real tracking, but there isn't time if we have any hope of catching the suspect. Granted, by this time, Hawk should recognize the suspect's scent because it's been comingled with the victims' all along. How much longer until we get there?"

Webb checked the map on his phone. "Twenty-four minutes."

"That's too long." She pressed down on the accelerator. "How fast will everyone else get there?"

"About the same. And they'll be pushing the speed limit." She glanced at the dash clock. "Every second that ticks by is a second he could be slipping through our fingers. This could be our one chance to catch him. We can't miss it."

CHAPTER 21

Crater: An unplanned and possibly unprotected fall from a significant height.

Saturday, November 10, 12:39 AM
Old Montgomery County Jail
Germantown, Maryland

The teams assembled just down the road from the county jail, pulling off to the side of the road in a line, taking care to stay out of sight around the corner and uphill from the jail property. They didn't want to blow their one chance to catch the suspect by coming in with lights blazing.

Stealth was definitely called for.

Craig was the final person to arrive. He pulled his car last into the line of the handlers' SUVs and Smaill's Jeep and jumped out with a handful of papers.

"I need everyone over here," he called. "And I need light."

They grouped around the hood of Craig's car, shining their flashlights down on the papers he laid out on the warm metal. Meg moved in to study the aerial photo showing a large property with a number of sprawling buildings spread out inside a forested area. The image had been captured at a slight angle, so the buildings themselves were partially visible rather than just rooftops from overhead.

The November night chill ran down her spine, and she pulled her jacket collar in closer.

"I took the time to call someone I know who has satellite access and can call up previously captured data." As Craig spoke, his breath misted out in the frosty beams from the flashlights. "He got to work getting me the layout of the property, and while he was doing that, I did some research so I could tell you what was where." He pointed to the large, rambling brownstone structure at the front of the property. "This is the original men's cell block from the mid-nineteenth century. These are the two original wings out front, the medical facility was behind it, and this"—he circled a smaller building tucked behind the western wing—"is the auditorium-slash-cafeteria that was added on in the early twentieth century. This concrete structure behind it is the more modern cell block for the men, dating from the 1930s." He tapped the next building. "This is the women's cell block, complete with its own medical facilities."

"What's that?" Lauren asked, leaning in for a closer look. "Is that a house just in front of the women's building?"

"It's the warden's house. He lived on-site."

"It looks . . ."

"Ornate and ostentatious? Even from an enlarged satellite photo? I agree."

Meg focused her flashlight on it. "White stucco with a red-clay tile roof. Because nothing says Maryland jail like Spanish Revival architecture." With her index finger, she circled a building off to one side with a smokestack at one end. "What's that?"

"The powerhouse," Craig said. "It was a big-enough

complex to need its own generator. And these are garages." He tapped two buildings on the outskirts of the property.

Brian crowded in for a better look. "This is a lot of ground to cover."

"That's why I wanted all of us here," Meg said. "A lot of territory, and he's here, too. It's our chance to end this now."

"And save the victim. What's his or her name?" asked Scott.

"Vikram Pillai. According to local authorities he's sixty-five and was abducted off a neighborhood street while he was out walking his dog. He's also likely the strongest victim the suspect has taken, so, if we're lucky, Mr. Pillai is giving the perp a hard time and slowing him down."

"We should be so lucky." Scott's tone held the doubt of many unsuccessful searches.

"Can I make a suggestion?" Smaill interjected. "While we're outlining the search?"

"Of course," said Craig.

"Urbex is rarely done at night because of the risk of serious injury. A lot of these places are already dangerous, and any misstep could be possibly fatal. Now put that exploration at night when there's no natural light. Then make it a situation where you're trying to track a killer and don't want to be waving your flashlights around in the dark to attract attention to yourself. We need to be *extremely* careful." He turned to look directly at Webb. "That goes double for us. Yeah, we're used to hazardous situations, but I've seen guys get into trouble simply because they're overconfident that it can't happen to them." At Webb's single nod of *message received*, he turned back to the group as a whole. "We need to at least be in pairs. No one should be alone in this situation. If you run into trouble, you'll need a buddy to help or at the very least sound the alarm. I have emergency equipment in my pack,

Webb has the med supplies. We can do a lot on-site, but if we don't know there's a problem, we can't help."

"What do you know about this particular site?"

"I've been here once before, but it was over a year ago, so it's probably deteriorated since then. The building that's actually in the worst shape is the modern cell block."

"They don't make 'em like they used to," Brian muttered.

"The lower floor was condemned after only about forty years of use, and they used the upper floors for a while, but then started moving prisoners to newer facilities. The women and some of the men were moved off-site. The original building may be in the best shape. Built solid. The powerhouse didn't get as much wear and tear, but the smokestack looked like it was falling apart back then. Depending on when this image was taken, it may be a pile of rubble by now. The warden's house was relatively safe. And it's small compared to the other buildings, so it'll be easy to strike that off the list."

"Thanks, that's good intel," said Craig. "This is how we're going to set up our searches. Todd, you're with Meg. Chuck, you go with Brian. Scott and Lauren, I want you two to stick together." Lauren started to interrupt him, and Craig cut her off. "I know, we're doubling up the dogs this way, but I need you both safe. Do you each have your service weapon? Meg, you have Brian's extra firearm?"

"Yes."

"Then let's get started. Everyone set their radios to channel twelve, but keep the chatter down to a minimum. We have to assume the suspect is somewhere in this complex and we don't want him disappearing because he overhears us. Flashlights are also going to be a problem, but we can't help but use them, so do your best to keep the light down on the ground. Hopefully, he isn't being so careful, so keep your eyes open for light coming from him." Craig looked up at the half moon overhead, brilliant in the cloudless sky. "Not hugely bright, but at least it's not a new moon." He turned to the aerial view of the complex. "Lauren and Scott, I want you to start at the warden's house, then cover the powerhouse. After that, loop around to the women's block if there's still no word. Brian, you take the original building, starting at the near wing and working your way down. Meg, you take the 1930s block. I want regular communications. Keep it short and quiet, but I want to know where you are in the buildings. I'll answer with a single click so you know I've received your message. If anyone finds him, or the victim, at that point we'll have more communication. Any questions?"

Meg glanced at Webb, who shook his head. "We're good to go."

Everyone else confirmed they were ready, and the teams shouldered their packs and readied the dogs. Meg set her radio to channel 12, ensured the volume wasn't too high, attached it by its belt clip at her left hip, and checked the holster at her right hip. Then they left Craig in Meg's roomier SUV to track and support the teams while also being able to watch the road for any sign of a vehicle or someone on foot. When Meg questioned that he would be okay on his own, he patted the holster under his left arm and assured his team he could handle whatever came his way.

They walked down the access road in silent pairs, Lauren and Scott with Rocco and Theo in front, followed by Meg, Hawk, and Webb, and finally Brian, Lacey, and Smaill. They hugged the side of the road and carried their darkened flashlights, depending on the light of the moon to illuminate their path. As they approached the dark buildings, they silently broke off in pairs with Lauren and Scott heading for the ghostly white form of the two-story warden's house and then Meg and Webb cutting behind the sturdy brownstone Victorian in the direction of the four-story concrete structure.

They did their best to keep their steps quiet as they crossed crumbling and cracked asphalt that stretched between the buildings, Hawk heeling to Meg's left. His head was up, actively scenting the air, but Meg didn't sense that he was onto any particular scent. She knew that for all Smaill's warnings, the site could still be used by urbexers or the homeless, so there could be residual scents lingering. Tonight, it was a matter of trying to track the freshest, and hopefully strongest, scent.

They approached the plain concrete building, and Meg looked up the rows of barred windows to the scant crenellation detail that some Art Deco architect added to dress up an otherwise drab, utilitarian exterior. *He'd failed.* Down below, someone who considered himself a street artist had tried to do the same with spray paint in multiple colors, a jumble of bubbled or angular letters spelling out faded words pointing to a gaping doorway leading into inky blackness.

Ready? she mouthed at Webb, and he gave her a nod. She stepped over the threshold, Hawk at her side, and paused for a moment inside the door, letting her eyes adjust to the darkness as she waited for any sign of artificial light or any hint of a sound—a moan from the victim, or the scrape of the suspect's boot.

But there was only darkness and quiet.

However, the longer she stood there, the lighter the space became. Up above, a huge section of the ceiling had collapsed inward, and a wide swath of sky was visible through the gap. Moonlight filtered into the building, and Meg was slowly able to discern the internal structure.

They stood at one end of a huge space, the roof soaring four stories overhead. The outer wall comprised vertical lines of barred windows stretching nearly from floor to ceiling; the building was designed so daylight would stream inside, cutting down on the need for electric lights at a time when only half the country had them. The cell block rose as a huge brick tower attached to one end of the building to touch part of the existing roof. The cells were constructed of sturdy brick walls, broken at regular intervals in layered levels up to the roof by gaps where cell doors once stood. A single railing lined some of the walkways above that stretched along each row of cells; some areas were an unimpeded straight drop to the floor below.

Meg looked down at the motionless dog at her side—his head was high, his nose actively sampling the air, his attitude one of focus and interest. Meg touched Webb's arm and pointed down at Hawk. He nodded in understanding.

Hawk detected fresh scent.

She wished she could radio Craig to let him know they might have a possible scent trail, but she didn't dare. In the silence of the huge, echoey building, her voice would carry, giving away both their presence and their position. They would risk losing the man they tracked and would make themselves targets. She would let Craig know when she had more definite information. Not wanting to risk a clearly transmitted radio message from anyone else, she turned the volume dial on her radio down to nearly zero.

Bending, Meg unclipped Hawk's leash to give him freedom to maneuver without restraint, then gave him the hand signal for "find." Hawk started into the cell block, Meg following closely, and Webb bringing up the rear. Meg held her dark flashlight in her left hand, but she was conscious of the weight of the firearm at her hip near her free right hand. She sincerely hoped she wouldn't need to use it tonight, but she would if given no other choice. In the meantime, she needed that hand for climbing.

The first floor was littered with long, heavy wooden beams and trusses from the collapsed roof, mixed with tar paper, shingles, and bricks. Clambering over a bulky beam, Meg glanced upward, the small, niggling concern at the back of her mind for the stability of the structure growing exponentially.

It's seriously falling apart.

Smaill wasn't wrong.

Hawk slipped under a fallen truss that lay propped against the second-floor walkway, and Meg had to duck to follow him. He headed for the far end of the building; as they got closer, Meg realized that double, opposing sets of open metal stairs climbed the block at that end. The staircases met at a single shared platform on the second level that then joined the catwalk hugging the end of the cell block, running to either corner, where the next flight of stairs rose to the third level, repeating again up to the fourth floor. One of the flights of steps leading to the upper level had come free from the concrete walkway that should have anchored it and instead sagged, untethered, into thin air from the third floor.

Hawk overshot the stairs, circling a tangle of wood and mangled rebar, but then paused, his nose down, scenting the floor. He explored the ground toward the back of the cell block for a few feet and then turned, sniffed around the pile of debris, and climbed it without hesitation.

The scent trail led upward.

Meg did her best to ignore the gut punch of fear that threatened to knock the air from her lungs as she looked up to the cracked and broken concrete platforms, many of which lacked railings, and to those barriers that did exist but couldn't be trusted.

She turned sharply to the nudge at her back. Webb pointed over her shoulder to where Hawk was now six steps ahead of her. She met his gaze, knowing he could read her thoughts in that moment, and then turned away, climbing up onto a truss to step onto the stairs. The stability of her first step told her that this part of the staircase was intact and would support the three of them, so she followed her dog toward the moonlight.

Hawk paused only briefly on the second level, decided on a direction, and then trotted to the far flight of steps to continue his upward climb. Meg followed him, taking care to keep her steps as quiet as possible. She avoided looking down but took comfort from the graffiti that flowed across the brick wall beside her, a testament to the stability of the stairs that street artists had used as a platform for their murals.

Up to the third floor. This time Hawk didn't hesitate, and followed the scent across the platform to the only remaining flight of stairs.

They were getting closer. The scent was stronger.

Hawk started up, Meg behind him, but when Webb mounted the steps, the staircase gave an ominous grinding sound up above. Looking up, Meg caught the faintest sprinkling of dust visible from the contact point. If she could see the concrete actively disintegrating in light this low, it must be close to giving way as it had on the other flight of steps. She held up an index finger to Webb. *Wait until we're up. Too much weight.*

He nodded and stepped off the steps, onto the concrete floor of the third-level platform.

Hawk climbed to the fourth floor, and Meg glanced up nervously. A painted tin ceiling, remarkably similar to the one she'd seen in the Massaponax Psychiatric Hospital, sagged just overhead, white paint peeling off to reveal darkness beneath. Wooden boards, still partially attached at one end of the roof, drooped like grasping fingers down toward the walkway. The entire roof looked as if it could cave in on their heads at any second.

But Hawk was unmindful of the threat of his surroundings. He had the scent, and his drive directed him to find it at all costs. He left the staircase and immediately trotted to the catwalk leading to the far side, heading for the far corner of the cell block.

Meg lightly tapped the staircase railing twice, hoping Webb would hear the quiet sound and know that was his signal to come up, and then followed her dog. He'd have to catch up to them; she had to have her dog in sight at all times in an environment as treacherous as this. Turning the corner, she saw that the roof opened to the sky and stars shone softly overhead. She exhaled heavily with exertion, her breath forming a diaphanous cloud in the frosty moonlight. The catwalk was a mere three feet wide, and she hugged the line of cells, refusing to look down, so far down to where debris that had already tumbled from that floor lay broken and mangled.

Even so close to the outside air, the atmosphere seemed deadly still, with only the barest whisper of wind as it fluttered over the gaping edge of the roof. But the back of Meg's neck prickled. *We are close.* She jammed her slender flashlight in her coat pocket, freeing her left hand, and drew her firearm with her right. So high up, the moonlight was enough to guide her way now.

Up ahead, Hawk trotted faster. She wanted to call him back but didn't dare without attracting attention. He paused for a moment outside a cell, almost seeming unsure of his direction, and then disappeared into the darkness within.

With a breathless spurt of fear for his safety, Meg abandoned silence and jogged after Hawk, focusing on the dark doorway where she'd lost sight of him.

Meg never saw the blow coming. As she paused in the

doorway of the cell where Hawk had disappeared, fumbling in her jacket pocket for her flashlight to find her dog in the dark, a man appeared out of the blackness of the adjacent cell, slamming full length into her. They both crashed sideways into the ancient metal railing that was the only barrier between the walkway and a fatal drop onto brick, wood, and steel below. The guardrail shrieked at the pressure, but held, stopping their sideways momentum with an abrupt jerk. But with one hand tangled in her jacket pocket, Meg was forced to let go of the gun so she could free her right hand to clutch at the railing to keep from going over. In a distant corner of her mind, she registered Brian's gun spinning off to smash against the barred windows twenty feet away and then plummet to the floor four stories down.

Freeing herself, she pushed off the railing with both hands to stand upright and planted her elbow in the stranger's solar plexus, hearing his grunt as he exhaled heavily. But he snaked his arm around her neck, cranking her head toward him at a brutal angle and taking him with her as he toppled backward. She managed to brace one leg, keeping them upright, but that left the man's full weight wedged against her windpipe, cutting off her air.

She had only seconds to act.

Send him over the edge before he does it to you.

Years of self-defense training kicked in, and rote actions took over. Pushing up straighter, Meg clamped down with both hands locked on his forearm and pitched forward, gasping cool night air into her lungs as his weight shifted, freeing her throat. She tucked into a crouch, levering downward with all her strength on his arm, and sent him flying over her head. But at the last second, his weight shifted, so instead of going over the railing, he crashed to the concrete platform at her feet.

There was an earsplitting crack, like a gun exploding in her ear, and the solid concrete floor disappeared from beneath her feet.

She heard Webb bellow her name over Hawk's frantic barking, and then she was falling.

CHAPTER 22

Hacking: The clever use of an urbex setting or materials.

Saturday, November 10, 1:18 AM
Old Montgomery County Jail
Germantown, Maryland

Meg crash-landed on her right hip with a force that shot bolts of blinding pain through her body and stole the breath from her lungs, just before her head struck a solid surface. As chunks of concrete rained down, she curled self-protectively into a ball, her arms looped over her head. But the sounds of scrabbling quickly reminded her she wasn't alone in the fall, and she jerked upright, taking in the scene in a single glance.

Twelve feet above, a six-foot span of the level four platform had disintegrated and she was now lying on the third-floor walkway directly beneath, which—thank God—remained intact despite both the weight and the force of the materials falling from above. A man was struggling to his feet about ten feet away. He looked back at her quickly—she got an impression of light hair and fair skin, although they were both covered in concrete dust, so she couldn't be sure—and then hobbled as fast as he could for the stairs.

"Meg!" Webb's head appeared over one edge of the platform, Hawk at the other. *Thank God no one else was hurt.*

"Find Mr. Pillai!" She tried to shout it, but she still fought to get her breath back and the demand came out as a croak. She tried again as she struggled to her feet, louder this time, hoping Webb heard, and then staggered after the suspect. Her legs weren't working quite right, and she nearly fell trying to climb over the concrete debris from the collapse. Then she lurched onto the open platform, but by that time, the suspect had a twenty-foot lead on her.

She tried to sprint after him but was wracked by pain and had trouble focusing her eyes in the dim light, so she had to settle for a stumbling half jog, her left hand out against the bricks, her right extended to grab the railing if she wavered too close to the edge. She took the corner at the end of the cell block as fast as she could, nearly falling but catching herself at the last moment. The man was clattering down the stairs, almost at the landing, as she dove for the steps, clutching the railing to stay upright.

She wasn't going to be able to manage this on her own. She needed help.

She ripped the radio off her belt, dialed the volume back up, and hit the talk button. "It's Meg. I found the suspect." She hit the second level and lurched down the platform to the next set of steps. He was nearly at the bottom. Was he getting farther away? "We're in the new cell block. I'm in pursuit." She stopped talking to drag in a breath with lungs that felt sluggish and half-frozen. "Need assistance. He's hurt. I'm hurt. He won't be able to run fast. Need assistance." In the back of her mind, she knew she was repeating herself, but she couldn't get her brain to fire correctly.

"I copy," Craig replied. "All teams, do you copy?"

Clutching the radio in her hand, Meg climbed over the pile of debris at the bottom of the steps on the ground floor, squinting at the shadowy figure running for the exit. One by one, the teams reported in with their positions.

"He's exiting the building. Still in pursuit."

The suspect disappeared out the door, turning left. Meg jogged after him, clearing the same doorway only about fifteen seconds behind, but in that period of time he'd disappeared. She circled the building and spotted him again, running past the women's cell block, straight for the trees lining the rear of the facility.

Meg knew without a doubt she wasn't going to catch him. He was already too far ahead, and she was too unsteady. She leaned against the concrete outer wall of the building, panting, and raised the radio to her mouth again. "I can't keep up with him. He's headed north, toward the forest behind the complex. Is anyone near? If not, send the dogs, they'll pick up his fresh trail. I don't have Hawk, he's still inside, possibly with the victim. I'm going back in."

Turning, she staggered into the building, slowly retracing her steps up the stairs. Her vision was starting to stabilize and, although she was in pain, nothing hurt badly enough to hint at a fracture. Banged up, but not out of the game.

Which was better than she could say for Brian's gun, lost somewhere in the debris of the first floor.

She was panting in jagged breaths by the time she got to the fourth floor. She jogged down the platform, not sure what she'd find other than Webb trapped on one side of a gaping hole and her dog on the other, but the platform was empty. However, a glow came from one of the cells on the far side, and two heavy wooden beams lay across the gap, forming a makeshift bridge.

Leave it to a firefighter to find a way to jury-rig a bridge.

Bracing one hand on the bricks, she fixed her eyes firmly on the far side and stepped onto the beams, testing her weight. When there was no play under her feet, she carefully started across the gap. She was halfway across when Hawk appeared on the far side, his dark eyes fixed on her, his body still as if sensing her concentration. "Hey, Hawk. I am beyond glad to see you. Give me a second. I'll be right there." Four more steps and she was on solid concrete with her arms full of her dog, who went up on his hind legs to lick her face and to sniff her everywhere as if to confirm she was still in one piece. "I'm okay, buddy, I'm okay. Settle down. Todd?"

"In here . . ."

Webb's unnaturally forced voice came from the second cell on the right, and she ran in to find him on the floor between a hinged metal bunk and the remnants of a sink and toilet unit at the far end of the cell. He crouched on the dirty floor over an elderly man, his hands layered as he administered CPR. His cell phone lay facedown on the bunk, the flashlight app throwing a cold blue-white light over the narrow room. Webb looked up as she came in, his gaze piercing as he scanned her for injury, taking in her scrapes, developing bruises, and the way she held on to the edge of the doorway for balance.

"How bad are you hurt?" he asked.

"I've been worse."

"Meg." The word came out as a half growl.

She sank down to kneel beside him, conscious of Hawk shadowing her every move. "Everything hurts, but I don't think anything's broken."

"Did you hit your head?"

Meg simply stared at the man on the floor and didn't say anything.

"I'll take that as a yes. You know the concussion you got in July makes that a problem."

"It's not that bad. I didn't lose consciousness this time."

"Small favors."

"I consider it a small miracle I didn't fall all the way to the ground floor, so I'll happily take this. Is he going to make it?"

He simply looked at her as he bobbed up and down with the compressions, then stopped and felt for a pulse at the man's throat. Eyes closed, he held his fingers there for too long; then he sat back, his hands falling to brace on his thighs. "He's gone. He was gone before we got here, but I had to try."

Meg drew back as if he'd slapped her. "What? I thought we had a chance this time. He was taken only two hours ago. The difethialone should have taken longer than that to work."

"Maybe this time it's a different dose. Maybe it's a different poison. Or maybe he was already in fragile health and couldn't take the combined strain of the kidnapping and the poison."

"He was out walking his dog. He can't have been *that* fragile." Frustrated, Meg slapped her hands to the filthy floor and pushed upright to stand, swaying with the sudden change in position. Hawk jumped up, pressing against her legs.

Webb shot to his feet, grasping her by both shoulders to hold her still. "Whoa, steady." He bent to peer into her eyes, his expression torn between clinical assessment and a lover's concern. "I want to check you out. Find out if you're concussed." He glanced over his shoulder.

She followed his gaze to the grimy, rusted bunk. "I am not sitting there. If you want to check me out, it can wait until we get back to my place." Even held between his hands, she felt unsteady and grabbed at his belt to anchor herself. "Maybe you can drive home?"

"That goes without saying. I assume you didn't catch him, or you wouldn't be back so quickly?"

"He got a head start on me, and I was a little bleary. I'm better now," she blurted in response to his intense stare. "Anyway, he was headed for the forest around the facility, so I called in the other teams. The dogs will follow the fresh scent, and Theo is a master tracker. If there's anything to find, they will. Hopefully there'll be an update soon."

"You need to call Craig. Tell him about Mr. Pillai."

She sagged slightly. "Yeah, I do." She tried to pull away, but he resisted, holding on tightly. "It's okay, you can let go."

He released her, but his hands hovered over her shoulders until he was satisfied she was steady.

She pulled the radio off her belt again. "Where did you get the wood you used to build the bridge?"

"Right off the roof. A bunch of boards were still partially attached, and I yanked two of them off. Lost the first one down below because I wasn't prepared for how heavy it was. Got the next two. They were solid enough for me to cross. That's when I found Mr. Pillai. He didn't have a pulse but was still warm, so I tried CPR." He looked down. "No dice."

"Thanks for trying." She raised her radio to her mouth. "Craig, it's Meg. We lost Mr. Pillai. He was dead before we found him. We're going to need an ambulance. Given where we are, I'd recommend calling in firefighter paramedics because it's going to be a tricky extraction."

"Copy that," said Craig.

"Anyone found the suspect?"

"We're tracking him." It was Brian's voice coming over the radio this time. "The dogs are agreed on the scent trail. Meg, are you okay? You said you were hurt. You sound steadier than before, though."

"Fell about ten or twelve feet when the concrete platform I was on collapsed. Rang my bell pretty good. But Todd is with me and will make sure I'm okay."

"And will drag you kicking and screaming to the ER, if required," Webb muttered.

She sent him an irritated glare. "We're going to stay here until Mr. Pillai is removed. Keep me in the loop. Meg out." She attached the radio to her belt, sudden exhaustion weighing her achy limbs with lead, her muscles protesting even the tiniest movement. She took in the filthy bunk—no way in hell was she going to sit there—and turned and limped out of the cell, Hawk on her heels. She glanced at the railing overlooking the four-story drop and opted to lean against the opposite wall, tipping her head back to stare up at the moon and stars through the gaping hole in the ruined roof. She felt the warm press of Hawk's body as he sat down close to her.

Webb came out of the cell, took one look at her, and leaned against the wall beside her. He stayed silent for a full minute, waiting for her to say something, until it became apparent she intended to remain silent. "You okay?"

She didn't look at him. "I told you, I don't think anything's broken."

"That's not what I mean, and you know it. I know you. You're going to consider this a failure."

"Well, it's not exactly a win, is it?" She could hear the bitterness and self-recrimination in her own voice but couldn't hold it back. "We had the best chance we're probably going to get in this whole case of finding a victim alive, which didn't seem to matter. I let him get the drop on me—"

"He didn't get the drop on you."

"He nearly put me over the railing. That fall would have been fatal. I'd call that getting the drop on me."

"You notice he didn't put you over the railing? By the way, I caught part of that fight. You totally had him, and I was flat-out impressed the way you flipped him over your head." He paused for a moment, as if weighing his words. "And then you scared the hell out of me when the floor disintegrated under both of you."

The sound that escaped her was dark with a biting edge. "You think it scared the hell out of you? I thought I was dead. It's a miracle the walkway below us held."

"Speaking of which, I want a look at you." Turning to her, he pulled the ponytail elastic out of her dust-covered hair, jamming it in his pocket, and then gently slid both hands into her hair, running his fingertips over her skull, carefully testing for lumps or anything that gave her pain. "Where did you hit?"

She was stiff momentarily, not wanting his touch or his comfort. *Can't he see I don't want his help? That I need a few minutes inside my own head to process what happened?* But when he continued his examination in the face of her silence, she slumped, giving in to his persistence, and covered one of his hands with hers, sliding it up to a spot on the back of her head. "Here." She groaned as his fingers probed, her nails biting into the back of his hand. "Yeah, that's it. It hurts, but it's not that bad."

His gaze fixed blankly on the wall beside her head as he concentrated on the scalp and bone under his fingertips. "No big goose egg, but I still want to check you out once you've had a chance to clean up." His hands slid away. "Any blurry or double vision, dizziness, nausea?"

"I was definitely wobbly right after, and the trip down the stairs was seriously tough. Like, I thought I'd pitch over the railing kind of tough, but that was bad only for maybe ten minutes. Once I stopped trying to push it, it got better."

"Might be a grade one concussion at worst, maybe not even that, but I'm still going to take a better look once we get out of here. What about the knee? Did you tear it open?"

Meg shrugged carelessly. "Honestly, I'd forgotten about it." She gave it a trial bend and winced. "It hurts, but I think that's just the original injury." She dropped her boot to the floor with a broken, cynical half laugh. "I'm a mess."

"This one's been rough on you, no doubt about it. But I sense a trend."

She shot him a questioning sideways look. "Meaning?"

"If there's anything I've learned about you since I met you last April, it's that when you get involved in a case, you give it your all, and your own physical well-being seems to come secondary. If—"

Meg's radio came to life with a spurt of static, then Brian's voice said, "The dogs lost the scent trail. It looks like he did the same thing as before and parked at the side of a rear access road. He's gone. We've lost him again."

"Copy. Come on back," Craig replied.

"Roger. We're on our way."

Meg sagged against the wall in utter defeat. Vikram Pillai was dead, the suspect had eluded them, they had no additional clues as to his identity, and he now knew they were hot on his trail, which would only make him more cautious than before.

They'd failed in every way possible.

Now the question was, who would pay for that failure with their life?

When Webb wrapped his arms around her, she reflexively pushed back, hissing a protest.

But he ignored her, pulling her in. "Stop fighting me. Let

go for a minute. No one will see. There's no one here but us." He touched his forehead to hers and simply held on until the stiffness left her body and she let herself lean on him.

Together, they waited in silence for help to arrive to take away the dead.

CHAPTER 23

Catch Basin: A low point beneath the street where water collects before flowing into a drain.

Monday, November 12, 6:32 AM
Rock Creek Park
Washington, DC

"Are you sure you're up to this?"

Meg sent Brian a sidelong, slit-eyed glare, then turned back to the leaf-strewn path, picking up her pace slightly, forcing him to work harder to stay with her. Hawk and Lacey, running alongside, enthusiastically joined the race, easily staying with her while Brian fell a pace behind.

Running was part of Meg and Brian's regular routine with their dogs. Their job required that both handler and dog be in top physical condition, and that included long-distance stamina. Meg hated running with a passion, but she knew it was a necessary evil for the long, strenuous hours of search-and-rescue. Since misery loved company, she and Brian met at least once a week to jog together with the dogs. When she'd called him last night to confirm their previous arrangement to meet this morning, he'd pressed her to ease off for a few more days, considering the beating she'd taken on Saturday.

It had been past three o'clock in the morning when she and Webb finally got to her place in Arlington. Once she'd showered off the concrete dust and the grime, Webb had checked her from head to toe, not letting her rest until he was satisfied that she didn't need professional medical care.

"You're a paramedic. You are *professional medical care."*

"Don't be an idiot. I wasn't kidding when I said I'd drag you kicking and screaming to the ER if it's required."

"Come to bed."

"Not until I'm sure you're okay."

In the end, he was satisfied that she wasn't badly hurt, even though she was a mess of scrapes and bruises. She slept like the dead for six solid hours and then woke up wondering how to climb out of bed when every muscle felt as if it were on fire. Webb got her upright and then Cara had coaxed her through a gentle yoga routine centered on stretching, which she admitted left her more limber and less burdened by pain. She was a sight to behold, though, her body a blooming mass of angry purple and black bruising.

But she was convinced she'd manage the jog this morning just fine. Her only concession to her injuries was a shorter route—a three-mile loop instead of their usual five- or six-mile minimum. It was bad enough that she'd agreed to that. Now to have Brian second-guessing her again was pissing her off.

She pushed away her frustrations, trying to recenter herself in nature. Dawn had lightened the cloudless sky, and the sun's burgeoning rays burnished the leaves with the glowing tones of flame. She struggled to concentrate on the beauty around her, but Saturday's failure still weighted every step, darkening the brightness of the day.

Just as the sun broke over the horizon, she and Brian had parked in the practically empty lot near the Boundary Bridge, where Rock Creek flowed from Maryland into the District of Columbia. The temperature hovered around fifty degrees, and Meg had dressed in her usual athletic leggings but had donned a sweatshirt to ward off the cooler temperatures until the jog warmed her. As usual, by tacit mutual agreement, they said little and immediately got to the job at hand; the sooner they started the torture, the sooner it would be over.

Meg almost immediately regretted her own insistence that she was fit to jog in the early morning chill over an asphalt trail. Every step vibrated pain up her legs, shooting through her right hip and straight up her spine. Even her shoulders felt locked into place, inhibiting her usual easy arm swing. Fluid motion of any kind seemed beyond her, so she put her head down, clenched her jaw, and pushed through the pain.

By this point they'd crossed the charming bridge with the arching wooden railings and followed the winding trail through the partially denuded forest in a curve that took them away from the creek, though she could hear the rush of the water ahead of them and see the glint of light flashing off cascading streams.

Brian caught up to her, tossing her a nonplussed raised eyebrow. "You're awfully cranky this morning."

"I'm always cranky in the morning."

"Well, yeah. But you've dialed it up to eleven this morning."

"So you're trying to make me crankier? Is that wise?"

"Babe, you know I would walk through fire for you. I will always have your back. But I will also always tell you when you're being an idiot. And right now, that's exactly what you're being."

Meg stopped dead in the middle of the path. Brian and both dogs went on several steps farther before they realized she wasn't with them.

Spinning around, Brian held out both arms in question. "What?"

"Me being an idiot seems to be a trend lately."

"Who else called you that?"

"Todd."

"Good man. He doesn't take anyone's crap."

"He really doesn't."

Brian walked back to her. "What's going on?" When she turned away, he grabbed her arm, earning a startled cry of pain. He snatched his hand away, letting go of her as if she were made of molten metal. "Sorry, that was a reflex. I forgot you're hurt."

He took a moment to study her, and Meg assumed she looked lousy from the concern that darkened his face.

"You know what?" he said. "I know loser buys coffee, but I'm going to buy the coffee this morning even if we don't take one more step. You look awful. Why are you pushing yourself like this?"

Meg started to say something, then threw up her hands and walked down the trail to the river. A warm brush of fur touched her leg, and she looked down to find Hawk beside her; he'd follow her anywhere, without question. His loyalty made her feel slightly better.

The trailed curved left ahead to flank the creek, but instead of following it, she angled off the trail to a wooden park bench near the edge of Rock Creek. She sank down onto the bench and slumped, her hands dangling loosely between her knees as she stared at the water tumbling over craggy rocks as it raced downstream.

Brian sat down beside her, carefully leaving a few inches between them but not allowing her any significant distance. "Can I make a suggestion?"

She turned her head to fix him with a flat stare. "What?"

"You're moving like an automaton. You could really use a chiropractic adjustment, because there's no way your alignment isn't out of whack after that fall. I go to a miracle worker of a chiropractor. Let me call him for you this morning and try to get you in."

"How is that going to help?"

"Then you won't be in physical pain, which will help you focus on the task at hand. Because I know what's going through your mind right now, and it's not that."

"You know better than I do?"

Brian slung his arm across the top of the bench, slipping his hand over her shoulder to chafe it companionably. "How many cases have we worked together?"

"Too many to count."

"And in all that time, there's not many times the case gets to you right here." He lightly tapped her temple with his index finger. "I mean, not counting the Garber case, because that was the whole point. But for normal cases, when you aren't a target, you stay objective. Yes, we get pissed or frustrated, but you always keep your head in the game. But something changed for you on Saturday morning. I could see it then, and I can see it now."

Meg didn't say anything, just stared straight ahead, her jaw set, her shoulder still under his hand.

But Brian wouldn't let her shut him out. "What was it? You're pissed because the walkway disintegrated? Because you couldn't keep it intact with the power of your mind? Because, of course, that was totally in your control as a woman who can do everything. Maybe if you'd used that power to—"

"I got distracted for a moment, okay?" she snapped at him. "I would have had him, but Hawk disappeared into a cell and I couldn't see him and I was focused on getting to him before anything went wrong and I wasn't there to stop it. I should have known something was off, simply from the way Hawk was acting. He paused at that first doorway before going in. Normally, he wouldn't do that, he'd go right in, but he must have been detecting the separate scent trails. The suspect and the victim going into one cell and then the suspect leaving to go hide in the next cell. But Hawk went after the victim—possibly because he was picking up on fear pheromones—and I was totally focused on going after him and nothing else. That's when the guy came out of nowhere. I had him, Brian, I had my hands on him, and I probably could have held on to him if I'd been ready. But I wasn't, and now, instead, he's still out there and someone else is going to die and—"

"So help me, if you say it's your fault, I'm going to slap you." Brian ruthlessly cut her off. "And you're going to deserve it. Let me get this straight: You were searching a building that was falling apart, with the roof literally caving in. Your dog, your *partner*, disappears from view, and you think he might run into trouble and you wouldn't be there to keep him from getting hurt, or worse. That's why you got distracted for a millisecond. It was bad timing, and that's all. I would have done the same thing. So would Lauren or Scott." He looked down to where Hawk and Lacey lolled, panting, at their feet. "These dogs are our whole world." His voice softened, the harsh edge gone. "You lost Deuce, and that's a nightmare I can't even imagine." He dropped his free hand onto Lacey's head and stroked it lovingly. "You would do anything to keep something from happening to Hawk."

The image of her Richmond PD German shepherd K-9 partner Deuce filled Meg's mind. Shot in the line of duty by the perp she was pursuing, he'd died in her arms as they'd huddled together in the rain, and she'd thought her world had ended. Until she'd returned to her parents' rural animal rescue to find a sickly black Lab puppy that had taken all her time and attention to pull from the brink of death. And in saving him, he'd saved her in return.

Hawk nudged her hand with his nose, as if sensing her thoughts. She ruffled his ears, and he licked her hand in return. "Yeah, I don't think I'd make it a second time. Maybe that played into it."

"Of course it did, on a totally subconscious level. You didn't stop to analyze it, you just reacted. It was bad timing that the guy went for you just then. But from how you and Todd described it, you totally had him, and if the walkway hadn't collapsed, he'd be in a cell right now. Want to blame something? Blame the crumbling infrastructure, not yourself. Distracted or not, you were getting him under control, until you both went into free fall."

Meg blew out a long breath and sat back against the bench, coming into the circle of his arm. "I guess." She looked up at him. "Leave it to you to pull me out of a funk."

"I knew if I was irritating enough, you'd talk to me. And I can do irritating, let me assure you."

She tipped her head onto his shoulder. "You're a pain in the ass, do you know that?"

He planted an overly dramatic, smacking kiss on the top of her head. "I'll be whatever you need me to be, as long as you don't shut me out. We work better together when you actually talk to me."

She laughed. "We sure do." A thought occurred to her, and she jerked away from him. "Oh no. Your gun."

"What about it?"

"I had it that night, and the guy knocked it out of my hand and it dropped four stories onto the floor below. I didn't even think of it. We need to go find it. Anyone could pick it up and use it."

Brian patted her knee. "No worries there. A Germantown PD officer found it later that morning once the sun rose and they had daylight to search. Though I'm pretty sure it will never fire a bullet ever again with any kind of accuracy. It's kind of banged up."

Meg winced. "I'm sorry, I'll replace it."

"Don't give it a thought. Craig's already taking care of it. Uncle Sam will replace it. So . . . want to finish the run?"

She ducked her head as her cheeks heated. "Would you mind if I took a rain check? I'm actually a little sorer than I originally thought."

"A little?"

"Okay, a lot. I'm not as up for a run as I thought I'd be. But I'm up for coffee if you're still buying. And I'll tell you about Todd asking me to move in with him."

Brian's eyes popped comically wide. "No way. I definitely want all the dirt. But yes to coffee. I'll slap myself if I don't get some caffeine soon. And because I'm a prince among men, I'm even going to spring for a scone for each of us."

They stood and slowly started up the path toward the cars.

"What's the plan for after the coffee and the scones?" Brian asked.

"Apparently, you're taking me to the chiropractor. After that, we're going back to work." Meg's voice was rock hard. "He won this round, but I'll be damned if he's going to get the next one."

CHAPTER 24

Dirty Shot: A photograph taken using maximum aperture (minimum f-stop) and high electronic gain (ISO) to capture action in low light. The resulting image is grainy and blurred.

Monday, November 12, 11:16 AM
Forensic Canine Unit, J. Edgar Hoover Building
Washington, DC

Craig regarded his entire team as they squeezed their rolling desk chairs into every nook and cranny of his office, leaving only enough room for the dogs to flop at their feet without the risk of rolling over a vulnerable tail, ear, or paw. "Thanks for making time for this impromptu meeting." He fixed Meg with an expectant look. "You said you wanted to regroup."

Meg looked around at the teams of humans and dogs crowded into Craig's office. "I feel like we need a plan moving forward after Saturday morning's f—" She jerked slightly and cut off the description "failure" when Brian kicked her chair and nailed her with an icy look. "Incident," she finished, earning a satisfied nod from him.

"Before we start beating ourselves up," said Craig, "because I know you guys and how you forensically analyze every case, I'd like to review what went right." With his index finger, he started counting off points, starting on his opposite pinkie. "One—the kidnapping got reported almost immediately. Two—we had a slight delay when the recovered dog had no tags, but we got full ownership information from the microchip. Three—the case got referred to us from the local PD immediately. Four—we had expert identification of the search location. Five—everybody, including our rescue and medical resources, hit the ground running and bugged out with their dogs and equipment in minutes flat."

"You're running out of fingers," Brian commented dryly.

"I love it when so many things happen like they're supposed to that I run out of fingers," Craig shot back. "Six"—he looked pointedly at Brian and started at his pinkie again—"everyone arrived promptly, we paired up for safety, organized effective search quadrants, and had the search underway just over an hour after the initial call. Seven—we had the suspect located within twenty minutes of starting the search." He looked directly at Meg now. "Say what you will about the fact that we were unable to apprehend the suspect, but the discovery of him was textbook. I couldn't have asked for a better response, so thank you all for a job well done."

Meg gave him a reluctant smile she knew didn't reach her eyes.

"Now," Craig continued, "let's look at what happened on-site. Meg, I know you're not happy the suspect got away from you."

"Not especially." She fought to keep the sour tone from her voice.

"I talked to Webb that night," Scott said. "In his opinion, you had him contained. He was down, and you would have had him cuffed and subdued in another ten seconds, but the walkway collapsed. Since he was already flat on the ground, he probably didn't get hurt as badly as you. You were on your feet and went down and hit your head. It's no wonder he managed to get away."

"I'm pretty sure none of the rest of us would have fared as well as you did," Lauren interjected. "If he'd jumped me, well, it wouldn't have been very pretty and I might have ended up going over the edge. You had the skills and the strength to fight him off, saving your own life. It's damned unlucky the apprehension went south after that, but that's not your fault."

Meg looked from Brian to Scott to Lauren. "Did you have a meeting ahead of time and agree to boost my ego?"

"Nope." Lauren's hand flick said she was having none of that. "We're just telling it like it is. You did the best any of us would have done, and we're lucky no one was killed. It's not good you got hurt, but even that could have been worse."

"For a minute there, I thought I was going down, so I agree, it could have been a lot worse."

"Agreed all 'round." Craig sat back in his chair and observed his team. "And, yes, some of the incident didn't go as planned. Let's start with Mr. Pillai. He was the victim in the best mental and physical condition so far, and yet he was dead when we arrived."

"There must have been a different poison in play," Brian said.

"Mrs. Devar was found alive and is currently recovering," Lauren added. "This case has made media headlines, and they trumpeted that win. And you remember what Rutherford said about how the suspect would be following media headlines? He's revised his methodology so it doesn't take as long, but that might have simply involved increasing the dose of the difethialone. Maybe he increased it because the kidnapping didn't go as planned and the dog raised an alarm, so he didn't think he'd have as much time before the victim was found. How long until we find out what was used?"

"It's usually at least three or four weeks," Craig replied, "but I can see if I can speed that along."

"I always wondered about that." Scott leaned forward so he could see Meg around Lauren. "How did we get that first tox result on Mr. Roth? That was less than a week."

"Officer Turner called in a favor so they'd get the results run quickly," Meg replied. "And I guess the poison wasn't a low-enough yield or complicated enough that it needed extensive testing, or even the favor wouldn't have helped."

"I'm not sure that getting these test results faster will make the difference to us. The important thing to know is that our search times are cut to a fraction of the original window." Scott looked down at Theo, snoozing at his feet, his heavy canine head centered between paws hidden by his draping, floppy ears. "We're going to need as many dogs as possible at every scene to cover all the ground, and we're going to need them to work faster. Then we might have a chance."

"Is any forensic evidence going to come from the jail scene?" Lauren asked. "Anything that might lead us to a suspect ID?"

"Crime scene techs have swept the jail cell where Mr.

Pillai was found as well as the stairwell railings and the third- and fourth-floor platforms, but there's substantial smearing, and the concrete dust following the collapse just complicated matters."

"And then I went staggering down the stairs after him, probably obliterating anything usable." Meg shook her head in disgust.

"You'd just been clobbered over the head," Brian pointedly reminded her. "If you hadn't held on, you would have fallen down the entire flight of steps. They'll have your prints on file, so if they get anything, they'll disregard yours. Here's a question I've been meaning to ask: Did you get a look at him?"

Meg gave a half shrug. "Sort of? Nothing to pin an identification on. When he originally came at me, I got an impression of size and strength that lines up with what we already knew from the Hampden Manor security tapes, but that was about all I got while fighting him. I will say, he was strong. If I hadn't had training that kicked in on pure instinct, he probably would have tossed me over the railing to die down below. But it was dark and he came out of the shadows, so I didn't get a look at him; then he was behind me, and then by the time I'd flipped him over my head and he was on the floor at my feet, the walkway was giving way, and cataloging his features was the last thing on my mind. Afterward I got a bit of a look at him, but he was covered in concrete dust. I think he was fair with light hair, but that's the current suspect description, so I might have assumed that was what I was seeing. Really, considering how much dust I had on me, and how it made my hair kind of a ghostly gray, what I saw might not have any similarity to his real appearance."

"You couldn't swear it was the same man from the security feed and the description?" Craig asked.

Meg shook her head. "I'm sorry, no. Given the lighting, the circumstances, and my knock on the head, there's nothing reliable for us to go on." Meg caught a flash of movement behind Lauren. Standing, she spotted Kate Moore by her desk. "What is she doing here? Kate," she called, waving. "We're in here."

Kate strode to Craig's office door but stopped in the doorway at the sight of the entire team sandwiched inside. "Am I interrupting a meeting?"

"We're reviewing the case," Craig said. "Please join us."

Brian stood and offered Kate his chair. "Sit. I'll get another one from the bullpen."

"Thanks." Kate sat down and shifted her chair closer to Lauren. "Good thing we're all friendly."

"This is why I need a conference room," said Craig. "I'm sorry about the crowding. This is what our impromptu meetings always look like." He waited while Brian pulled another chair in and sat down in the office doorway, Lacey coming to sit at his feet. "Do you have something new for us?"

"I do," said Kate. "Forty-five minutes ago, a man posing as a hospital orderly tried to get to Bahni Devar. We think he was trying to finish the job."

There was silence for one second, and then everyone started talking at once.

"Whoa!"

"Did they get him?"

"How did he find her?"

"Is she okay?"

Kate held up a hand for silence. "First of all, he did *not* finish the job. We've had one of the hospital security guards stationed outside her door since she arrived, so anyone who wants to enter has to be on a list provided to the security staff daily, and their photo ID must be shown each time. As far as how he found her, that was the hospital's fault. My instructions were that her name not be included on any public patient lists, but it was. He simply called Baltimore area hospitals until he found her by name. Then he showed up, dressed as a volunteer with what looked like a hospital ID and carrying a large flower arrangement, and he tried to enter the room. However, he wasn't on the list and the guard blocked him. He jammed the flowers into the guard's hands and power walked away. The guard checked the flowers for a card, but there wasn't anything. He called down to the flower shop, but they didn't have an order for that room. He called the security office and they tried to track the guy down but were unsuccessful. He just . . . disappeared."

Tension arced through Meg as if by an electric charge. "This changes everything. He has a purpose."

Kate nodded. "Exactly."

"Hold on," Scott interrupted. "What do you mean, a purpose? Of course he has a purpose, or else why would he have gone to all this trouble?"

"It's not quite the same." Meg stood and turned to face the map still tacked to Craig's wall. "It makes me wonder how many of these are really his. Because what he did today proves that he's not just doing this for kicks. He's taking specific people, and it's not just for the thrill. He actually wants these specific people dead."

Kate picked up the thread. "And when Mrs. Devar survived her abduction, he returned to finish the job. To make sure she ended up dead. So now the question is, why?"

A sudden chill filled Meg, and she whirled back to face Kate. "You need to beef up security on Mrs. Devar."

"Already done. There will be an agent on her door twenty-four/seven until further notice. Before, it was a precaution. Now, it's a requirement. Oh, I need to show y'all something." She pulled out her phone and brought up a photo. She turned it around to face the room. It was a police sketch.

"Is that him?" Meg stepped forward for a better look. She held out one hand. "Can I take a closer look?"

"Of course."

Meg took the phone and studied the sketch intensely.

"Is that the guy you saw on Saturday?" Brian asked.

"Still really hard to tell. I wouldn't have been able to describe him well enough to create a detailed sketch. That being said, nothing strikes me as being out of place from what I saw that night, in the low light and under a coating of dust. I assume you showed this to the guard who stopped him?"

"Yes. He says the man purposely tried to stay half-hidden behind the flowers and then tossed them at him so he was scrambling to hold on to them while the guy turned and walked away. So he never got a full view of him."

Meg handed the phone to Brian. "You have to think he did that on purpose, too. No one is getting a full look at him."

Brian handed the phone to Lauren so she could see the sketch. "Except the one little old lady he assumed had dementia but was actually sharp and aware and cataloged every aspect of his appearance. That one little old lady could be how we bring him down." He stood and joined Meg at the map and stared at the flags. "Back to the victims—there has to be a connection between them. Well, between some of them, if we assume that we've included some deaths that aren't involved."

"We need to do a seriously deep dive on the victims we know are involved. Even if we look at only these four victims, the ones we can directly connect to this suspect, what connects *them*? McCord's initial work didn't lead to anything tangible. Then again, there are additional players now."

"And the goal is the death of the victims." Lauren passed Kate's phone to Scott. "What about life insurance? Any way they could all have the same beneficiary?"

"They don't even all have life insurance," Kate said. "I looked into that with their families. You know the rule—you don't insure your dependents. Many of these people were totally dependent on family and caregivers, so there was no need to insure them to care for those left behind. Some had modest policies to cover funeral expenses only, but most had nothing. That's not our motive."

"Could they all share some secret?" Brian asked. "Something so terrible they all needed to die to keep it hidden?"

"But then Mrs. Devar doesn't make much sense," Meg reasoned. "Her memory is mostly gone, and what's left is disappearing by the day. She simply isn't a reliable witness in any way."

"Still, we should keep it on the list of possibilities." Kate took her phone from Scott and started making notes. "It's possible the killer didn't know how advanced her dementia was."

"Will you update Rutherford with these new details?" Craig asked.

"As soon as I get to my desk. He needs this new information for his profile."

Meg shifted uncomfortably in her chair, knowing her next request was pushing her control of this case. "Kate, with your approval, I'd like to put McCord back on this. He's done some research on these people, but I'd like to see if he can find more. In conjunction with our work, of course. But sometimes, with his connections and investigative reporting skills, he can pull facts out of seemingly thin air."

Kate paused for a moment, considering, but then nodded her assent. "As long as he continues to sit on the story until I release him to go public with it, I don't have a problem with that."

"I'll call him today and get him back on track. If we can figure out a connection, we can maybe figure out who the next victim or victims might be. If we can do that, maybe we can beat him to the punch." Her smile was full of determination. "It's time we started calling the shots. Let's make it happen."

CHAPTER 25

Light Painting: Moving a handheld light source within a dark space while the shutter of the camera is left open.

Monday, November 12, 1:22 PM
S Street Dog Park
Washington, DC

"This feels like old times."

Meg looked up at the sound of McCord's voice and grinned. "You mean like when I stalked you in this very park posing as an innocent dog owner but was really fishing for information?"

"And here I thought it was my boyish good looks that won you over." McCord sat down beside her on the iron bench encircling one of cherry trees lining 17th Street NW. He unclipped Cody's leash, and the golden retriever took off in a blur of frenetic motion to join the pack of dogs racing around the open green space.

Tucked into a compact triangle between S Street NW, New Hampshire Avenue NW, and 17th Street NW, the dog park was a green oasis surrounded by rows of Victorian brownstones and neat apartment blocks. In the middle of bustling Washington, DC, it was a spot for dog owners to safely let their dogs run free while they breathed in the fragrant garden air.

It was also conveniently close to McCord's brownstone apartment. And it was here that Meg had tracked McCord down last April when a serial bomber terrorized the eastern seaboard and had used McCord and the *Washington Post* as his own personal mouthpiece. After a rocky start, Meg and McCord had agreed to work together to solve the case. That success had led to other cases, and they'd been working together when a case required it ever since.

Meg looked up at the graceful tree branches stretching wide overhead. Back when they'd met, the trees had been a glorious pale pink profusion of DC's iconic cherry blossoms; now they were resplendent in tones of crimson, gold, and topaz.

She turned her attention back to McCord. "I've always been attracted to your wily mind, McCord."

McCord let out a bark of laughter. "Good thing your sister loves me for my mind *and* my body." He waggled his eyebrows comically.

Hawk and Cody raced up to them, and Cody dropped a bright green tennis ball at McCord's feet. He picked it up and lobbed it into the middle of the green space. Hawk and Cody tore off after it, and were joined by another four dogs as they barreled toward the far end of the park.

McCord was chuckling as he turned to Meg. "He really loves it here. Loves to kick up his heels with whoever happens to be handy."

"He looks great now." Meg followed the pack of dogs, her gaze locked on Cody. "He's filled out nicely, and Cara says his manners are almost flawless."

"Yeah, she's done a great job with him."

"*You've* done a great job with him," Meg countered. "Cara is a great teacher, don't get me wrong, but I know how much work the dog owner puts into training their dog. You live with him day in and day out. The instructor is your support system, but you're doing all the work. And it's paying off. He's a great dog."

"Thanks." McCord grinned, gazing after his dog as Cody rolled on the ground with one of the other dogs. Then they were both up and racing to the far end of the park, Hawk sprinting behind them. "And as much as I love to hear you singing Cody's praises, I know you're here for something. So, what's up?"

"I was actually going to stop downtown. You know, at the office where you work?"

"Working from home today on an exposé for next week, hopefully. If I know I'm going out for research, I'll often start my day that way. And Cody loves it when I work from home."

"I'm sure he does. Are you too busy to do some snooping for us?"

"I'm never too busy for snooping when the story is good, and this one is. I can make the time for this and the exposé."

"Look at you, multitasking like a woman. I'm so proud."

"This is how you convince me I should be helping you?"

"You know as well as I do you'll jump through hoops to get an exclusive on a big case. You in?"

"That goes without saying. I'm just giving you a hard time because I can. What's new with the case?"

"We need to kick up the investigation." She paused as Hawk trotted over, snuffled at McCord's leg's, stood still for a stroke from Meg, and then bolted toward to the pack. "Something interesting happened this morning. He went after Bahni Devar at the hospital. We think he intended to finish the job."

McCord's eyebrows shot straight up. "He went back to try to kill her a second time?"

"Yes. He wasn't successful."

"I'm glad to hear that. You went through a lot so she'd survive. I'd hate to see him win now. But he needs her to die. It's not just about taking them and leaving them to die at his handpicked sites. He actually needs them to die. Why?"

"I knew that you'd see the significance without my having to spell it out. The why is where you come in."

"How?"

"The Bureau is full of agents, but sometimes you're better at digging deep and pulling out investigative angles no one else can manage. We have a group of victims, and maybe more if we go back to Agent Moore's potentials list. You've sketched out some possible connections in their ethnic backgrounds, but I don't think we're convinced your thalaikoothal is the motive. So what else connects them?"

"Considering their connected ethnic background, it seems likely there may be some basis in that. I assume you're in a rush."

"Lives could depend on it. I missed him on Saturday and—" She broke off at McCord's narrowed stare. "Okay, we all missed him on Saturday, so he's out there and still a threat. Unless he has a specific list and that list is complete, he's going to be on the hunt. Even if the list is already established, as long as people are on it, he'll be hunting."

"What about Mrs. Devar? Is she still under guard?"

"Now more than ever. Kate is keeping an agent on her door twenty-four/seven. He won't get to her again. Whatever his end game, we've already got him beat there. But if we can figure out what it is, we'll have a chance at tracking him down before he goes after someone else."

"Or providing protection to anyone else who might still be a target." McCord scanned the dog park, stopping when he found his dog. "I'll give him ten more minutes to play, then he should be ready to nap for a few hours and I can work in peace."

"Do you need to go into the office now?"

"Nope. Anything I need there, I can access from home. I can put off the other story for a few days and work on this full time so you get an answer sooner."

"Your editor isn't going to be upset that you put an existing story to the side?"

"Not when we get the exclusive on this one. This one is time sensitive, the other isn't." He glanced at his watch. "If something pops sooner, you'll hear from me, but I'll update you on how I'm doing Wednesday morning no matter what."

"That sounds perfect. Thanks."

"No problem. Someday I'm going to have a Pulitzer for investigative reporting sitting on my shelf, and it could very well come out of work like this. But even without that incentive, you know I'd be in the trenches with you." A speculative gleam came into his eye, and Meg knew he had the scent every bit as much as her dog did at a search site. "Making that second attempt so soon on Mrs. Devar was a tactical error, because now we're on his trail. And we're going to make damn sure he's going to regret it."

CHAPTER 26

Holy Grail: A high-risk, high-reward exploration that requires extensive research, planning, and sometimes collaboration and teamwork.

Monday, November 12, 8:29 PM
Jennings residence
Arlington, Virginia

McCord's first text had come in Monday night:
Can I bring someone else in on the case?

Is it absolutely necessary?

Yes. Having language issues. Multiple dialects.

Do you trust this person?

Yes. She's solid. An editor here. Have worked with her for years.

Meg made the executive decision based on the fact that Kate had already given her permission to bring in whatever resources she needed.

Keep it confidential but do it.

The next text from McCord had come on Tuesday just as she got home from work.

Need more time.

How much more?

Can we push the update to Thursday?

Is this good news?

Yes. I'm onto something.

Thursday it is.

She knew he really was onto something from the way he dropped out of sight.

Even Cara hadn't heard anything from him other than the briefest of texts. They'd only been together for six months, but she was already accustomed to his blackout investigative reporting sprints. "He's caught the scent," Cara said. "It's radio silence because he's probably working around the clock and not eating or sleeping." She frowned down at Blink as he ambled around her feet. "I hope he's feeding Cody."

"Don't worry about Cody," Meg replied. "That dog won't let anyone starve him or not take him out. Though I admit he's likely not being walked and is mostly being left to his own devices." She could see her sister fretting, not about the man—he could take care of himself—but the dog. "Cody will be fine. A few quiet days won't kill him. And if you're really worried about him, bring him here for a few hours or overnight. He'll be happy as a clam with us."

Not surprisingly, an hour later, Cara walked into the kitchen with Cody, who proceeded to dance joyously from human to dogs and back again in an excited circle.

Meg pushed through the canine frenzy to open the sliding door that led out to the deck and their fenced backyard, and then stood out of the way while four dogs shot through. "How's he doing?" Meg asked. "McCord, not Cody." She stepped through the doorway into the rapidly fading twilight, watching the retriever bullet around the backyard, stubby little Saki admirably keeping up with him. "Cody is clearly in his element."

"I got a mumble, two grunts, and the most distracted good-bye kiss ever." Cara joined her sister on the deck and slid the door shut behind her. "He's really on the trail of something. Not that I got any details, but he had about sixty tabs open in his browser, several files of notes, and a Slack window going on his phone, so he's actively working with someone."

"That part I knew. Not that I know who it is." Meg leaned on the deck railing. Hawk raced by with a knotted rope dangling from his mouth, kicking up a plume of multicolored leaves behind him, Cody close on his heels. "He'll let us know when he's ready, I guess."

"You can't rush him. He'll resurface when he has something. In the meantime, I'll feel better knowing Cody is getting some attention."

Meg poked her sister in the arm. "Look at you, caring more for the dog than the man."

Cara poked her back. "Not true. McCord can take care of himself. I have no doubt there'll be a stream of delivery food arriving around the clock. Our having Cody will actually make his work easier because he can stay focused."

"And most of the time you like dogs more than people." Meg held up her hand, palm out.

Cara high-fived her with a grin. "You got that right."

McCord's next text came after ten o'clock Wednesday night.

10am at the Post. In my editor's office. Martin Sykes. Bring Agent Moore.

Aye aye, Captain.

A gif of *M*A*S*H*'s Hawkeye Pierce giving a saucy salute was his only response.

Thursday, November 15, 9:57 AM
The Washington Post
Washington, DC

The next morning, Meg, Kate, and Hawk arrived at Martin Sykes's office. Kate knocked on the door, and a sharp voice barked, "Come in!" from the other side.

Kate entered the office with Meg behind her. The room was spacious and well-lit from a wall of windows that looked over K Street to Franklin Square beyond. Framed stories and awards covered every open inch of wall space. A square-jawed man with steel gray hair and assessing eyes sat behind a desk covered with paper printouts and sheets of newsprint. A Washington Capitals mug with multiple coffee rings stacked up the inner surface sat beside an older-model desktop computer.

McCord rose from one of four chairs in front of the desk; two chairs clearly belonged there, and two more had been brought from the small meeting table near the windows. "Meg, Agent Moore, thanks for coming in to meet with us." He held out a hand toward his editor. "This is Martin Sykes, my editor. Sykes, this is Meg Jennings and Agent Kate Moore, both of the FBI. And this is Hawk, Meg's search-and-rescue K-9." He waited while Sykes shook hands with Meg and Kate, and then he stepped back to reveal a woman sitting in the adjacent chair. "And this is Priya Chari, one of our best multiplatform editors."

The petite woman stood and held out her hand with a warm smile. Dressed in black dress pants and a simple black sweater, she set off the outfit with a stunning scarf in vivid tones of indigo and silver with dangling silver earrings to match. "It's nice to meet you," she said. "Please, join us."

Meg took the chair next to McCord while surreptitiously studying the newcomer. Her facial features and fashion accents spoke of her ethnic heritage, but her vocal inflection was born-and-bred New York City. Her name was unfamiliar, but she trusted that McCord wouldn't have brought her into the case if he'd had any other choice.

"Thanks for coming down to meet us," McCord said. "We wanted to bring you up to speed as soon as possible, and I thought it would be best if you could meet Priya personally and could ask her any questions directly." He glanced at Kate, but then his gaze settled again on Meg. "I know you wanted the circle kept as close as possible, but I couldn't do the research I needed, and I'd trust Priya with anything. She's been here at the *Post* for six years now—"

"Seven," Priya corrected.

"—seven years now," McCord continued, without missing a beat, "and she's thorough, efficient, and dependable. And a damned good editor."

Priya leaned on one elbow to stare at McCord. "I'm already on board to help. You can stop pumping up my ego."

Meg stifled the laughter that sprang into her throat at McCord's disconcerted expression. She liked this new colleague already. Tempering the smile that twitched at the corners of her lips, she turned to Sykes. "Mr. Sykes, thank you again for your willingness to give Clay the freedom to work with us. You've been flexible several times in the past few months, and the Bureau has noted that flexibility and is appreciative."

"We're happy to do it." The rasp in Sykes's voice spoke of years spent in smoky newsrooms, flavored with what Meg bet was a tendency toward scotch. "The stories are always worth the extra effort. Including this one." He picked up a folder off the desk and held it out. "McCord, bring everyone up to date."

"You got it." McCord took the folder, laid it on his lap, and opened it. "We've previously talked about the South Asian connections between the victims found by the Human Scent Evidence Team. Donna Parker was adopted at age six into the Achari family, Indian immigrants in New York City, and she took their family name. Fourteen years later, she married Harry Parker and moved to Virginia, and her name changed again. But she stayed in close contact with her family, as have her children and grandchildren. Warren Roth was married to Jovita Peera for nearly fifty-five years until she passed away two years ago, leaving him in their house in the retirement community. Jovita was born in India, in the southwestern coastal city of Kochi, and came to the US as a baby. Bahni Devar was born in Maryland, but her parents were from Chennai, the capital of the Indian state of Tamil Nadu, and immigrated to the US shortly after they married. The newest victim, Vikram Pillai, also had ties back to India. He immigrated with his children to the US from Madurai when he was in his forties. They moved around the country a lot, but he was retired and living in Germantown. We've also got three other victims who are a potential part of the pool."

"You mean the three seniors found in abandoned buildings before the case started for us?" Meg asked.

"Yes. First there's the gentleman found in the mansion near Trenton, New Jersey. Norman Stanley. At first, I couldn't find any Indian connection for him, until I finally discovered that his daughter married into an Indian family. Then there are the two individuals who SSA Beaumont tracked down. Iniya Pearson was found in the Martinsburg movie theater. She's a second-generation American, but her family hailed from Thanjavur in southern India. Kathir Nadar is the one I'm having trouble finding information on. We have his name because his wallet was found with him in the abandoned brewery, but we don't know much else. He was a recluse, kept very much to himself, and had no family in the area. So I need to do more work there and simply ran out of time with everything else I had going on. But if you look up the genealogy of his family name, it has Tamil origins."

"Were you able to find a connection between the victims?" Kate asked. "None of our research turned up any links between them that could be related back to business or family relations."

"At first, I couldn't find anything either. Life insurance was a mixed bag with no common beneficiaries for those who had it. They didn't live near one another, and as far as their families know, they didn't know one another. There was no overlap in jobs or careers. From the research and interviews I did, the Indian connection is the only one I've found that seemed relevant, so I dug deeper there. The families were eager to help in any way that would advance the case, but I admit at the beginning I had little hope we were going to get anywhere. And then one of Roth's grandkids, a guy who's one of those business whiz kids who had his eye on an MBA before he even started his undergraduate degree, mentioned what he described as the 'weird annuity' his grandfather received. The kid apparently helped his grandpa do his taxes every year and knew about this single fund that paid out in rupees that were converted to American dollars for deposit here. That's the main reason it caught his attention—the foreign currency. But his grandmother was Indian, so he didn't really dwell on it until I really started asking questions. When I asked Vikram Pillai's son, he said his father had a similar investment. And that's when I knew I was onto something."

"And that's when he realized he needed help," Priya said.

"I'll say." He pulled a pamphlet out of the folder and handed it to Meg. "You see my difficulty."

The paper was blocked out in bright tones of gold and orange and covered with an array of letters comprising curving lines and bars. She met McCord's eyes and took a wild guess. "Sanskrit?"

"Devanagari." Priya answered for McCord. "It's Hindi. I translated it for him."

"I see why we needed you." Meg turned to McCord. "You recognized it as a South Asian script?"

"That was about as far as I got with it. Once I had your okay, I took it to Priya, who speaks Hindi and several other languages."

"Tamil, Telugu, and a smattering of Malayalam," Priya said. "I can understand it much better than I can speak it."

Meg extended the pamphlet. "What is this?"

"It's an investment advertisement. For the specific annuity in question."

Kate plucked it out of Meg's hand and looked at it. "I thought English was the language of business in India?"

"It is, especially for international business. But there are plenty of citizens who don't speak it fluently. This is for them. This isn't a multibillion-dollar, multinational deal, this is an investment for regular people who are looking to make some money to retire on."

"It's an IRA?"

"Not exactly." The gleam was back in McCord's eye. "Are you familiar with the term 'tontine'?"

Meg glanced at Kate, who shrugged. "Apparently neither of us are. It's a financial term?"

"Yes. It's an annuity fund that is set to pay out annually to the shareholders in the fund at the time. Everyone buys in at the beginning to a joint fund, investments are made, and then dividends are distributed as expected. They tend to be low-risk, high-yield investment funds that can be paid in installments. However, a tontine has the provision that the annuities are paid out only to surviving investors. As the investors age and die out of the fund, the remaining surviving investors receive higher payments."

Meg opened her mouth, closed it again when nothing came out, and swiveled in her seat to stare at Kate, who wore a dumbfounded expression that mimicked how Meg felt.

McCord leaned toward Priya. "I told you she'd get it inside of about three seconds."

Meg finally found the words. "They're killing each other off in a race to the final payout?"

"I think so, yes. Or a variation on that theme. And before you ask, yes, we've done the legwork. In India, only insurance companies offer annuity plans. This one comes from Kalidasa Life Insurance Company. Most of their annuity funds are the traditional kind that pays annually, settles with the beneficiary after the fund holder's death, and then closes. But a tontine is a group annuity that pays out to all the investors every year."

"So it's a race to see who can survive the longest," Kate said.

"Until the one person left is getting all the income." Meg sat back, shaking her head in disbelief. "What a scheme."

"It's better than that," McCord said. "When there is only one person left, the tontine dissolves and the final investor gets all the income as well as all of the original investment."

Kate whistled. "That's a hell of a motive. How is this even legal?"

"It's not," Priya clarified. "At least not in America. It is legal in several European countries, like France. It is also legal in India."

Hawk, lying at Meg's feet and doubtlessly feeling the tension in the room, pushed his head against her knee. She stroked his head until he relaxed and lay down again. "The fund is based in India, which is where they invested the money?"

"Yes. From what I can gather, the most important issue was the low buy-in value of the initial investment. The rupee is not a strong currency, and the poverty rate at that point was quite high, so the insurance company itself was looking for an infusion of US dollars. The company set up this specific fund as an investment initiative for Indian diaspora living in America, and investors went looking at members of Indian diaspora cultural associations, essentially recruiting them to invest. This is why we couldn't connect the victims—they didn't belong to the same associations or communities, but the company paid to send employees to the US to entice Indian diaspora to invest." McCord flipped through a couple of pages until he came to a specific one. "And I don't know if the insurance company was extremely savvy or they happened to get in on the ground floor of a gold mine by chance, but they invested in technology stocks." He stopped and looked at them expectantly. "The fund started in 2000."

Meg glanced from McCord to Kate—who shook her head—and back again. "Does that mean something?"

Sykes leaned forward over his desk, as if for emphasis. "Before outsourcing became what it is today."

Meg understood then. "Before some of this country's biggest tech companies started outsourcing their technical support lines and coding teams. Before those businesses started employing huge numbers of people, and likely raking in some pretty big profits."

"Blessing their early investors with a portion of those profits."

"So you're saying this fund did well. If they reinvested some of the profits into additional shares, then the profits have continued to grow," Kate stated.

"And when you're talking about winner takes all," Sykes said, "the last man standing is going to have a very, *very* nice payout."

"Yeah, I did a little research on that to see what kind of investment it is, and has been. Did you know that outsourcing is nine and a half percent of India's GDP and that they provide sixty-seven percent of the world's information technology? All while hiring workers at a starting salary of a whopping eight thousand dollars a year."

Meg winced. "Ouch."

"You can say that again. So the fund made a very nice profit. From what I understand from the families of the American investors, the income from these annuities made a big difference in the comfort of their retirement." McCord pulled out a pile of papers consisting of smaller bundles paper-clipped together and stacked. "Business whiz kid provided several years of statements from the annuity. But not everyone kept statements, or at least the family doesn't know where they are at this point."

"They must still be shell-shocked," Meg said. "Some of the victims might have been less stable as far as their health was concerned, but some were fairly healthy for their age, so the loss is jarring."

"Can I take those?" Kate asked.

McCord extended the papers to her. "He scanned and sent them to me, so you can have these copies."

"And all the victims were enrolled in this fund?"

"Yes."

Meg grabbed Kate's forearm. "We need to find out who else is in the fund. That could quite literally be the kill list."

"We'll have to get cooperation from the Indian authorities, but I'll get to work on that now. One thing is clear, though—it doesn't sound like whoever is doing the killing is one of the investors. You said the fund started in the year 2000?"

McCord nodded. "Yes."

"Then we're looking at someone who likely hadn't even reached the age of majority at that time, let alone had money to invest."

Meg had a brief flash of the man struggling to his feet on the cell block platform. "I agree. He's too young. Maybe he's a friend or relative of one of the investors?"

"Or maybe he was hired by one of the investors so he or she kept their hands clean," McCord suggested. "But either way, I agree, he's killing on behalf of someone else in the fund, not himself."

"Maybe not," Sykes said, "but if he's killing for a relative, he may be waiting for the money to come to dear ol' grandpa before ol' grandpa becomes the last tragic death."

"And we still don't have any idea why the urbex locations." Meg considered the search sites they'd explored. "You want these people to die and you're not going out of your way to hide their identity. But then you're not leaving them where they can be easily found. What if someone got missed? Then there's no big final payout because the fund is ongoing."

"What if he's trying to give himself some space?" McCord proposed. "What if he will ensure the bodies are found, he just wants some time to go by so his fingerprints aren't all over the killing, so to speak. If he's familiar with urbex sites, he may know how often they're explored, so he knows that the bodies will be found within a matter of weeks. I still think he's there, in that community. That's where we need to go looking for him."

"These are good questions." Kate considered the flow of numbers down the statements. "Questions we need to answer to finish this. The circle is closing in on him, though. We're getting closer. It's only a matter of time now."

CHAPTER 27

Texta: A marking pen with a thick writing point made of felt or fiber used to paint graffiti.

Thursday, November 15, 7:53 PM
Jennings residence
Arlington, Virginia

"What are those? Crime scene photos?"

Meg had been so involved in her work, she hadn't heard her sister come back from walking all three dogs, and she jumped at the sound of Cara's voice in her ear. She turned her head to find Cara's chin practically on her shoulder as she leaned in to study her laptop screen. "Hello to you, too. How were the dogs?"

"Fantastic, as always. Starting to be a serious nip in the air, though." Cara circled the sofa and plopped down beside Meg as Hawk and Blink vied for space on the dog bed. Saki followed Cara to curl up beside her with a satisfied sigh. "What are we looking at?"

"*I* was looking at the photos from the urbex sites. Because *I* work for the FBI."

"And you know very well *I* would never tell anyone *I* looked at them. Besides, so far all I'm seeing is a picture of peeling paint, rust, and a metric ton of grime. Even if I was going to talk to someone, that information would tell them nothing they couldn't find in a Google image search. Which site is that?"

"The psychiatric hospital in Fredericksburg. More specifically, it's the front lobby." Meg flipped through a sequence of photos. "These are the stairs we could only barely climb. Some of the exam rooms. The basement. And this is where we finally let Hawk have his head and start the search he'd been telling me about all along, only I wasn't listening at first."

"From the looks of this place, it could be dangerous, and you'd think people would leave it alone. But look at the graffiti. Clearly a number of people are exploring it."

"Urbex is apparently a bigger pastime than I ever imagined. Chuck Smaill says there are entire online communities devoted to it. People share exciting urbex sites and stories, give warnings about dangerous locations, teach rookies the ropes, give tips about how to evade security measures, etcetera. They try to keep a lot of what they do on the down-low because as soon as a site becomes public, people outside the community flock in to see what the fuss is about and pretty much destroy the place."

"Don't the urbexers do that?"

"The way Chuck described it to me, people get into urbex because it's fascinating to see the slow-motion dismantling of civilization by nature and the elements. For them, the gradual degradation of these sites is what makes them fascinating. They can go to the same site for years, and each time it's a different experience as sections of it fall apart, revealing new elements. They respect the sites and want to share them with their community. They do *not* want outsiders who are just going for a lark, destroying and vandalizing the sites."

Cara studied the photo displayed on the monitor. "These are the furnaces where you found the first victim?"

"Yes."

Cara pointed to the rolling garage-style door near the coal bin. It was covered with graffiti in multiple colors and styles, some words, some stylized drawings. "And that's not vandalizing the sites?"

"Actually, no, not in the sense they mean. For them, vandalizing a site is ripping it down, speeding the destruction. Pulling stuff off walls, taking materials out with you. I asked Chuck about graffiti, because I thought of it as vandalism, too. But that's not how they see it. They're leaving their mark, an *I-was-here* totem, often at the farthest point of their exploration. If you can reach a point like that, and there's no graffiti, then you have the honor of being the first explorer and being the first to leave your mark."

Cara zoomed in on the image. The rusted steel door was covered with multicolor images and words, some bare bones, some in plump bubble letters in shaded tones. Some signatures were simple initial pairs, and some were clearly screen names—FreeLancer536, Captain Blackhawk, Tunneldigger—because you wouldn't want to leave your real name in a place covered in No Trespassing signs. "Got to hand it to these guys, they do some interesting work. Look at this one." She blew up the image of a monkey's face with glowing red eyes and a furious snarl. "Or this." A grinning skull sporting a set of headphones. "Or this one." It looked like a bug with twin antennae. She resized the image to its original proportions. "Have you considered—"

Meg grabbed Cara's wrist. "Wait. Go back."

"Back to what?"

"That last symbol."

It took Cara a moment of moving through a section of graffiti before she found the symbol again. "This one? The bug?"

"Yeah." Meg leaned in and studied it. Spray-painted in a vibrant electric blue, the body took on the shape of an upside-down teardrop, the lower part of the body halved and then crosscut into segments leading down to a curving, whiplike tail. Twin antennae sprouted from the head and curled down to flank the body on both sides. "That . . . bug. I've seen it somewhere."

"At that site?"

"No." She minimized the photo and held still for a moment, her eyes closed, trying to remember where she'd seen it. That shape, that color of blue on a dark background. *Black . . . no dark red. Brick.* Her eyes flew open. "The smokestack. On the roof."

"Where was that?"

"Bowie Meat Packing. On the roof where I did the balance beam routine. The smokestack is built out of dark-red brick." She selected a folder and scrolled through thumbnails of photos. She opened a photo. "Wrong angle." Another photo, then another. "This one." It was an image of the open space of the roof. The shattered skylight was on the right, stretching back toward the middle of the photo, with the smokestack behind it, rising high into the sky, disappearing out of view of the camera. She zoomed in on the base of the smokestack. "There."

Cara leaned in, her nose only a few inches from the monitor. "Well, I'll be damned. That *is* the same symbol. Do you think he's leaving a signature for the killings?"

"No. I think he's exploring places to compile a list of where to leave the bodies and leaving his mark like he probably always does. But how many places are out there, over how many states that carry his mark? Assuming that it is him, of course, and not some other urbexer who happened to hit the same two locations. Now, if we can find this specific mark in every place that's been a dump site, that could help tie them together. And if we can connect the suspect to this individual mark, then we'd have definitive proof that he'd been there at some point." She stared at the photo on-screen, restlessly tapping her fingers on the palm rest. "But I don't remember seeing it at any of the other sites."

"Doesn't mean it wasn't there. Maybe you just missed it because of where it was situated or the light level. Or because the floor collapsed under your feet. Come on, I'll help you look through the pictures again."

They strategically searched through the other two sites, starting with Bethlehem Steel, where Cara spotted the symbol high up on blast furnace D, behind one of the upper walkways.

"I never saw it," Meg admitted. "We came to furnace D because Brian found Warren Roth, so first he had my attention, and then the wannabe cop did. Once we'd found the victim, we didn't pay any more attention to the site itself."

"What's left, the jail?"

"Yes. And we were purposefully doing that search by moonlight, so I won't be surprised if it's there."

"My gut says it is. This is him, I can feel it." Cara caught Meg's pointed look. "Not that we're looking at these pictures or anything. I'm pretty sure I'm at my dog training school finishing off a private lesson."

"I'm pretty sure that's exactly how this evening has gone." Meg opened the final site folder and the pictures from the cell block structure. "All these pictures were purposely taken the next morning, by daylight." She flipped through a number of photos. "This whole incident would have been so much easier in the light. I bet we could have ended it then and there."

"Wait!" Cara pushed Meg's hand away and went back to the previous photo. It was shot from the ground floor of the cell block, looking up toward the upper levels. In the photo, the jagged gaping hole on the fourth level was starkly visible, twin boards still stretching across the chasm. "That's where you went through?"

Meg's stomach curdled just looking at the photo and remembering the terror of the floor falling away from under her feet, and the certainty that her death lay below. "Yeah."

"Damn. I mean, you told me about it, but seeing it . . . That's completely different. That must have been terrifying."

"That's putting it lightly." Meg, not able to look at the image anymore, steered the topic back to the investigation at hand as she flipped to a new photo. "There's lots of graffiti on this lower level, but I don't see much up top. But now that I think about it, I did see some at the stairs as we were going up. Just a few flashes of color. It had to be graffiti."

They found the graffiti exactly where Meg remembered it. Then they found the symbol on the upper level at the top of the staircase.

Cara flopped back against the couch cushions. "There you are. Four for four. Think it's a coincidence?"

"In four sites, spread across Virginia, Pennsylvania, and Maryland? I can't say that it's not, but I'd say the chances are significantly smaller. At least it gives us a place to start. I'll pass it on to the team first thing tomorrow, but I want to show this symbol to Chuck Smaill and see if he recognizes it." She reached for her phone but froze with her hand suspended over it.

"What?" asked Cara.

"He's on shift with Todd right now at the firehouse."

"You talk to Todd when he's on shift as long as he's between calls and not busy with firehouse business. Could you talk to Smaill?"

"Maybe." She grabbed her phone. "I'll text Todd and find out if they're available. If I don't hear from him, then they're on a call or doing firehouse duties."

"At this time of night?"

"Well, the calls can happen anytime, but I agree, they're likely not washing down the trucks."

She typed in a message for Webb and was rewarded with an answer only minutes later.

"They're just back from a two-alarm fire," Meg reported. "They're hitting the showers to wash off the soot, but then they'll be sticking around the house unless something else happens. He's suggesting I come by." She glanced at the time on her phone. "Seems kind of late for that."

"He says to go in, so go in. He wouldn't have suggested it if it wasn't okay. You've been there before?"

"A few times. Hawk's a big hit there."

"Then take him with you. If you're nervous about it being late, Hawk will be the icebreaker."

At this name, Hawk's head shot up from where he was curled around Blink on the dog bed.

Meg closed the lid of her computer and stood. "Come on, Hawk. It's back to work. But not really for you. You'll have fun at the firehouse."

"Pics or it didn't happen." Cara flashed her a wide grin. "You know what they say about firefighters. Do a girl a favor?"

Meg rolled her eyes at her sister and called her dog. But Cara had lightened her mood, which Meg suspected was exactly her goal.

Thursday, November 15, 9:08 PM
Engine Company 2, DC Fire and Emergency Services
Washington, DC

Twenty-five minutes later, Meg pulled her SUV up to the curb in front of the blocky monstrosity that housed the District of Columbia's Fire and Emergency Services Engine Company 2. She glanced up at the shapeless poured-concrete square and grimaced. For someone with a love of classic architecture, anything built after about 1950 had an excellent chance of offending her sense of taste, and this building certainly qualified. But in the end, the only thing that actually mattered was what and who it housed. DC's fire department, after a bumpy few years and some major budgetary problems, was trying hard to get back on its feet with a substantial overhaul.

She got out of the SUV, shouldered her laptop bag, and let Hawk out of his compartment. He stood still on the sidewalk as she clipped the leash onto his collar, and then they climbed the short flight of steps to the glass door leading off the street. Meg pulled open the door and let Hawk precede her into a small vestibule. Unlocked during the day, the door leading into the firehouse was locked after hours, so she pushed the buzzer to alert the company to her presence.

Webb's voice sounded over the intercom. "Engine Company 2, can I help you?"

"It's Meg."

"I thought it might be you. Be right there."

Thirty seconds later, Webb appeared on the other side of the glass door. He shot back the deadbolt, held the door open for her, and then he closed and locked it behind them. She grinned up at him, neatly dressed in his navy DCFEMS uniform, and touched her fingertips to the edges of his still-damp hair. "Looking good, Lieutenant. I don't often get to see you in uniform."

"You should have seen me half an hour ago, in filthy, wet bunkers and covered in soot."

"You clean up good, though."

He flashed her a grin. "Thanks. But I'm assuming you didn't come to ogle me in uniform."

Meg let out a sigh as her smile faded. "Sadly, no. I'm

here on business. I think I made a breakthrough tonight, and I need to talk to Chuck."

"Really? What?"

"Let me brief you both together. Where is he?"

"In the kitchen. He was helping Ox with dinner. The call came in just as we were about to start meal prep, so no one has eaten yet."

"Ox?"

"You'll see."

He led her through the darkened firehouse admin office and toward the company living quarters. They passed windows that opened out to the giant garage housing a line of shiny red trucks—an engine, a rescue squad truck, a mobile command unit, an ambulance, and the fire chief's SUV. Farther down the hall, they entered a brightly lit shared kitchen and eating space with long tables flanked by chairs. A mixed group of men and women either lounged at tables or prepared dinner. A huge man with shoulders twice as wide as Webb's stood at the stove stirring a massive steaming pot.

"What's tonight's special, Ox?" Webb called.

Ox waved a tomato-sauce-stained wooden spoon at him. "Firehouse chili. Keep your hose handy. You're going to need it." He chuckled at his own joke as he turned back to his cooking.

"Now I see why you call him Ox," Meg said under her breath.

"He's a mountain of a man, but he's light on his feet when he's dancing around flames. On top of that, he's an amazing cook. His chili is a thing of beauty. Feel free to join us."

"I'm kind of afraid it might blow my head off after that warning. There's Chuck. Can we grab him for a few minutes?"

"Sure. Smaill!" Webb waited until Smaill looked up

from the chopping block where he was preparing veggies. "We need you for a few."

"Will do. Rafe, you're up!"

A tall Latino man seated at the table looked up from his phone. "I helped out at lunch."

"And now you're helping out at dinner. You want to eat or what?"

"Well . . . yeah."

"Then get over here. I have a meeting." Then Smaill ruined the serious nature of his order by squatting down and patting his thighs. "With this handsome boy. Come here, Hawk."

Meg quickly unclipped his leash and gave Hawk the hand signal to go. Hawk raced over to happily greet Smaill while Meg turned to Webb. "Where do you want to do this?"

"How private do you need this to be?"

"It's an active case, so more private than this."

"No one will be using the briefing room at this time of night. Smaill! Briefing room!"

"Yes, Lieutenant."

Webb led Meg back the way they'd come. She gave a low whistle, and Hawk immediately trotted after her, Smaill following behind. Webb stepped through a dark doorway and flipped on the light switch to reveal a room with rows of tables, each table backed by a row of chairs, all facing forward toward the whiteboard on the front wall. Framed newspaper stories of the company in action lined the walls spaced between a few faded safety posters. "This is where we do training and the Morning briefing." He dragged a couple of the chairs over so a group of three was arranged around one end of a table.

They took their seats, Hawk settling between Meg and Smaill as she lowered her laptop bag to the floor, leaning it against a chair leg.

"Thanks for letting me pop in like this," Meg said. "I hate to interrupt your shift."

"Not a problem," Webb said. "The chief knows we've been involved in this investigation. As long as it doesn't interfere with an active call, he doesn't object. If the alarms go off—"

"Hawk and I will get out of the way and we'll pick this up later. Let's get to it before that happens. I noticed something tonight while I was reviewing the pictures of the scenes. I started with the Massaponax hospital, and I took note of the graffiti this time around."

"There's always graffiti," Smaill said. "Remember, it's what we do. How we mark a site as explored."

"I haven't seen you do it."

"Definitely isn't something I'm going to do at a crime scene. And, by and large, I'm not that competitive about it, though I do carry a can of spray paint in my bag. I occasionally leave my initials if I'm in a place where it's clear I haven't followed in the footsteps of two hundred other guys. I am also not artistic, so my mark isn't anything impressive. Some of the guys are pretty creative."

"Yes, they are." She pulled her laptop from the bag, opened it on the table, and woke it up. "Like this symbol, for example." She turned the laptop around so the men could see the image better. "This was on the garage door in the furnace room, near the coal bin where we found Donna Parker."

Webb's expression didn't change as he studied the drawing, but Smaill leaned in to stare at it, his eyes narrowed, his shoulders tensed.

"Do you recognize it?" Meg asked.

"I think . . . I . . ." Smaill slouched back in his chair. "Maybe. I can't be sure."

"I want you to think about it. Because when I saw it at this site, I realized it looked familiar, but it would be familiar only to me, because I was the only one on the rooftop at the Bowie Meat Packing Plant." She brought up the photo of the roof and smokestack of the plant. "This was on the roof near where Bahni Devar was found alive."

"Well, I'll be damned," Webb said. "He's leaving a signature?"

"Maybe, maybe not. Chuck?"

He shook his head, his eyes still fixed on the image as if he couldn't look away. "No, not a signature. Look at the paint. It's weathered. It's been there for some time."

Meg turned the laptop toward her to look for herself. "I didn't even see that part of it. I was just focusing on the symbol itself. But you're right, that's not fresh paint. Definitely not made that day."

"You need to be careful here, though." Smaill finally looked up, his eyes full of caution. "Some guys mark every place they go, so this could be someone unrelated who's been at both sites. Could also be months ago and he hasn't been back. This is circumstantial at best."

"I agree. But then I looked through the other sites." She met Smaill's eyes. "That same mark is at every one." She showed them the photos of furnace B at Bethlehem Steel and at the top of the stairway on the upper level of the cell block. "I know it could still be unrelated, but the more places it shows up the smaller that possibility gets."

"Good eye," Webb said. "I was at three of those four sites with you, and I missed it every time."

"I think we need to give ourselves a break at the Montgomery jail. We were purposely keeping our flashlights down or off and navigating by moonlight. We never would have seen it. Also, you were in rescue mode."

"Rescue mode?"

"It's like me in search mode. You're trained to do that job. I've seen you turn it on like flipping a switch. You go from relaxed to focused, intense, and intent on only one task. That's how it should be when a life is on the line. But sometimes when you have blinders on like that, you miss a detail like a paint splotch on the wall." She looked down at the photo. "And sometimes you catch it after the fact, when that focus is gone."

"Can I take a closer look?" Smaill asked.

Meg slid the laptop toward him and watched as he flipped from picture to picture, zooming in and studying each one in contemplative silence. Finally, he pushed it away and sat with arms crossed, his brow furrowed, and his lips a thin line.

"What are you thinking?" she asked.

"That I might have seen it before. In other sites, or in photos posted in one of the online forums. I'm not sure where, though. I need to think about it. I can go through my own photos and see if I can find it. I can also go back through the forums. Can you send me those shots?"

"I'll do it right now." Meg hot spotted her phone, connected her laptop to it, and sent him the photos attached to an email. "Just remember, those are crime scene photos and can't be shared. If you need to post one or ask any of your urbex connections if they've seen the mark, I need to get permission from Agent Moore before we take that step. I don't think she'll say no, but we have to keep everything documented and transparent."

"Understood."

"Do you think you can find the guy based on this bug?" Webb asked.

Smaill wobbled his head back and forth in an uncertain gesture. "If I'm lucky I might be able to narrow it down to a screen name in a forum. I think it's really unlikely I'll be able to find someone who can give me the guy's real name, but I guess you never know."

Meg closed the lid of her laptop. "We need to be careful

here. If this evidence gets us anywhere close to him, we can't let him rabbit because of it. This can't warn him that we're onto him."

"Yeah, that would be bad. Maybe I can come up with something for you. I'll certainly have better luck than you would. If a stranger came onto the forums looking for information, everyone would shut down. Remember, those of us who do urbex are usually breaking the law by trespassing on every outing. We don't take kindly to strangers looking for more information than how to get started."

"So you'll be a proxy for Meg," Webb said.

"Yup. They've known me for years and won't be suspicious of my questions. And I know some of the guys personally. Let me see if I can shake this case loose for you."

CHAPTER 28

Viewing Hole: An eye-level, rectangular hole cut into the boards surrounding a construction site so curious passersby can see what's happening inside.

Monday, November 19, 10:27 AM
Forensic Canine Unit, J. Edgar Hoover Building
Washington, DC

Kate's message to the team came through Craig: **1 PM in the fourth-floor conference room. Bring the map.**

Meg looked up at Craig as he stood between her desk and Brian's. "What do you think that means?"

"Besides the obvious? Not sure. I find it hard to believe with the time difference and the international red tape that she's received information from the Indian authorities about the tontine investor list, so she must have a lead on something else. Maybe some information that will reduce the potential list of twenty-three down to a smaller victim pool."

"We should map the known victims as well." Brian leaned back in his chair, his fingers linked over his abdomen. "We only put the original twenty-three unknown potentials on it. But if we're going to make a new list of everyone involved in this case, then we need to add in our known victims."

"We should also add the three possible past cases. Until we know or can prove otherwise, they're a part of this case," said Meg. "That pushes the possible victim pool up to thirty."

"I'll leave that to you two." Craig looked at his watch. "There's no way Scott and Lauren are going to be back today."

"They're still tracking those abducted children in South Carolina?"

"Yes. It will be good news if they have it wrapped up today, but I think that might be a miracle. It's probably more likely going to be a couple of days, so we'll update them when they return. In the meantime, move the map from my office and have it up in the conference room with the known victims added by one o'clock. I'll meet you down there."

Monday, November 19, 1:05 PM
Fourth-floor conference room, J. Edgar Hoover Building
Washington, DC

Craig rushed into the conference room, glancing from side to side, his shoulders sagging with relief as he realized only his teams were in attendance.

"She's not here yet," Brian said from where he sat at the table with his feet propped on the empty chair beside him. Lacey and Hawk curled up companionably behind it.

Meg smacked him lightly on the shoulder. "Way to state the obvious."

"Hey, maybe she'd just stepped out."

"She texted me saying she was running a few minutes late. I expect her any time."

As if on cue, the door opened, just narrowly missing Craig still standing near the entrance. Kate sidled in, her arms full. "Oh, sorry. On the run because I'm late again."

"I just got here myself." Craig pulled out a chair opposite Meg and Brian and sat down. "Lauren and Scott send their regrets. They're off-site on an active search. I'll update them when they're back."

"Sounds good." Kate took the chair beside him, setting a folder and a covered coffee cup on the table in front of her. She took a deep breath and then let it out, her shoulders falling low on the exhale.

"Been that kind of day?" Meg asked.

"It really has. But it's been good, as you'll see." She craned her head to see the map tacked to the wall. "Great, you brought it with you. If I'd known it would just be us, we could have done this in Craig's office, but in case we had everyone, I wanted to make sure we had enough room." She opened the folder and pulled the first document off the top of the pile, brandishing it in the air. "Because the Indian authorities came through for us. This is the list of the Kalidasa Life Insurance Company tontine annuity fund investors."

Brian's feet fell off the chair with a *thump*. "No way. How did you manage that so quickly?"

"I got lucky right off the bat, contacting an investigator on Thursday after our meeting at the *Post*. Last thing at night for us, first thing in the morning for him, and I stayed up for a while making sure he had all the information he needed. We played email tag for a few days going through the weekend—each of us emailing the other in the middle of the night their time and returning the email in the middle of the night for the other. But it got the job done. He got me the list early this morning our time. Guess who's on it?"

Meg squelched the urge to whisk the sheets out of Kate's hands for instant access to the information. "Our four victims."

Kate leveled an index finger at her with one eye closed as if she was training her sights on Meg. "You got it. Plus the victim Mr. McCord remembered and the two Craig found."

"Out of how many in total?"

"When the fund started in the year 2000 there were originally forty-five investors. Once the fund got off the ground, it was closed to incoming investors and the number stayed constant for a few years. Then some of the older ones died out of the fund."

"Had the fund taken off by then?" asked Craig.

"It had, so even if they were only in the fund for three or four years, they still got a nice return. Of course, not as nice as those who stayed on through the Indian tech boom years."

Finally, Meg thought, *we can go on the offensive on this case*. "Now the real question. Who's left as a likely target?"

"We need to run them down to make sure they're still with us at this point, but as far as the fund administrators know, there are nine living investors still in the fund." Kate flipped to a list of names on the second page.

Meg could see from across the table that some of the names had a bracketed "deceased" beside them. "They can't know about the recent victims in our case yet."

"No, they don't. So Donna Parker, Warren Roth, Bahni Devar, and Vikram Pillai are all included in this list."

Meg rose to stand in front of the map. "Which missing or deceased persons on this map aren't on the list? If they aren't included, we should remove them to see what the real distribution looks like. And you can add the 'deceased' tag to anyone on the list they don't know about yet."

"I'll do that. Read them to me one by one."

One name at a time, they reviewed the list of thirty missing or deceased possible victims.

"Speaking of the victims list," Craig said, "from your list of twenty-three individuals of which ten were burials, you were going to request exhumations for tox screen testing. Were you successful?"

"I was, for all of them. I haven't got results for any so far, but it's a little soon. Oh, and while we're on the subject of tox screens, I have the results for Donna Parker."

"Difethialone?"

"Difethialone, so we're consistent there. Still waiting on Bahni Devar's results. Give me the next name."

One at a time, flags were removed from the map. Then a flag pair remained in place. Then another. Until nine pairs remained.

Meg stepped back to study the map. Instead of being spread from coastal New Hampshire to Illinois, there was now a concentration of flags in Maryland, Virginia, West Virginia, Pennsylvania, Delaware, and New Jersey. "That's all seven of our known or suspected victims, plus two more. It looks like the rest of the original twenty-three suspicious deaths or disappearances are unrelated to this case."

"We need to update Rutherford with this information, but if he was here, he'd be happier with this spread," Craig pointed out. "It's a smaller geographic area—six contiguous states instead of ten—which could be driven in a matter of hours rather than nearly a whole day."

"Not to mention that now instead of a four-year period of killings, we're down to just over six months for the deaths on which we have full information. Also notice how spread out the first kills are, at least for those we know the date or an approximate date. First came the victims we suspect are part of the case. Norman Stanley disappeared on April eleventh. Iniya Pearson was reported missing from her retirement home on June twenty-fifth. Kathir Nadar disappeared sometime during June or July but was discovered on September nineteenth. Then we get into the recent disappearances with known dates. October fifth. Then October twenty-sixth, November fifth—unsuccessful, but it still counts—and then November ninth."

"Is he devolving?" Brian mused. "Or something else is artificially speeding up his time line?"

"Maybe whoever is ordering the hits is getting greedy and impatient that the process is taking so long." Kate underlined two names on the investor list. "As you noted, we have two more victims, one that the fund administrators listed as deceased and one they still thought was alive."

"And if they thought nine investors remained alive, then we actually only have five remaining. And if you take Mrs. Devar out of the mix, as the killer is certainly trying to do, then we only have four left."

"Out of those four, one is likely safe because he or she is the one calling the shots," Brian hypothesized. "So that leaves three targets."

"Which is where things get sticky." Kate set down her coffee cup. "Four investors are left, one who intends to receive the entire fund simply by being the last man or woman standing. We don't know which one that is, so my gut instinct is to protect all four of them. But if we inform them of their risk—"

"You're informing the person who hired the killer that we're onto him and his motive, and he'll stop the killings cold," Craig finished for her.

"That's it. We can't tell them to be cautious because in

doing so, we risk terminating our own case. Maybe then the one person hoping to collect the money doesn't succeed, but if we can't link the killings to anyone, we don't find justice for the existing victims."

"What about putting protection on them without their knowledge?" Meg stepped over Hawk, where he stretched out dozing on the floor, and took her seat again. "Tricky for sure, but at the pace we're going right now, hopefully it wouldn't be for more than a few weeks. We know the suspect isn't one of the investors, simply because of his age, but if we can find him, we can find which of the investors hired him to do his dirty work. We need to arrest them both for either premeditated murder or conspiracy to commit murder."

"Not that the older investor will likely do much jail time at his or her age, but I'd really like to see it, anyway. As would the victims' families. I think assigning protective details will be our best way to protect the investors without raising suspicions. It wouldn't be foolproof by any means, but it will be preferable to letting them fend for themselves."

"What do we know about these four new names?" Craig looked at the map on the wall. "Maybe we should be adding those as well?"

"That's a good idea." Meg pushed back from the table again.

Brian stopped her with a hand on her arm. "I got it." He crossed to the map. "Give me the first location."

They went through them, one at a time.

Lukesh Baldwin, Newark, New Jersey.

Simona Kavarai, Harrisburg, Pennsylvania.

Mani Ramachandaran, Dover, Delaware.

Peter Stevenson, Blacksburg, Virginia.

Brian stood staring at the altered map, his hands on his

hips. "If that's all of them, then we're still within the same geographic boundaries."

"If McCord is right about the way they recruited investors—through Indian diaspora cultural associations—then this is what I'd expect. They probably worked with a limited number of specific associations until they got as many investors as they needed, which is why everyone is in a relatively limited geographic area. If anyone has moved, they haven't gone too far. Not to the West Coast or anything. Kate, if you have no objections, I'd like to give these names to McCord so he can continue his research."

Kate nodded her assent. "As long as he does nothing, *absolutely nothing*, to give them a heads-up that they may be in danger, then I'm fine with it. He's deep in this case already and has proved his discretion. We'll investigate from our end as well, since this is brand-new information and we don't know anything about them yet. I'm going to get more information on the living arrangements of these individuals. Do they live on their own, with family, or in retirement or nursing homes? Then I'm going to arrange for protection right away. If we're lucky, we'll catch the suspect in the act of trying to grab one of them. I don't think we'll need to protect them for long, though. Considering our sped-up time line, and the fact that we're now nine days since the last killing, I suspect he's going to strike again soon."

CHAPTER 29

Trojan Horse Exploit: Infiltration of an urbex site via a public space by an explorer dressed as if he or she belongs there—for example, an explorer dressed in casual business attire who slips off a subway platform and gains access to the abandoned train or service tunnels.

Wednesday, November 21, 7:21 AM
Jennings residence
Arlington, Virginia

Meg's phone rang just as she was sitting down at the kitchen table with a cup of coffee and a toasted bagel. "Jennings."

"Meg, it's Chuck. I figured something out last night, but it was so late I didn't want to give you a call."

She grabbed the sugar from beside Cara's empty place and scooped up a rounded spoonful. "Did you find anything?"

"I think I have him."

Meg froze with the spoon suspended in midair, grains of sugar sliding off to sprinkle the table. "You have . . . our suspect?"

"I think so. I found him on the boards at about two this morning. All because of that bug. Except it's not a bug. It's a trilobite."

"A tribble?"

"A trilobite."

"I have no idea what that is. Something that's not a bug?"

"It's a prehistoric arthropod."

"And we're back to bug." After realizing she was spilling sugar all over the table, Meg dumped the rest of the spoonful into her coffee.

"Only if you consider an underwater bug really a bug."

Meg poured cream into her coffee and stirred. "I guess not. So this prehistoric sea critter is what the killer is spray-painting at all the crime scenes? Isn't that a little . . . off the beaten path?"

"Just a little. But that's what led me to him. Or at least to his screen name. He's 'Trilobite' on multiple boards."

"I guess I should have seen that one coming, considering the not-bug." She took a moment for a sip of coffee while she turned over the information in her head. "How sure are you on this?"

"The guy's screen name is an obscure sea creature I had to look up to find out what it was. And before you ask, some of the fossil forms match his cartoon drawing. They're way more complex and they evolve over time, but he's working with spray paint and a short time frame, so what he does is enough to get the point across and leave his mark. I've seen that calling card in a bunch of pictures he's posted to show his explorations. So, yeah, it's him."

"Great job. I'm not sure we'd have even known where to start looking for him. Can you send me information on the boards and on him?"

"Already done, including my user ID and passwords for the sites so you can get in and nose around freely and no one will suspect anything. Check your email. Can you get the computer wizards at the FBI to track him down based on his IP address or whatever it is they use to trace people?"

"Maybe. I'm certainly going to find out. Can I give you a call if I have any questions?"

"You sure can. Happy hunting." He hung up.

Meg jammed a bite of bagel into her mouth, washed it down with a slug of coffee, and picked up her phone again, speed-dialing McCord.

"Morning." His voice was still sleep-slurred.

"I need you to wake up."

"I am awake. I'm talking to you, aren't I?" Sleep-slurred shifted to slightly surly.

"I have a lead. Maybe *the* lead. I need my researcher awake."

The was a momentary pause. "I'm awake." His voice was clearer now. "Though I can't promise any miracles until after I've had at least one cup of coffee."

"I hear you. Got a pen and paper handy?"

She heard a low groan she translated as McCord pushing himself out of bed. "Okay, shoot."

She quickly outlined the information she'd learned from Smaill. "I'll forward you the email he sent me. But considering what we know about this guy, we need to figure out who he is. I'm about to call Kate and get agents on it, but I want you on the scent first. Not that they're not great at what they do . . ."

"But they don't have my investigative chops and some of my contacts who would never talk to law enforcement. Are you trying to butter me up?"

"I don't need to. Just the promise of this story is enough to light a fire under you."

"How well you know me."

"By this point, yeah. I need this as soon as you can, McCord. This is when things are really going to start to move."

"Then stop talking to me so I can get going." He hung up.

Meg picked up her plate and her mug, chugging the cooling coffee as she walked to the sink. Then she called her dog and gathered her things. She'd call Kate from the SUV.

It was time to go to work.

It was time to end this.

CHAPTER 30

Cracking: Being the first explorer at a site.

Wednesday, November 21, 8:17 AM
Forensic Canine Unit, J. Edgar Hoover Building
Washington, DC

Never one to sit with her feet up waiting for others to do the work, Meg dove into her own research as soon as she got to the unit office.

"You got coffee."

She looked up at the sound of Brian's voice as he and Lacey entered the bullpen. "We were supposed to jog this morning," Meg said, "but I canceled so we could be in earlier. I thought it was only fair."

"I don't need fair, but I'll gladly take the coffee. Lacey, go hang out with Hawk." He watched the two dogs happily greet each other, and then he pulled out his chair and sat down. "What's with the Glock?" He indicated the gun she wore tucked into a belt holster at her hip.

"I could ask you the same thing. You don't normally come in with your service weapon."

"Maybe it's wishful thinking, but I feel like the guy's going to try again. *Soon.* And I want to be prepared for anything."

"That's exactly how I feel."

"While we're waiting, what do you need me to do? You look like you're already into something."

"I am. McCord is on the scent, and Kate is working on her leads, so I'm trying to give them a hand." She picked up her laptop and rolled her chair to his desk, perching it on top so they could both see. She took him through Smaill's email and some of the sites. "I've gone through the first two links he sent and I'm working on the third. Can you take the fourth and keep going?"

"Can do. We're looking for anything that might lead to his identity? Maybe hints about where his home base might be based on a concentration of urbex searches in the vicinity?"

"Actually, that's a really good idea. I've been trying to pick up on anything about his personality and profession that might indicate his identity, but geographic centralization is a great angle. Life is busy, and when you want to spend an afternoon doing some exploration, you don't want to waste four hours of the day driving there and back." Meg stretched out a hand to her desk and grabbed her notebook. "I've been making notes, including all the sites he's listed here." She handed him the notebook. "Want to make a copy?"

"Yeah, I'll do that."

Brian copied Meg's existing notes, and then they both settled in to work at their desks. Craig came in, and they both looked up only long enough to give him a nod and get back to work.

More than an hour later, Meg's phone rang. She ignored it for the first two rings as she finished reading a post on a location in Virginia. She reached for it blindly and hit talk. "Jennings."

"It's me."

Meg's head snapped up at McCord's voice to find Brian staring at her expectantly. "That was fast."

"When you're good, you're good. Is everyone there?"

Her pulse kicked into overdrive. "Do we need everyone?"

"Yes."

"Call me back in three minutes at this number." She rattled off Craig's office extension and hung up. She picked up the handset on her desk and dialed Kate's extension.

She picked up the call. "Agent Kate Moore."

"It's Meg. Can you get to the unit in three minutes? I think McCord has a break in the case. He's calling into Craig's office."

"I can be there in two." The line went dead.

Kate made it in just over two minutes, but her heavy breathing told Meg she'd skipped the elevator and opted to run the stairs for speed. She paused in Craig's doorway, one hand braced on the jam. "Did I make it?"

"You did." Meg stood up from the chair in front of Craig's desk. "He—" She broke off as Craig's phone rang.

Craig hit the speaker button to answer the phone. "SSA Craig Beaumont."

"It's Clay McCord of the *Washington Post*."

Meg leaned low to speak into the phone. "We're here, McCord. Craig, Kate, Brian, and myself. What have you got?"

"I have your suspect. I mean *really* have. His actual identity."

Meg met Kate's skeptical gaze and then motioned to the phone. *Take the lead.*

"Mr. McCord, this is Agent Moore. Can you explain in detail who this man is and how you reached that conclusion?"

"Sure. Meg shared Chuck Smaill's research into the urbex community following her discovery that a common graffiti image was discovered at all four body dump sites.

As an urbexer himself, he had access to some closed forums and could contact other members personally as a trusted community member. He also supported this by going back through some of his own photos of previous explorations. He came up with a screen name, which also happens to be his signature image. Trilobite."

"Hang on a second, McCord." Meg brought up an image of a trilobite on her phone, showed it to everyone in the room, and then followed it with the crime scene image from Massaponax Psychiatric Hospital. "They've seen both the fossil and the spray-painted version. Keep going."

"As you might imagine, this is kind of an obscure reference, both the name and the image. I started doing some digging as to who works on this kind of research. I mean, I'd never even heard of this critter before this morning, and I bet most people haven't. This guy not only uses it as his graphic representation, it's his screen name. They're clearly a fascination for him. I felt that particular aspect had to minimize the suspect pool. So I pulled a string to start the process." He cleared his throat. "I contacted Ryan Bennett."

Meg whipped around to stare at Brian, who blinked at her with his mouth agape.

After a second of silence, Kate said, "I don't understand. Should I know who that is?"

"That would be my husband," Brian said. "McCord, were you looking specifically at what the Smithsonian had in its collection?"

"That, and I was looking for a springboard to a connection with a Smithsonian paleobiologist or geobiologist. I met Ryan at Meg's get-together after the Garber case closed. I really liked him, and he said if I ever needed a contact within the Smithsonian for a story to talk to him. So . . . I did."

"My husband, the confidential informant," Brian muttered. "Did he connect you to someone?" he asked so McCord could hear him.

"Actually, yes. He was extremely helpful."

"He's a walking encyclopedia, so that doesn't surprise me."

"He connected me to Dr. Collette Boucher. Called her himself, at home considering the time, to make the introduction, then gave her my number so she could call me. I had her on the line inside of ten minutes. When I told her about the critter, she knew about it. But it's not her particular field of expertise and the Smithsonian doesn't have any trilobite fossils in its collection."

"But someone must," Meg said, "or else you wouldn't be calling."

"Nailed it. She didn't have any fossils, but she knows who's working on these little guys. And that would be Virginia Tech."

Brian held up a finger and darted out of his chair, running back into the bullpen.

"Hang on a second, McCord. It looks like Brian's onto something."

Brian returned, holding the photocopy of Meg's notebook list. Several more locations were listed on the page after Meg's list in blue ink. "McCord, Virginia Tech, that's in Blacksburg, right?"

"Yes."

Brian stood and went to the map, quickly finding the location to the west of Roanoke on the eastern edge of the Jefferson National Forest. "This is it here." He brandished the single page. "I thought it would be Virginia, though I thought it might be more centralized. The majority of the urbex sites I've been compiling are Virginia, West Virginia, and North Carolina."

"What sites are those?" McCord asked through the speaker.

"Meg and I split our research workload. She was looking for anything directly related to the guy's identity or career. I was working on the hypothesis that if he's been doing urbex for a while, the majority of the sites will naturally be closer to his own home base. And I'm finding a concentration of sites in that area."

"Nice." McCord sounded pleased. "Then this fits right into that theory. There's a paleobiology and geobiology group at Virginia Tech. Dr. Boucher referred me to Dr. Göran Nilsson, one of three researchers in this group. And when I described the man I was looking for—around six foot two, white, strawberry blond, light eyes, freckles, and the crescent-shaped birthmark on his neck—he immediately knew who I was talking about. Brett Stevenson, a postdoctoral fellow in his own lab."

"Hold your horses," Kate interrupted. "Stevenson? One of the remaining investors is Peter Stevenson."

"Grandson maybe, based on his age?" Craig suggested. "If he's a postdoctoral fellow, he's probably in his late twenties. These investors are all midsixties and up."

"We've been thinking all along that one of the investors was orchestrating this with an outside killer to make sure they got the money. What if this guy has made a deal with his own grandson to make sure he gets a big inheritance? He must have found out who the other investors are, maybe through the cultural associations, and then the grandson does the killing? Maybe he gets a portion of it now and is promised an even bigger portion when his grandfather dies? That kind of thing?"

"Or maybe the grandson is doing all of this with an eye to his grandfather being the final victim in his spree so he gets the windfall as his inheritance," Meg said. "McCord, was this guy willing to work with you? If he's a paleobiologist, the eastern seaboard isn't exactly the La Brea Tar Pits. He must be sending his people out somewhere else."

"Actually, there's more in this area than you'd think, but most of it has been discovered already because of population centers and urban growth. A lot of paleological research in the US is now out west, like New Mexico and Arizona. And that's where Dr. Nilsson's research is, in Arizona."

Kate leaned forward in anticipation. "And his people go out there? They do research in the state of Arizona?"

"They sure do. And I have dates. And every single one of them is outside of the abduction dates. In fact, Dr. Nilsson is willing to state on record that Stevenson was in Virginia during all of those times. And he promised not to mention our conversation to Stevenson so he won't get tipped off and make a run for it."

Meg turned to Kate. "We've got him." She couldn't keep the excitement out of her tone.

"Sure looks that way. Good work, Mr. McCord. Can you—" She broke off as her cell phone rang. She read the name on her caller ID. "Sorry, hang on, I need to get this. It's one of the agents on protective duty." She answered the call.

Meg glanced at Brian, who grinned back at her as they listened to Kate's end of the call.

"Agent Kate Moore. Yes, hi. You're where? And that's where he is?" Suddenly she went ramrod straight in her chair, her voice going sharp. "You're sure about this? Who did you talk to?" A long pause. "And that's the official prognosis? Thank you, Agent Esposito. Combined with other new information learned today, this case just broke wide open. I expect a full report on my desk later today. Thank you." She hung up and looked at the group. "That was the agent covering Peter Stevenson on protective duty.

He just followed Mr. Stevenson to the LewisGale Medical Center in Salem, Virginia. Mr. Stevenson is there for treatment because he has terminal pancreatic cancer."

Craig leaned back in his chair thoughtfully. "That's the whole game right there, isn't it? Pancreatic cancer is terrible, and the recovery rate is in the single digits. He's dying. He's going to be taken out of the investment as a result."

"And that's the key," Meg said. "He may have no idea what's going on around him. He could be just living what's left of his life. His grandson, on the other hand, has his eye on the prize. If his grandfather is the only one left standing, the tontine closes. And when he dies, which sounds like it could happen imminently, then all the riches will go to the beneficiaries of his will, which the grandson might inherit eventually if his parents are still alive. Or he might be the direct beneficiary. We need a better picture of that family."

"On it," Kate said, typing something furiously into her phone.

"And we have to go after Brett Stevenson," Brian said. "You have enough to call him in for an interview."

"I absolutely do. Today. I want him either here or in a field office today. And I want to handle the interview myself. Mr. McCord, did Dr. Nilsson say if Brett Stevenson is currently in state?"

"He is. But his hours are flexible. He doesn't see him in the lab on a daily basis. Sometimes he works from home doing analyses. They have a flexible working arrangement because of all the time he's required to spend out of state."

"Handy for when you need time during the workday to abduct and kill a senior citizen." Brian's tone was sour.

"That's exactly what I thought."

"I'm going to find his home address and send agents out there now. I want him locked down before—" Her phone rang again. "Sorry. It's apparently going to be one of those days." She accepted the call. "Agent Kate Moore. Yes. Yes,

I . . . *What?*" She surged to her feet. "When? Did you double-check that? Yes, I have it. Do that." She disconnected the call with an angry press of her thumb. "Mani Ramachandaran is missing. The agent on protective duty got nervous when he didn't see any activity this morning in her house. He also had the shift yesterday morning, and she was up by seven and pottering around the kitchen. This morning, he saw activity around that same time, but for the last hour, nothing."

"Maybe she's taking a nap?"

"He wasn't sure about that, so he walked up to the front door and rang the doorbell. Nothing. He went around the rear of the house to investigate and found the back door's been forced and the house is empty."

Now Meg and Brian were on their feet.

"Where was this?" Meg asked. "If he has her, then we need to get the search started. He may already have her at whatever site he's selected."

"Dover, Delaware."

"That's going to take us hours to get there. We're going to be too late. If that's even where we think he's going." Meg turned to Brian. "I need Chuck. I need him to tell us where he thinks Stevenson is taking her."

"You figure that out," Craig said. "Give me a location. Then head for Ronald Reagan Airport. I'll fly you guys out there. Clock's ticking—we don't have time for you to drive it." He threw up a hand in Kate's direction before she could say anything. "Yes, I know it's an expense. But this is their case, and it would take too long to bring a local field agent up to speed. And we need the dogs. It has to be them."

Kate simply leveled a raised eyebrow at him. "I'm not arguing with you."

"Oh. Sorry. We get pushback sometimes from people who don't understand the crucial nature of the dogs."

"Not from me. If this case has taught me anything, it's that we have zero chance of finding the victim alive without them."

Craig turned to Meg. "How many are going?"

"Brian and me, with the dogs. Chuck. I'm going to ask Webb to come, too, as medical backup."

The sound of a throat clearing came out of the phone speaker.

Meg looked at Kate, eye brows raised.

"Fine," Kate said. "Mr. McCord, you're in. You got us here, I'm fine with you being a witness to the end, but you have to stay out of the way the second you're ordered. You are not to be involved in the takedown. Everyone else who is there has a specific search-and-rescue task."

"Understood. I'm headed for Ronald Reagan right now. Meg, let me know where you need me to be."

"Will do."

"See you there." Then there was dead air, and McCord was gone.

"I'll call Todd and Chuck from the car. Brian?"

"All I need is my go bag from my desk."

"Me too. We'll head for the airport, too, and update you en route."

Kate nodded. "Go. Good hunting. Take this guy down once and for all."

Meg, Brian, and the dogs left the unit at a run.

CHAPTER 31

Topping Out: A construction ritual celebrated after the installation of the last piece on the highest part of a large structure like a bridge or skyscraper.

Wednesday, November 21, 12:40 PM
Over Maryland

True to his word, Craig had a chartered plane waiting for them at Ronald Reagan Airport, and they were in the air less than fifteen minutes later. Their destination was New Castle, Delaware.

They had time while flying to update the group as a whole and to review Smaill's choice of sites.

"I got a text from Kate just before we took off," Meg said from where she leaned on the back of Webb's chair. "Brett Stevenson is Peter Stevenson's only living relative. Brett's parents were killed in a car accident four years ago."

"That clinches motive," said Webb, half turned in his seat to look up at her. "He's after a massive payout when his grandfather dies. He just needs to make sure his grandfather is the only investor standing at that point."

"Kate got a little more information about that. Peter was diagnosed with pancreatic cancer last February."

"The first kill was April." Brian was kneeling side by side with McCord on the seats in front of Smaill and Webb, turned around to face the rear of the plane, leaning on the headrests with their elbows. "He hatched the plan sometime after the diagnosis and put it into action by April. But his first kills were sort of spaced out. What happened in September that kicked it up a few notches by October?"

"Peter Stevenson had surgery to try to remove the tumor . . ." Meg glanced at the text message again. "In July. But in September it was clear the cancer had spread anyway. He was given three months to live."

"Which explains why the abductions have been practically one on top of the other since then," said McCord. "His initial time frame got compressed."

"In spades," Meg agreed. "Which leads us to today's abduction. Chuck, tell us where we're going."

"I know I've picked a site that's a fair distance from where the victim was taken," Smaill said.

"About forty-five minutes away by car," Meg said. "Why nothing closer?"

"That whole area of Delaware, it's mostly farmland and small towns. There aren't any big urban centers there, and Kent and Sussex counties—Dover is in Kent county—are agricultural areas. There aren't large or complex urbex sites in those two counties that would work for us. Smaller sites, like old manor houses, but nothing big. And yes, Maryland is the east side of the Delmarva Peninsula, but it's also agricultural. For big sites, you have to go north into New Castle. And there are a couple of spots there. An old hospital, a shoe factory, a school. But they're all really urban. It would be harder to get in and out with a victim in the middle of the day and not be seen. But the New Castle Coal Dumper is different. It's right on the Delaware River, in an industrial area, and tucked in directly behind the parking lot of a transport company. Most of the time that parking lot is full of empty semitrailers waiting to be loaded. So it's almost like there's a wall between the main road and the coal dumper. It's isolated, and that makes it perfect." He paused momentarily, his mouth working as if unsure of his next words. "But what if the killer doesn't think it's perfect? What if we're headed to the wrong location?"

"Then he's won and we've lost," Meg replied. "But we can't blame ourselves for that. We're making the best decision we can in the time we have." She couldn't help but remember the gut-wrenching choice she'd made during the Garber case when two victims went missing at the same time and she had to choose between them. One of the victims being her own sister might have made the decision more obvious but only added to the guilt of making an emotional call instead of a logical one. She was forever grateful that Webb had been with her that day, his medical skills saving the lives of both women in the end. "But we can't let that cloud our judgment. We make the best call we can with the information we have, we commit to it, and then we carry it through. And if it's the wrong choice, we know we did our best."

"I have to ask." Brian looked a little sheepish. "What's a coal dumper? I mean, besides the self-explanatory dumping of coal. But how? I don't have any idea what we're walking into, and I'd like to, from a safety standpoint."

"You don't see them often anymore. This one was built during World War I but was closed in the eighties. Basically, it was a transfer station. Back in the days when coal was one of the main industrial fuels and electricity was produced at coal-fired power stations, the trick was getting the coal from mining locations to the individual states."

"Didn't they do that by train from start to finish?" McCord asked.

"Rail was great for that, but often it was easier to run barges up and down the coastline. Coal was brought to the coast by rail, but then they had to come up with a way to get it onto the ships. Enter the coal dumper. It was a pretty ingenious system, built on a pier out into the river to allow access by both rail and boat. An open hopper railcar full of coal would be brought into the dumper on the tracks, then the rest of the train would move away. Through a massive system of weights, the car was lifted up in the air to the loader, which was essentially a giant chute. The car was carefully tipped against a series of steel beams that held it in place but allowed the coal to pour out into the loader, down the chute, and be funneled into the waiting barge below. Lower the car back down and then bring in the next car of coal, apparently at a rate of about one car every two minutes."

"That's fast." Webb made a circling motion with his index finger. "So then they'd keep repeating the process until the barge was full. How did they get rid of the railcars if the dumper is built on a single pier out into the water?"

"The new car coming in bumps the first car out of the way and it rolls downhill to the kickback. The kickback is essentially a mini ramp, so the empty railcar runs up the ramp and then back down it. In the meantime, when it went over the exit track, it threw a switch so that when the car runs down the kickback, it gets shifted to an entirely different track that runs alongside the dumper. Those empty cars are then reattached and taken away by the engine once the entire train has been emptied. It's an entirely closed-loop in-and-out system on a narrow pier."

"That is ingenious," Webb said. "How do you know all this?"

"Actually, most of it is pretty evident just standing there. Well, maybe not now, but when I first explored it, it was in better shape and all the tracks and the kickback were intact. You could follow the track to see how the whole thing worked."

"What do we need to look out for?" McCord asked. "Every site seems to have some pretty dangerous areas."

"This one will definitely be dangerous. The biggest issue is straight-up disintegration of the structure. Last time I was there was probably two or three years ago. And even then, all the metal components of the site were starting to fall apart. It's more than a hundred years old and has been entirely neglected for over thirty years, and that's ample time for metal to rust and become unstable. Not to mention a large portion of the structure is on a wooden pier sticking out into the river, though some of it is on concrete pylons. The wood is waterlogged and rotting. The whole thing was in better shape before Hurricane Sandy roared through in 2012. That did a ton of damage to the existing structure, hastening the degradation."

"Hurricanes," McCord muttered in a sour tone. "Great."

At Smaill's questioning look, Meg explained, "The four of us went through Hurricane Cole in July, or came in right afterward for victim rescue and recovery."

"And then a bonus human trafficking case," Brian added.

Smaill nodded in understanding. "I heard about that. I had no idea that was you. Guess you're not a fan of hurricanes."

"Absolutely not," McCord said.

As a reporter sent in to cover landfall, McCord was the only one of them who'd lived through the fury of the storm. Meg imagined it was an experience he never wanted to repeat. "Any tips on managing the site safely?"

"Second-guess every structure," Smaill replied, looking up at her. "Don't assume that because something looks solid, it is. Floors can give way, bolts that look secure can snap under the slightest stress, wood can shatter. Especially on the upper levels, where the structure has been exposed to the elements with absolutely no maintenance for about thirty-five years. I have ropes and harnesses in my pack, but if Stevenson is on-site, you're not going to have time to use them. Safety first at all times, because this place is deadly. And one other complicating factor—I checked the weather. It's supposed to be pouring rain there, which is going to make every foot- and handhold slippery. So, as I said, second-guess everything."

Meg ducked low, peering out the small aircraft window to the east. "Lots of cloud cover out there." She straightened. "A storm coming in off the ocean is going to stack the deck against us."

"How?" Smaill asked.

"It's going to complicate the search for the dogs. A little rain isn't a bad thing in a search—it can even concentrate the scent on the ground, making a clearer path for the dogs. But a big storm with pouring rain can simply wash the scent away. Then we're essentially going in blind. How is this place set up?"

Smaill pulled his phone out of his pocket and started flipping through pictures. "I downloaded some photos so you know what to expect. Ah, here's a good one." He brought the photo up full screen and handed it to Meg, who studied it for a minute and then passed it to Brian.

"That shot is from one of the urbex boards. You can see that whoever took the photo is standing on the shoreline, looking out onto the pier. The railroad tracks on the right go up to the dumper. The set on the left comes back from it. There's a walkway there on the very right, to get to and from the dumper."

"And that massive structure is the dumper? It looks like a box on spindly legs."

"Not so spindly when you are standing next to them. And that structure is easily five or six stories tall. See how the tracks go uphill to the dumper? What you can't see is the structure under the tracks. That houses the giant engines and winches for the weight and pulley system that moved both the railcars and the loader, because the loader would have to be winched up into the air to allow the boats to move in or out from beneath it; then it had to be lowered into position to dump the coal. All the works are underneath. It's possible your victim could be there, but I doubt it. If you want to leave someone where they can't possibly get away, up top is the way to go."

McCord took the phone from Brian. "From what I see here, the dumper is basically steel struts, looks like four on each side, with a platform up above, the loader hanging on one side and the weights on the other to counterbalance it. The top platform—that's where the pulleys are, I assume?"

"Yes."

"Is that a control room on one side of the dumper, three quarters of the way up?"

"Yes. From there, the site manager could see everything—where the cars are coming in and going out, where the boats are on the water. And there was a second control room on the loader itself, so there would be communication going on between those two rooms."

"The victim could be in either control room."

"Maybe, but I doubt she would be in the loader control room." Smaill held out his hand for his phone, then selected another photo and turned it around to show everyone. "The loader itself hangs in midair, winched up about halfway, sticking out over the water. The control room tilts upward at a crazy angle at the end of it. It would be incredibly treacherous to get out there, even harder to get into the control room itself, especially dragging a victim along with you. One fall and you'd be three or four stories down into the water. Depending on how you landed, the fall could kill you or you could drown."

Meg plucked the phone out of Smaill's hand to study the picture. "That doesn't make sense, then, going with the theory that this is one of the investors' grandsons trying to kill off all the investors except his grandfather so that when the grandfather dies, he inherits everything. You can't inherit if you're dead. He's already taking chances, but why take that kind of chance when there are other options available?"

"I think he's going to go straight up," Webb said. "Can I see a picture of the whole site? From a distance?"

Smaill took the phone from Meg, scrolled through to another picture, and handed it to Webb.

He took a moment to study the layout. "Here's my concern. Yes, the site is going to be dangerous. But Stevenson is also going to be dangerous, too, once it becomes clear we're on-site with him and we know who he is. It's the entrance to this place that bothers me." He pointed to the long open area of the pier leading out to the dumper, twin runs of railroad tracks on disintegrating wood bordered on one side by the concrete walkway. "I don't like how exposed this is. There's no way to hide our approach. If he's up top, he's going to see us coming in. And if he's armed, we're going to be sitting ducks."

"I thought about that, too," Smaill said. "And you're right. This section here"—he pointed at the section of the pier closest to the shore—"is definitely going to be problematic. Once we get to the point where the track curves upward, we'll have some shelter, but for the first two hundred feet or so, the best we're going to be able to do is come in as quietly as possible at a dead run. If he starts shooting at us, we'll have to hope we're too far away and moving too fast and that he's a lousy shot. On the bright side, if it's pouring rain, it's going to make visibility the pits, so that will increase our chances of coming in undetected. Let's review once we get there, but I think that's our only option. We can't go by water, because we'll be slower and just as visible. Speed is the only solution, I think."

"Unfortunately, I agree with you," said Meg. "The layout of this site gives us an opportunity to trap Stevenson. But that's going to make him desperate, so we need to be ready for anything." Meg glanced from Smaill to Brian. "Same teams as last time? You guys have paired up a few times and that seems to work."

Brian held out his fist and Smaill bumped it in camaraderie over the seatback. "Sure does. Lacey likes him, too."

Smaill held out his arms in an encompassing gesture. "What's not to like?"

"Exactly. We're good."

"Perfect. Todd, you're with me." Meg turned to McCord. "Now . . . you."

"What about me?" McCord's expression said he already knew what she was going to say.

"I know Kate cleared you to be here. I also know you want to be able to finish this story off with every detail down to the smell of the salt breeze and the crumble of rust under your boots. But you're not law enforcement. Or our expert guide. Or medical."

"No, but I can watch the dogs."

"Watch the . . . what?"

"Look at this site. Most of the structure is in the air, and that's where you think he'll be. What if you can't get Hawk up the stairs or ladders? Or the struts, if that's your only way up? You'd never leave them alone where they might be in danger."

Meg opened her mouth to argue, and then realized McCord was absolutely right. "If that happens, you're going to watch the dogs?"

"Let me come with you. I know how to stay clear of a situation, you know that. I wouldn't have survived Iraq without that sixth sense and the ability to run like the wind if needed. If you have to go vertical and can't take the dogs with you, you can hand them off to me and do your job. You know I can keep myself and them safe. They know me now. They trust me."

Jaw tight, lips a thin line, she studied him. "Anything happens to you and I'm going to be murdered by my own sister."

"Who is a gem of a woman I'd lay down my life for, but nothing is going to happen. There's nothing to worry about."

Meg glanced at Brian, who nodded his agreement. "Okay, fine. But you do everything Brian and I say." She leveled an index finger at both Webb and Smaill. "That goes for you two as well. I know you're trained, but not specifically for this. And you're our responsibility."

"Tell us what you need us to do, and we'll get it done," Webb said.

"We're all set, then." She glanced at her watch and then out the window. "We should be on the ground in about ten minutes. With a little luck, we'll have Stevenson in handcuffs within the hour."

CHAPTER 32

Tankcatting: Breaking into a site overcoming locks, obstructions, and decay.

Wednesday, November 21, 1:24 PM
New Castle Coal Dumper
New Castle, Delaware

They came in at a run through a miserable, stinging cold rain, down the narrow concrete walkway that hugged the train tracks. Meg led the way, with Hawk, unleashed, galloping at her side—then Webb, Smaill, Lacey beside Brian, and McCord bringing up the rear.

They had parked their rented vehicles in the transportation lot near the shore, tucking them in between parked semis behind the transport company's warehouse. Except for McCord, they'd each donned a pack—Brian and Meg their SAR packs; Webb his medical pack; and Smaill a rescue pack stuffed full of climbing cables, harnesses, and tools. Due to the nature of the site, and the degradation of the structure itself, Brian and Meg left their dogs unleashed. If one of them went down, they needed their dogs to be able to save themselves.

On the way toward the shoreline, McCord had spotted

the dark SUV through the pelting rain, similarly pulled out of sight between the trailers.

He was here.

Meg sprinted down the cracked and broken concrete pathway, alternately scanning the way ahead for obstacles and the structure above for any sign of movement. The hood on her jacket was tugged over her head, and she peered out from under it, squinting up at the dumper, partially obscured by weather.

If we can't see him, hopefully he can't see us.

To her left, the train tracks ran alongside, their wooden platform built above concrete footings that disappeared beneath the surface of the river. Puny trees and shrubs sprouted from between the rails, growing from a wooden base toward the sun around iron rails unused for decades.

The blustery northwest wind drove the rain at a sharp slant over the railroad ties, sluicing water onto the concrete walkway. Meg glanced at Hawk, noting his head-up posture—he was alert but wasn't focused on any specific scent. Without a victim-specific scent to search for, he'd be looking for the freshest scent, and the rain paired with the creosote-soaked railway ties, leaching their clingy, oily scent all over the concrete walkway, likely masked any human scent.

Heavy, twisted ropes lay across the concrete walkway, trailing over the uneven surface to tumble into the water below, and thick wood crossbeams, blown or ripped from the railbed, lay tangled with the ropes. But Meg never paused, simply lengthening her stride to leap over the obstacles, Hawk mirroring her every move.

As agreed, the group split partway down the pier, Meg, Hawk, Webb, and McCord taking advantage of a break in the railing to jump to the wooden railway platform before it rose above the engine room, and Brian, Lacey, and Smaill continuing on down the walkway as the railbed rose over their heads. They would make their way into the engine and winch room, ensuring it was empty before meeting the rest of the team on the upper level.

They had to slow their pace as soon as they climbed onto the wooden platform. One quick look told Meg their footing was precarious, since many of the railway ties were shattered where they'd been pierced by spikes, and the weathered wood was splintered and cracked over its entire length. The wood groaned and occasionally cracked underfoot, so she slowed as much as she dared to minimize the force of every single step. To their advantage, the uneven surface provided traction over the soaked wood.

They sprinted up the incline, staying close to the railing as it rose above the walkway below. As they neared the top, Brian ran directly underneath them to cross under the tracks and into the building below.

They reached the top of the incline, and Meg slowed to a halt beneath the platform high overhead. Temporarily out of the rain, she pushed her hood back to be able to see and hear the site more clearly.

The railroad ties here were in worse shape, with entire support beams missing and gaping holes showing the drop to the concrete platform below. In front of them, the track ran onto the steel loader, the long platform the length of the railcars that would have been rolled onto it for dumping. One side of the loader was solid steel, though badly rusted, and it was here that each car was raised and tipped. To their left, a narrow set of open metal stairs ran up to the spidery steel structure overhead. In the first flight, several steps were simply missing, the contact points having rusted and the stair treads fallen away.

She bent down to Hawk, running her hand over his soaking fur. "Hawk, buddy, do you smell anything? Find, Hawk. Find."

As Hawk put his nose down and started to explore this

level, Meg scanned the area for any sign of life. One quick glance told her that Stevenson and Mani Ramachandaran would not be easily found. Only twenty feet above the waterline, the wind whistled around them as it blew off the river, and the sound of rain striking metal was a constant drumbeat.

Hawk had moved to the stairs and now started to rapidly climb up the rusted mesh treads. His trail stopped abruptly as he came to a gaping section missing three consecutive steps, and he sat down and turned to look at Meg.

He's alerting. Someone recently took those stairs.

She turned to find McCord standing behind her, breathing hard, his blond hair plastered to his head and his glasses speckled with rain. He stood with his head tipped up, toward the levels overhead. She touched his arm, and when he looked toward her, she pointed up and he nodded.

She swallowed, hard. *No choice for it. Hawk is saying they're up there, so that's where we go.* "Hawk, come." Reaching into her navy FBI jacket pocket, she pulled out Hawk's leash, coiled it, and jammed it into McCord's hands as Hawk clambered back down to her. She squatted down in front of her dog, dropping her voice down to a bare whisper over the wind and rain. "Hawk. Stay with McCord. Stay." She ran a quick hand over his head, taking comfort in the trust in his dark gaze, and then she stood and turned away from him. Meeting Webb's eyes, she jerked her head toward the stairs.

When he would have stepped in front of her to go first, she grabbed his arm, shaking her head. She met his gaze. *FBI operation. You can't go first.* She knew he understood when he stepped back a pace, letting her precede him.

She set her foot on the metal mesh step, testing its firmness, then trusting her weight to it. Climbing as quickly as she dared, she tested each tread, skipping any that seemed unstable. Halfway up the first flight, she came to the section of missing steps that signaled the end of Hawk's search. Grasping both railings, feeling the chill and the roughness of the weathered metal beneath her palms, she stepped up onto the side supports of the staircase. She set her other boot on the far side, thankful for her nearly six feet of height that allowed her a stride wide enough to traverse the space, and used her arms to drag herself up. Once her boot slipped on the wet, slick metal, but she held on with both hands, pulling herself up until she gratefully stepped off onto the next intact stair tread and then the next. As Webb stepped back onto the staircase, she looked down to catch McCord's encouraging nod. Hawk's eyes stayed locked on her, his body looked tense as if he was ready to spring after her, but McCord had him leashed and held the shortened lead tightly.

She turned away from her dog and continued up the stairs.

At the top of the first flight of stairs, the bottom of one of the massive weights hung along a track down one of the rear struts of the complex. About twenty feet in length, it had to be at least several tons in weight, suspended by its original cables, and matched an identical weight on the far side of the structure.

They climbed up another two flights of zigzagging stairs, pausing just below the landing for the turn that led to the control room jutting out from the side of the structure. Glancing down, Meg saw that McCord now stood with two dogs, and Brian and Smaill had cleared the open section of stairs and were following them. After pulling her Glock 19 from her hip holster, Meg held it low against her thigh as she waited for them.

Brian took one look at her weapon and pulled his own, slipping into place behind her and giving her a nod. *Ready.*

They moved quietly up the stairs, faces turned up directly into the rain, and she and Brian stepped onto the control room landing and quickly moved to either side of the open doorway, the door having been removed long ago.

Meg pointed at Brian and then up; next, she pointed at herself and then down. Looking him in the eye, she mouthed *One . . . two . . . three!*

They swept into the control room, Brian going high, Meg going low, guns extended in a double-fisted grip.

The room was empty. It was lined with ancient consoles, and the remnants of the dumper controls lay scattered across the floor, but the room had mostly been picked clean. There was no sign of Stevenson or his hostage.

The long, windowless back wall was covered with graffiti, and tucked into the corner nearest the door was the now-familiar blue trilobite.

Five for five.

Smaill had guessed right.

They returned to the group and started upward again. Meg paused at the landing above the control room, holding out her free hand to stop the rest of the group as she froze to listen. Up this high, the wind rose to a scream, stabbing like chill fingers through her hair and driving raindrops against her exposed skin, painful like tiny knives.

But there it was—a scrape from above. And what she swore was a muffled cry.

She took off up the stairs, the rest of the group behind her. They came off the staircase onto the top platform, which opened out to a series of pulleys, thick, twisted metal cables, and crisscrossing catwalks.

Two people huddled in the rain on the far side of the platform. No, not huddled, Meg realized. Struggled. Meg recognized Stevenson immediately, even drenched and without a covering of concrete dust, and the woman he was holding down had to be Mani Ramachandaran.

Still alive.

"FBI!" Meg bellowed.

"Freeze!" Brian yelled.

Stevenson's head jerked in their direction, his pale face losing even more color at the sight of Meg and Brian, both armed and in FBI jackets. He pushed Mrs. Ramachandaran away and jumped to his feet, bolting for the far side of the platform, then ducking behind a giant iron wheel with a heavy cable looped over it to disappear from sight.

"Stay with the victim!" Meg yelled over her shoulder to Webb and Smaill.

She and Brian headed straight across the platform while Webb and Smaill tried to cut across it diagonally, heading straight for Mrs. Ramachandaran. A narrow metal mesh walkway rimmed the edge of the platform, but large sections of it were missing, leaving stories of empty space beneath. The wind howled around them, shaking the platform and driving the rain on a steep slant, seeming to set the entire dumper swaying.

How stable is this structure?

Meg grabbed for the railing, but her gaze fell on the water down so far, far below, the rain being blown over the surface in sheets. She pushed away the raw terror that rose in her throat, not only at the height but also the potential instability of any part of the structure.

Focus.

Where the mesh had rusted and rotted away, they were forced to cross on one side of the gap on the exposed I-beam, slowing their progress. It felt like an eternity to make it to the far side, though in reality it was only about twenty seconds; in that time, Stevenson was gone.

"Where did he go?" Meg held her hand over her eyes to shield them from the rain as she scanned the platform, but it was as if he'd disappeared into thin air.

"There was a ladder on the forward leg on this side."

Brian had to come close to yell over the wind. "Maybe there's one on the back leg, too."

There was, but as Meg leaned out, she could see that he never would have taken it, as a large number of the rungs were rusted out and missing. She spun around to where Webb and Smaill were kneeling over the victim, Smaill talking to her as Webb dug furiously in his pack for something.

Where did he go?

Then a flash of movement caught her eye, and she turned with a gasp.

Through the wind and the rain, Stevenson was climbing out on the support leg. About four feet wide, it was made of crisscrossing steel supports woven through a boxy square frame. The leg projected about ten feet out from the top platform, then ran directly down to the main concrete pad for the entire complex.

If he makes it to the ground, we've lost him.

"There!" She pointed after him. "He's headed down. If he makes it all the way to the ground, he'll even miss McCord on the track level. We need to split up. You take the stairs back down and cut him off from below." She started after Stevenson.

Brian grabbed her arm, jerking her to a halt. "Where are you going?"

"After him. Someone needs to follow him. This structure has too many levels. If he jumps onto the engine room roof, he could get past you on the ground floor. If I follow him down, I'll block his way back up here, and we need eyes on him at all times to see where he goes. Todd and Chuck are busy right now and can't help us. Now go!" She jerked her arm free and ran after Stevenson as fast as she dared across the ruined platform. Meg didn't look behind her to ensure Brian had followed her order but kept her eyes firmly on Stevenson. She knew she could hit him if she fired on him at this range, but that would likely mean certain death six stories below. Justice for what he'd done, for sure, but not her kind of justice. She'd let the courts deal with him and let him face the families he'd wronged.

She jammed her Glock in its holster and hoisted herself up onto the frame to follow him. Crawling off the platform onto the wet and slippery steel supports, she hesitated. This isolated metal structure swayed even more in the merciless winds and was so high in the air, her brain tried to simply short-circuit, leaving her frozen. Below her, what was left of the wooden pier that had once been part of the switchback stretched out into the river for sixty or eighty feet. There was less of the pier left than the dumper itself, and the mangled metal track, still attached to the remnants of the raised kickback, dangled over water studded with a forest of thick wooden support piles, weathered and exposed into jagged, knifelike edges.

She closed her eyes for a moment, gathering herself. *You can do this. Do not look down. Do not slip. One careful step at a time.*

She took a deep breath and opened her eyes straight ahead to take in nothing but the steel beams. She grasped the nearest crossbeam, hauling herself forward onto the strut. *Take it one move at a time.* Right foot and knee to a new position. Left hand. Breathe. Left knee. Right hand. Breathe.

Slowly she crawled out over nothing but a deadly drop as the man in front of her and the wind combined to shake her very foundations.

Three feet.

Five feet.

Breathe.

Seven feet.

Ten feet, to the vertical section, and she maneuvered

herself from horizontal to vertical, from the inside of the support arm to the outside, where she could climb freely and her way wasn't blocked by crossbeams every five feet. Now movement seemed easier, partly because she was now climbing to safety instead of away from it.

She could see Stevenson in front of her. Was she gaining on him?

"Brett Stevenson!" she yelled into the wind, hoping he could hear her. "FBI! You're under arrest. Stop and you won't be charged with evading arrest."

Stevenson didn't slow. In fact, he moved faster, but whether he was aiming for the engine room roof or the ground, she couldn't tell.

"Goddamn it."

Meg had to cling tight to a beam during a particularly brutal gust of wind, ducking her head and screwing her eyes shut as rain pelted her and she held on for dear life while her body was buffeted. She let out the breath she'd been holding when the wind died down slightly and reached down with her left boot when she heard the scream of tearing metal and a cry of terror. Craning her head over her shoulder, she looked down.

Stevenson was dangling from one hand as his other hand flailed and his legs kicked futilely in the air.

Dangling from one hand was bad enough, but the wet metal had plenty of slide and he wouldn't be able to hold on for long.

Her fear of heights dissipated in the face of his imminent death. Throwing most of her caution aside, Meg climbed down more rapidly, eschewing safer hand- and footholds for speed.

She knew she must be about fifty feet in the air still but opted to not look down. That way she could pretend it was only twenty feet.

"Hang on! I'm coming!"

Another metallic shriek meant she had to look to determine how close she was to him.

Not close enough.

"Hang on!"

"Help me!"

"Find a foothold!"

"I . . . can't . . ."

She was going to lose him.

She was now getting close enough to read the utter terror in his eyes. She had to figure out how to get a stable-enough handhold to be able to grab him without letting him jerk her into thin air, killing them both.

From below, she heard Brian bellowing her name, but she shut it out and simply concentrated on the task at hand.

Get your legs wrapped around one of the crossbeams. You'll need to support twice the weight.

She moved around to the side of the support column adjacent to Stevenson and slid her legs inside, slipping her boots underneath and locking her ankles for stability. Then, clamping her right hand around a crossbeam, she leaned out into the buffeting wind, her left hand extended to him. "Take my hand."

The blue eyes that turned to her seemed overbright in the starkly white face, the raindrops like tears against his cheeks.

"Take my hand," she repeated, stretching even farther.

He lunged for her, wildly, frantically. And missed.

"Again!" she ordered. "You can do this."

He surged upward, trying to pull himself up enough to make contact. His fingers touched hers, scrabbling for purchase. Then his hand slipped and he was gone, spinning off into the air, his scream following him down.

Meg stared down in horror, frozen, her hand still extended, reaching for him, the rain dripping from her fingers in a near-constant stream.

The scream abruptly cut off as he landed on one of the support piles jutting up from the river.

She turned away, pulling herself up and wrapping her arms around the nearest crossbeam she could reach, and tried to drag air into her shocked lungs as her entire body shook.

The crisis past, now all she could do was hold on.

She didn't know how long she stayed there, wrapped around the support beam, her head bowed and her cheek pressed against cold metal, rain streaming off her hood, too scared to move in case another crossbeam gave way or she slipped and joined Stevenson in an awful death.

Finally, the sound of her name being called penetrated her brain.

Todd?

It sounded as if he was nearby, but she knew full well he was on the platform, saving Mani Ramachandaran's life.

"Meg. Meg, it's me."

She raised her head, opening her eyes for the first time in minutes.

Webb was at eye level only a few feet away, swaying slightly in the wind.

She blinked at him. "What . . . ? How?"

"I'm here to take you down. Look up."

She blindly followed his instruction, tipping her face into the rain. Up above, Smaill and McCord were braced at the end of the platform, holding the rope she now realized supported the harness Webb wore.

"Brian's below with the dogs. McCord came up to help Smaill with the rescue gear. They're going to lower us down," he continued. He slid a rope around her and tightened the slack, snugging her against him, and clipped the free end onto his harness. "You're safe now. I've got you. You can let go of the beam."

She did then, letting go of her white-knuckled grip on the crossbeam and transferring it to him.

"You okay?"

Her face buried against the warmth of his throat, she nodded. "Just get me the hell down from here."

"With pleasure." Webb gave a thumbs-up to Smaill, and slowly, carefully, they let out the rope.

Two minutes later, relief swept through her as her feet touched solid ground.

Webb slowly unclenched her fingers to loosen her death grip around his neck and transferred her hands to his shoulders, where they latched on again hard enough to make him wince. "We're down. You can relax now."

"My brain knows that, but my body hasn't got the message yet. Give me a minute."

"Take as long as you need." Ignoring the harness and the carabiners that dug into their bellies, he gripped her hips, holding her close. "You know, that was a hell of a stunt you pulled up there. You scared the crap out of me. I didn't know if I'd get to you in time. We had to dig the equipment out of Smaill's pack, set it up, get me out on the ledge, and then down to you. I kept looking down expecting to see you floating in the river beside Stevenson."

Meg let out a laugh that cracked with strain more than humor. "You and me both. All I could do was hold on. Not very proactive of me."

"You'd been damned proactive up to then. While you had a life to save, you didn't give two thoughts to the risk you were taking."

"Until he went down, and then it was all I could think about." She looked up at him and finally released his shoulder to cup his jaw with one hand. "I haven't said thank you."

"No thanks required. I'm just relieved he was our only loss. The whole thing could have gone sideways in so many ways. As it is, Beaumont may put your ass in a sling for risking your life like that."

"It wouldn't be the first time. And likely won't be the last." She went up on tiptoe and pressed a kiss to his mouth. "That's all the thank you I can do here and now. But there'll be a much better one later. In private."

His gaze went hot. "I won't say no to that."

"Would you let go of her already." Brian's irritated voice sounded behind them. "I need to know she's in one piece."

Webb laughed as he unroped Meg from him and passed her to Brian so he could shuck off the harness.

"God Almighty, you scared about twenty years off me," Brian scolded, clamping his arms around her so tightly she had trouble drawing breath.

"Just think about how many it scared off me." The words bubbled up with relieved laughter. But the laughter caught abruptly as her gaze landed on Brett Stevenson. "Oh, Brian." She pushed away from him.

Stevenson had landed faceup about fifteen feet from the edge of the concrete platform, the pier support pile impaling him to protrude gorily from his abdomen. He lay limp, his hands floating on the surface of the river, his feet submerged in river water running red with blood. His eyes, open and glassy, stared up into the rain.

Webb came to stand on the other side of her, and the three of them stood silent for a moment, staring at the man who thought someone else's death was justified for his financial gain.

"I was willing to send him to jail for life, but I tried to save him this," Meg murmured.

"I know," Webb said simply.

"I watched from below as you tried to save him," Brian

said. "And I know how terrifying that must have been for you, but you did it anyway. You're not responsible for this. He went out there of his own volition."

Meg sighed. "Part of me knows that. The other part knows this isn't how it was supposed to end."

In the distance, the first wail of sirens pierced the air.

"On the bright side, Mrs. Ramachandaran is going to make it," Webb said.

That jerked Meg out of her contemplation. "She is?"

"Knowing what we were dealing with, I made sure I had intravenous vitamin K in my med pack. That's the antidote to an anticoagulant like difethialone. I had to assume that's still what he was using, so I had it on hand for when we found her. She's a fighter, that one. Fought him the whole way. Slowed him down, made getting her up to the top platform a nightmare. I administered it up top, and it's already working. Smaill and McCord will stay with her until we get a team up there."

"Local law enforcement marine unit, local field agents, and EMTs are on the way," said Brian. "I've already talked to Craig and Kate, and they're both waiting for a follow-up from you. But first, the dogs are back about twenty feet out of the rain, and Hawk must be going crazy right now waiting for you to let him know you're okay."

Later, after Meg's reunion with Hawk, after explanations and statements, and after the rain finally stopped, they made their way down the pier and onto the shoreline. As a group they turned and looked back at the coal dumper, standing tall against steel-gray clouds and the backdrop of the river that had been its purpose for decades.

Webb slung an arm over Meg's shoulders. "No need to stick around. We've done enough today."

As if to punctuate the sentiment, Hawk gave a hearty bark that was echoed by Lacey.

Brian laughed. "Sounds like Lacey agrees."

"I think we all agree," said Smaill.

McCord nodded. "I'll drink to that."

"That's because you want to head home and get this story written up," Meg accused. "You're already eyeing tomorrow's front-page headline."

McCord rolled his eyes skyward and innocently whistled a few tuneless bars. Then he grinned.

Meg laughed and looked down at Hawk. "You all set, buddy?"

Hawk simply gazed up at her with a canine smile and wagged his tail furiously.

"Me too."

Together, they turned their backs on the end of the case and the man who was responsible for so much death and pain.

Justice had been found.

It was time to go home.

Epilogue

Wednesday, November 21, 8:10 PM
Jennings residence
Arlington, Virginia

"Even after a shower and clean clothes, I swear I still feel chilled from all that rain." Brian knelt on the floor in front of the roaring fire that Chuck had built in the fireplace and held his hands out toward the warmth, letting out a satisfied sigh. "This should finally get rid of it, though."

With the headlong rush now over, Craig had the teams drive their rented vehicles from New Castle back to DC. Brian and Meg and the dogs had gone straight to the Hoover Building to debrief with Craig; Kate had still been out of the office, but they'd touch base with her later.

While Meg drove back to Arlington, Brian headed home but promised he'd be back at Meg's by eight o'clock for a late dinner.

One by one, the whole team arrived. Webb stopped at his apartment for a shower and dry clothes but had still beaten Meg back to Arlington. After picking up Cody, McCord had gone straight to the house to meet Cara and bring her up to date on the search. Meg got back with enough time to shower and change into leggings and a comfy, faded Richmond PD sweatshirt. Smaill and Brian met in the driveway and came in together.

Now the group was gathered around the fireplace in the living room. Webb slouched comfortably on the couch with Meg curled up beside him, her legs tucked under her. McCord sat in the overstuffed armchair, his stockinged feet propped on the coffee table and his laptop balanced on his knees. Cara sat with her back propped against his chair, Saki stretched out along her leg, snoring quietly. Smaill sprawled in Meg's ancient, much-loved recliner. The other dogs were scattered around the room—under the coffee table, on the dog bed, by the fireplace.

"When's the pizza getting here?" McCord asked, his eyes locked on his monitor as he typed.

"Any minute now." Cara tapped him on the knee. "Are you going to stop typing to eat?"

"Paper gets put to bed at midnight. I'm on the clock. This is going out for tomorrow's front page if it kills me."

"You can't be writing the whole thing from scratch. You must have had this story half written already," Meg said.

McCord stopped typing long enough to shoot her a sideways glance. "More than half. I'd never make it otherwise. I'll stop when the pizza arrives. A man has to eat." He started typing again.

"Amen to that." Webb stretched his long legs out under the coffee table, comfortably crossing his ankles. "I'm so hungry, I could eat a horse right now."

As if on cue, the doorbell rang.

"Perfect timing. Sorry, Saki, I need to get this." Cara climbed to her feet. Meg started to rise off the couch, but Cara waved her down. "Sit, I've got it."

"I'm buying."

"Nope. When I placed the order, I put it on Clay's credit card."

She waited, grinning at her sister, mouthing the words *One . . . two . . . thr—*

"Wait." McCord's head shot up. "You did what?"

"I did no such thing. But the pizza is here, and I thought that might be the only way to get your attention off your article. You said you wanted to eat," she tossed over her shoulder with a grin as she went to meet the delivery man.

Within minutes, McCord's laptop had been discarded to the kitchen counter and everyone resettled around the fire with their dinner, bottles of beer, and glasses of wine.

Brian took a big bite of his loaded slice and sat back with a sigh. "So good."

"And so needed after this case," Meg agreed.

"No kidding." Brian pulled a piece of sausage off his pizza and tossed it to Lacey, sitting next to him and tracking the slice's every movement with her eyes.

"You men," Cara scolded. "You insist on feeding the dogs during meals. You're a bad influence."

"I can't help it. She looks at me with those big brown eyes . . ." Brian looked at Lacey to find her staring at him, her head tilted quizzically to one side. "I just can't resist her." A piece of ham followed the sausage.

"Softie."

"Oh, totally. She knows it, too."

Meg's phone rang where it sat on the coffee table tucked between pizza boxes. She groaned and reached for it.

"Do you have to get it?" Webb asked. "After the day you've had . . ."

"If Craig even tries to put us back on the clock, he knows he's going to get an earful." Meg glanced at her phone screen. "It's not Craig, it's Kate." She accepted the call. "Hi, Kate."

She listened for a few minutes, occasionally asking questions but mostly staying silent. Then she thanked Kate for the call and hung up.

She put the phone down on the coffee table and just sat staring at it for a moment.

Webb rubbed a hand over her forearm. "Hey, you in there?"

"Yeah."

"Everything okay?"

"Yeah." She took a deep breath, let it out, and reached for her plate, buying a little more time as she took a bite of pizza, chewed, and swallowed. "That was Kate."

"So you said." Brian leaned back on an extended arm so he could look up at her. "What did she say?"

"She tracked down Peter Stevenson. In fact, she was with him when my text came through that we'd found Brett. That he was dead. So she broke the news to him right then. He was devastated." Setting her plate down on the table, she looked over and met Brian's eyes. "He had no idea his grandson was killing investors so he'd be the only one left. Kate has no doubt about his sincerity. It wrecked him. He couldn't talk for a full ten minutes after she told him. He just shut down."

"Damn."

"Unfortunately, this will likely be the end of Peter Stevenson," said Webb. "The cancer is killing him, and his systems are slowly shutting down. This kind of stress will weaken him even further."

"So many dead, and for what?" Meg could hear the bitterness in her tone but couldn't filter it out. "What a waste of life."

"It is," McCord agreed. "But don't forget that we saved the last three victims. Look at the way things were going. Since Peter found out in September that his grandfather's treatment had failed, he'd been on a mission. He'd been working his way through those he'd already planned and making plans for the few who were left. That's probably why we went nearly two weeks between the last kill and this one. I bet if he'd gotten past us and been allowed to continue, we would have seen the last two victims die inside of the next week. He was fighting the clock just as much as his grandfather was. But we stopped him. Take it from me as someone who spends way more time covering the dark side of the human condition than the light—you have to let yourself focus on the wins, not just the failures. Otherwise you'll go crazy."

"And you won't be ready to take on the next case," Brian added. "Which we don't really have to tell you, because you already know it." He tapped his temple, a private message just for her. *There's not many times the case gets to you right here.*

She gave him a half smile and nodded. "I do. This case just got under my skin. Usually at the end of a case, I'm happy about how it turned out, or at least satisfied. But this time . . . it's more than that. Sadness at the worthless loss of life. Rage that his payment for his crimes was over like—" She snapped her fingers. "Happiness that we stopped him before he could kill Mrs. Ramachandaran." She sagged back against the couch and against the warmth of Webb's body. "And so damn tired."

"Can I say something?" Smaill asked as everyone turned to him. "I'm new to this group, new to this kind of investigation. I know Webb's been with you a few times, but this was an eye-opener for me. Here's the outsider take on what I just witnessed: You guys are amazing. You've been working this case for about six weeks now. And from what I've heard from Webb, this wasn't your only case, and you've been called out on other searches. I've been witness to some of the setbacks, some of the victims you've lost, even when you thought you had a chance at them. But you also saved some victims you thought were beyond help. You made a real difference."

"*We* made a real difference," Brian interjected. "Don't downplay your part in it. We might never have gotten in front of him without you."

Smaill grinned. "Thanks."

"There's something else," Cara said. "This case ended so abruptly. There can't be the same kind of emotional justice that you got with Daniel Mannew, Derek Garber, or Marcus Fairfax, where the man responsible will be tried in a court of law, found guilty, and pay for his crimes. I think that's weighing on you more than you think."

"Maybe. We know Stevenson was guilty," Meg said. "At least we have that."

"Sure," Webb agreed. "But it's still not the same. At least not in my head. He should have been left to rot in jail for the rest of his long, miserable life to pay for the lives he took. Yes, his victims were older. Yes, they'd lived almost all their natural lives. But now they'll miss things—birthdays, Christmases, weddings, great-grandchildren. And they died scared and alone."

Meg pulled back to stare at him, surprised by the sudden venom in his tone. "You're pissed."

"You sound surprised."

"You always seem so steady when it comes to this stuff."

"That's the first responder in me. Just like you're steady when you have to be. But afterward . . ."

"Afterward, you get pissed."

"Sometimes. Just like part of you is. Just like you're also feeling the loss of the ones we didn't save. Sometimes the ones we lose stay with us, and we have to work through that."

"And you know what's best for that?" McCord lifted his beer bottle. "The company of people who feel the same way."

Brian lifted his bottle in solidarity. "And then putting it away because somewhere out there is someone who needs us, and we'll be ready for them."

"You're right. You're all right." She smiled at them. "Thanks."

"No thanks required," said McCord. "What is required is pizza. This article isn't going to write itself. I need to fuel up."

As he reached for the nearest pizza box, Meg sat back and took another sip of her wine.

She would give herself tonight to mourn the ones they'd lost.

Tomorrow, she'd be ready to save the next one.

Acknowledgments

It was many years ago that I stumbled over a website called Opacity that consists of photographs of abandoned places as shot by Tom Kirsch. I was fascinated by the atmosphere created by his photography and was impressed by the range of locations and types of structures. Years after I initially found the site, I came back to Opacity when I was planning this novel, as I realized that urban exploration would provide interesting, challenging, and potentially dangerous search locations for the K-9 teams. More specifically, the Opacity website provided the visuals I needed to write the manuscript. One site was named in the novel as it truly existed (i.e., Bethlehem Steel), but many sites were altered to be moved to convenient East Coast locations (i.e., Riverside State Hospital/Northam Manor Psychiatric Hospital, the Armor Meat Packing Plant, the Old Essex County Jail, and the McMylar Coal Dumper). Mr. Kirsch, we've never met, but I want to thank you for the time and care you put into your craft. It opened up a wonderful and imaginative world for me, and I couldn't have written this novel in the same way without your photographs.

As always, my critique team has been instrumental in producing a clean manuscript that required remarkably little editing afterward. Many thanks to Lisa Giblin, Jenny Lidstrom, Jessica Newton, Rick Newton, and Sharon Taylor for once again being first readers, logic testers, and a story clinic all in one. It's a lot of work, and you do it (repeatedly) with your trusty red pens and a smile, and I am forever grateful for your efforts.

Thank you to my agent, Nicole Resciniti, for your constant care and attention. You're always there for anything and everything, and I very much appreciate all you do.

And to my editor, Esi Sogah, thank you for your guidance, your collaboration, and your camaraderie throughout this project. As always, it's been a pleasure to work with you to make each story as strong as it can be, and I look forward to our continued partnership!